Thrilling
ADVENTURE STORIES

Thrilling
ADVENTURE STORIES

TREASURE PRESS

First published in Great Britain in 1984 by
Octopus Books Limited under the title
A Date with Danger

This edition published in 1988 by
Treasure Press
59 Grosvenor Street
London W1

Illustrated by Trevor Parkin (Linda Rogers Associates)

Arrangement and Illustrations © 1984 Octopus Books Limited

ISBN 1 85051 324 4

Printed in Czechoslovakia
52 169

CONTENTS

THE CURSE OF THE IDOL

Campbell Black

he jungle was darkly verdant, secretive, menacing. What little sunlight broke the high barriers of branches and twisted vines was pale, milky in color. The air, sticky and solid, created a wall of humidity. Birds screamed in panic, as if they had been unexpectedly trapped in some huge net. Glittering insects scurried underfoot, animals chattered and squealed in the foliage. In its primitive quality the place might have been a lost terrain, a point unmapped, untraveled – the end of the world.

Eight men made their way slowly along a narrow trail, pausing now and then to hack at an overhanging vine or slice at a dangling branch. At the head of this group there was a tall man in a leather jacket and a brimmed felt hat. Behind him were two Peruvians, who regarded the jungle cautiously, and five nervous Quechua Indians, struggling with the pair of donkeys that carried the packs and provisions.

The man who led the group was called Indiana Jones. He was muscular in the way one might associate with an athlete not quite beyond his prime. He had several days' growth of dirty blond beard and streaks of dark sweat on a face that might once have been handsome in a facile, photogenic fashion. Now, though, there were tiny lines around the eyes, the corners of the mouth, changing the almost bland good looks into an expression of character, depth. It was as if the contours of his experience had begun, slowly, to define his appearance.

Indy Jones didn't move with the same caution as the two Peruvians – his confidence made it seem as if he, rather then they, were the native there. But his outward swagger did not impair his sense of alertness. He knew enough to look occasionally, almost imperceptibly, from side to side, to expect the jungle to reveal a threat, a danger, at any moment. The sudden parting of a branch or the cracking of rotted wood – these were the signals, the points on his compass of danger. At times he would pause, take off his hat, wipe sweat from his forehead and wonder what bothered him more – the humidity or the nervousness of the Quechuas. Every so often they would talk excitedly with one another in quick bursts of their strange language, a language that reminded Indy of the sounds of jungle birds, creatures of the impenetrable foliage, the recurring mists.

He looked around at the two Peruvians, Barranca and Satipo, and he realized how little he really trusted them and yet how much he was obliged to depend on them to get what he wanted out of this jungle.

What a crew, he thought. Two furtive Peruvians, five terrified Indians, and two recalcitrant donkeys. And I am their leader, who might have done better with a troop of Boy Scouts.

Indy turned to Barranca and, though he was sure he knew the answer asked, 'What are the Indians talking about?'

Barranca seemed irritated. 'What do they always

talk about, Señor Jones? The curse. Always the curse.'

Indy shrugged and stared back at the Indians. Indy understood their superstitions, their beliefs, and in a way he even sympathized with them. The curse – the ancient curse of the Temple of the Chachapoyan Warriors. The Quechuas had been raised with it; it was intrinsic to their system of beliefs.

He said, 'Tell them to be quiet, Barranca. Tell them no harm will come to them.' The salve of words. He felt like a quack doctor administering a dose of an untested serum. How the devil could he know that no harm would come to them?

Barranca watched Indy a moment, then he spoke harshly to the Indians, and for a time they were silent – a silence that was one of repressed fear. Again, Indy felt sympathy for them: vague words of comfort couldn't dispose of centuries of superstition. He put his hat back on and moved slowly along the trail, assailed by the odors of the jungle, the scents of things growing and other things rotting, ancient carcasses crawling with maggots, decaying wood, dying vegetation. You could think of better places to be than here, he thought, you could think of sweeter places.

And then he was wondering about Forrestal, imagining him coming along this same path years ago, imagining the fever in Forrestal's blood when he came close to the Temple. But Forrestal, good as he had been as an archaeologist, hadn't come back from his trip to this place – and whatever secrets that lay contained in the Temple were locked there still. Poor Forrestal. To die in this godforsaken place was a hell of an epitaph. It wasn't one Indy relished for himself.

He moved along the trail again, followed by the group. The jungle lay in a canyon at this point, and the trail traversed the canyon wall like an old scar.

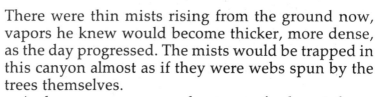

There were thin mists rising from the ground now, vapors he knew would become thicker, more dense, as the day progressed. The mists would be trapped in this canyon almost as if they were webs spun by the trees themselves.

A huge macaw, gaudy as a fresh rainbow, screamed out of the underbrush and winged into the trees, momentarily startling him. And then the Indians were jabbering again, gesticulating wildly with their hands, prodding one another. Barranca turned and silenced them with a fierce command – but Indy knew it was going to be more and more difficult to keep them under any kind of control. He could feel their anxieties as certainly as he could the humidity pressing against his flesh.

Besides, the Indians mattered less to him than his growing mistrust of the two Peruvians. Especially Barranca. It was a gut instinct, the kind he always relied on, an intuition he'd felt for most of the journey. But it was stronger now. They'd cut his throat for a few salted peanuts, he knew.

It isn't much farther, he told himself.

And when he realized how close he was to the Temple, when he understood how near he was to the Idol of the Chachapoyans, he experienced the old adrenaline rushing through him: the fulfilment of a dream, an old oath he'd taken for himself, a pledge he'd made when he'd been a novice in archaeology. It was like going back fifteen years into his past, back to the familiar sense of wonder, the obsessive urge to understand the dark places of history, that had first excited him about archaeology. A dream, he thought. A dream taking shape, changing from something nebulous to something tangible. And now he could feel the nearness of the Temple, feel it in the hollows of his bones.

He paused and listened to the Indians chatter again. They too know. *They know how close we are now.* And it scares them. He moved forward. Through the trees there was a break in the canyon wall. The trail was almost invisible: it had been choked by creepers, stifled by bulbous weeds that crawled over roots – roots that had the appearance of growths produced by some floating spores randomly drifting in space, planting themselves here by mere whim. Indy hacked, swinging his arm so that his broad-bladed knife cracked through the obstructions as if they were nothing more than fibrous papers. Damn jungle. You couldn't let nature, even at its most perverse, its most unruly, defeat you. When he paused he was soaked in sweat and his muscles ached. But he felt good as he looked at the slashed creepers, the severed roots. And then he was aware of the mist thickening, not a cold mist, not a chill, but something created out of the sweat of the jungle itself. He caught his breath and moved through the passage.

He caught it again when he reached the end of the trail.

It was there.

There, in the distance, shrouded by thick trees, *the Temple.*

For a second he was seized by the strange linkages of history, a sense of permanence, a continuum that made it possible for someone called Indiana Jones to be alive in the year 1936 and see a construction that had been erected two thousand years before. Awed. Overwhelmed. A humbling feeling. But none of these descriptions was really accurate. There wasn't a word for this excitement.

For a time he couldn't say anything.

He just stared at the edifice and wondered at the

energy that had gone into building such a structure in the heart of a merciless jungle. And then he was shaken back into an awareness of the present by the shouts of the Indians, and he swung round to see three of them running back along the trail, leaving the donkeys. Barranca had his pistol out and was leveling it to fire at the fleeing Indians, but Indy gripped the man's wrist, twisted it slightly, swung the Peruvian around to face him.

'No,' he said.

Barranca stared at Indy accusingly. 'They are cowards, Señor Jones.'

'We don't need them,' Indy said. 'And we don't need to kill them.'

The Peruvian brought the pistol to his side, glanced at his companion Satipo and looked back at Indy again. 'Without the Indians, Señor, who will carry the supplies? It was not part of our arrangement that Satipo and I do menial labor, no?'

Indy watched the Peruvian, the dark coldness at the heart of the man's eyes. He couldn't ever imagine this one smiling. He couldn't imagine daylight finding its way into Barranca's soul. Indy remembered seeing such dead eyes before: on a shark. 'We'll dump the supplies. As soon as we get what we came here for, we can make it back to the plane by dusk. We don't need supplies now.'

Barranca was fidgeting with his pistol.

A trigger-happy fellow, Indy thought. Three dead Indians wouldn't make a bit of difference to him.

'Put the gun away,' Indy told him. 'Pistols don't agree with me, Barranca, unless I'm the one with my finger on the trigger.'

Barranca shrugged and glanced at Satipo; some kind of silent communication passed between them. They'll choose their moment, Indy knew. They'll make their move at the right time.

'Just tuck it in your belt, okay?' Indy asked. He looked briefly at the two remaining Indians, herded into place by Satipo. They had trancelike expressions of fear on their faces; they might have been zombies.

Indy turned toward the Temple, gazing at it, savoring the moment. The mists were becoming denser around the place, a conspiracy of nature, as if the jungle intended to keep its secrets forever.

Satipo bent and pulled something out of the bark of a tree. He raised his hand to Indy. In the center of the palm lay a tiny dart.

'Hovitos,' Satipo said. 'The poison is still fresh – three days, Señor Jones. They must be following us.'

'If they knew we were here, they'd have killed us already,' Indy said calmly.

He took the dart. Crude but effective. He thought of the Hovitos, their legendary fierceness, their historic attachment to the Temple. They were superstitious enough to stay away from the Temple itself, but definitely jealous enough to kill anybody else who went there.

'Let's go,' he said, 'Let's get it over with.'

They had to hack and slash again, cut and slice through the elaborately tangled vines, rip at the creepers that rose from underfoot like shackles lying in wait. Sweating, Indy paused; he let his knife dangle at his side. From the corner of his eye he was conscious of one of the Indians hauling back a thick branch.

It was the scream that made him swing abruptly round, his knife raised in the air now. It was the wild scream of the Indian that made him rush toward the branch just as the Quechua, still yelling, dashed off into the jungle. The other remaining Indian followed, crashing mindlessly, panicked, against the barbed branches and sharp creepers. And then they were both gone. Indy, knife poised, hauled back the branch that had so scared the Indians. He was ready to lunge at whatever had terrified them, ready to thrust his blade forward. He drew the branch aside.

It sat behind the swirling mist.

Carved out of stone, timeless, its face the figment of some bleak nightmare, it was a sculpture of a Chachapoyan demon. He watched it for a second, aware of the malevolence in its unchanging face, and he realized it had been placed here to guard the Temple, to scare off anybody who might pass this way. A work of art, he thought, and he wondered briefly about its creators, their system of beliefs, about the kind of religious awe that might inspire something so dreadful as this statue. He forced himself to put out his hand and touch the demon lightly on the shoulder.

Then he was conscious of something else, something that was more disturbing than the stone face. More eerie.

The silence.

The weird silence.

Nothing. No birds. No insects. No breeze to shake sounds out of the trees. A zero, as if everything in this place were dead. As if everything had been stilled, silenced by an ungodly, destructive hand. He touched his forehead. Cold, cold sweat. Spooks, he thought. The place is filled with spooks. This was the kind of silence you might have imagined before creation.

He moved away from the stone figure, followed by the two Peruvians, who seemed remarkably subdued.

'What is it, in the name of God?' Barranca asked.

Indy shrugged. 'Ah, some old trinket. What else?

Every Chachapoyan household had to have one, didn't you know?'

Barranca looked grim. 'Sometimes you seem to take this very lightly, Señor Jones.'

'Is there another way?'

The mist crawled, rolled, clawed, seeming to press the three men back. Indy peered through the vapors, staring at the Temple entrance, the elaborately primitive friezes that had yielded to vegetation with the passage of time, the clutter of shrubs, leaves, vines; but what held him more was the dark entrance itself, round and open, like the mouth of a corpse. He thought of Forrestal passing into that dark mouth, crossing the entranceway to his death. Poor guy.

Barranca stared at the entranceway. 'How can we trust you, Señor Jones? No one has ever come out alive. Why should we put our faith in you?'

Indy smiled at the Peruvian. 'Barranca, Barranca – you've got to learn that even a miserable gringo sometimes tells the truth, huh?' And he pulled a piece of folded parchment out of his shirt pocket. He stared at the faces of the Peruvians. Their expressions were transparent, such looks of greed. Indy wondered whose throats had been cut so that these two villains had managed to obtain the other half. 'This, Barranca, should take care of your faith,' and he spread the parchment on the ground.

Satipo took a similar piece of parchment from his pocket and laid it alongside the one Indy had produced. The two parts dovetailed neatly. For a time, nobody spoke; the threshold of caution had been reached, Indy knew – and he waited, tensely, for something to happen.

'Well, amigos,' he said. 'We're partners. We have what you might call mutual needs. Between us we have a complete map of the floor plan of the Temple.

We've got what nobody else ever had. Now, assuming that pillar there marks the corner –'

Before he could finish his sentence he saw, as if in a slowed reel of film, Barranca reach for his pistol. He saw the thin brown hand curl itself over the butt of the silver gun – and then he moved. Indiana Jones moved faster than the Peruvian could have followed; his motions a blur, a parody of vision, he moved back from Barranca and, reaching under the back of his leather jacket, produced a coiled bullwhip, his hand tight on the handle. His movements became liquid, one fluid and graceful display of muscle and poise and balance, arm and bullwhip seeming to be one thing, extensions of each other. He swung the whip, lashing the air, watching it twist itself around Barranca's wrist. Then he jerked downward, tighter still, and the gun discharged itself into the ground. For a moment the Peruvian didn't move. He stared at

Indy in amazement, a mixture of confusion and pain and hatred, loathing the fact that he'd been out-smarted, humiliated. And then, as the whip around his wrist slackened, Barranca turned and ran, racing after the Indians into the jungle.

Indy turned to Satipo. The man raised his hands in the air.

'Señor, please,' he said, 'I knew nothing, nothing of his plan. He was crazy. A crazy man. Please, Señor. Believe me.'

Indy watched him a moment, then nodded and picked up the pieces of the map.

'You can drop your hands, Satipo.'

The Peruvian looked relieved and lowered his arms stiffly.

'We've got the floor plan,' Indy said. 'So what are we waiting for?'

And he turned toward the Temple entrance.

The smell was the scent of centuries, the trapped odors of years of silence and darkness, of the damp flowing in from the jungle, the festering of plants. Water dripped from the ceiling, slithered through the mosses that had grown there. The passageway whispered with the scampering of rodent claws. And the air – the air was unexpectedly cold, untouched by sunlight, forever shaded. Indy walked ahead of Satipo, listening to the echoes of their footsteps. Alien sounds, he thought. A disturbance of the dead – and for a moment he was touched by the feeling of being in the wrong place at the wrong time, like a plunderer, a looter, someone intent on damaging things that have lain too long in peace.

He knew the feeling well, a sense of wrongdoing. It wasn't the sort of emotion he enjoyed entertaining because it was like having a boring guest at an otherwise decent dinner party. He watched his shadow move in the light of the torch Satipo carried.

The passageway twisted and turned as it bored deeper into the interior of the Temple. Every now and then Indy would stop and look at the map, by the light of the torch, trying to remember the details of the layout. He wanted to drink, his throat was dry, his tongue parched – but he didn't want to stop. He could hear a clock tick inside his skull, and every tick was telling him, *You don't have time, you don't have time. . .*

The two men passed ledges carved out of the walls. Here and there Indy would stop and examine the artifacts that were located on the ledges. He would sift through them, discarding some expertly, placing others in his pockets. Small coins, tiny medallions, pieces of pottery small enough to carry on his person. He knew what was valuable and what wasn't. But they were nothing in comparison to what he'd really come for – the Idol.

He moved more quickly now, the Peruvian rushing behind him, panting as he hurried to keep up. And then Indy stopped suddenly, joltingly.

'Why have we stopped?' Satipo asked, his voice sounding as if his lungs were on fire.

Indy said nothing, remained frozen, barely breathing. Satipo, confused, took one step toward Indy, went to touch him on the arm, but he too stopped and let his hand freeze in midair.

A huge black tarantula crawled up Indy's back, maddeningly slowly. Indy could feel its legs as they inched toward the bare skin of his neck. He waited, waited for what seemed like forever, until he felt the horrible creature settle on his shoulder. He could feel Satipo's panic, could sense the man's desire to scream and jump. He knew he had to move quickly, yet casually so Satipo would not run. Indy, in one smooth motion, flicked his hand over his shoulder and knocked the creature away into the shadows. Relieved, he began to move forward but then he heard Satipo's gasp, and turned to see two more spiders drop onto the Peruvian's arm. Instinctively, Indy's whip lashed out from the shadows, throwing the creatures onto the ground. Quickly, Indy stepped on the scuttling spiders, stomping them beneath his boot.

Satipo paled, seemed about to faint. Indy grabbed him, held him by the arm until he was steady. And then the archaeologist pointed down the hallway at a small chamber ahead, a chamber which was lit by a single shaft of sunlight from a hole in the ceiling. The tarantulas were forgotten; Indy knew other dangers lay ahead.

'Enough, Señor,' Satipo breathed. 'Let us go back.'

But Indy said nothing. He continued to gaze toward the chamber, his mind already working, figuring, his imagination helping him to think his way inside the minds of the people who had built this place so long ago. They would want to protect the treasure of the Temple, he thought. They would want to erect barricades, traps, to make sure no stranger ever reached the heart of the Temple.

He moved closer to the entrance now, moving with the instinctive caution of the hunter who smells danger on the downwind, who feels peril before he can see signs of it. He bent down, felt around on the floor, found a thick stalk of a weed, hauled it out — then reached forward and tossed the stalk into the chamber.

For a split second nothing happened. And then there was a faint whirring noise, a creaking sound, and the walls of the chamber seemed to break open as giant metal spikes, like the jaws of some impossible shark, slammed together in the center of the chamber. Indiana Jones smiled, appreciating the labors of the Temple designers, the cunning of this horrible trap. The Peruvian swore under his breath, crossed himself. Indy was about to say something when he noticed an object impaled on the great spikes. It took only a moment for him to realize the nature of the thing that had been sliced through by the sharp metal.

'Forrestal.'

Half skeleton. Half flesh. The face grotesquely preserved by the temperature of the chamber, the pained surprise still apparent, as if it had been left unchanged as a warning to anybody else who might want to enter the room. Forrestal, impaled through chest and groin, blackened blood visible on his jungle khakis, death stains. Jesus, Indy thought. Nobody deserved to go like this. Nobody. He experienced a second of sadness.

You just blundered into it, pal. You were out of your league. You should have stayed in the class-room. Indy shut his eyes briefly, then stepped inside the chamber and dragged the remains of the man from the tips of the spikes, laying the corpse on the floor.

'You knew this person?' Satipo asked.

'Yeah, I knew him.'

The Peruvian made the sign of the cross again. 'I think, Señor, we should perhaps go no further.'

'You wouldn't let a little thing like this discourage you, would you, Satipo?' Then Indy didn't speak for a time. He watched the metal spikes begin to retract slowly, sliding back toward the walls from which they'd emerged. He marveled at the simple mecha-nics of the arrangement – simple and deadly.

Indy smiled at the Peruvian, momentarily

touching him on the shoulder. The man was sweating profusely, trembling. Indy stepped inside the chamber, wary of the spikes, seeing their ugly tips set into the walls. After a time the Peruvian, grunting, whispering to himself, followed. They passed through the chamber and emerged into a straight hallway some fifty feet long. At the end of the passageway there was a door, bright with sunlight streaming from above.

'We're close,' Indy said, 'so close.'

He studied the map again before folding it, the details memorized. But he didn't move immediately. His eyes scanned the place for more traps, more pitfalls.

'It looks safe,' Satipo said.

'That's what scares me, friend.'

'It's safe,' the Peruvian said again. 'Let's go.'

Satipo, suddenly eager, stepped forward.

And then he stopped as his right foot slipped through the surface of the floor. He flew forward, screaming. Indy moved quickly, grabbed the Peruvian by his belt and hauled him up to safety. Satipo fell to the ground exhausted.

Indy looked down at the floor through which the Peruvian had stepped. Cobwebs, an elaborate expanse of ancient cobwebs, over which lay a film of dust, creating the illusion of a floor. He bent down, picked up a stone and dropped it through the surface of webs. Nothing, no sound, no echo came back.

'A long way down,' Indy muttered.

Satipo, breathless, said nothing.

Indy stared across the surface of webs toward the sunlit door. How to cross the space, the pit, when the floor doesn't exist?

Satipo said, 'I think now we go back, Señor. No?'

'No,' Indy said. 'I think we go forward.'

'How? With wings? Is that what you think?'

'You don't need wings in order to fly, friend.'

He took out his whip and stared up at the ceiling. There were various beams set into the roof. They might be rotted through, he thought. On the other hand, they might be strong enough to hold his weight. It was worth a try, anyhow. If it didn't work, he'd have to kiss the idol good-bye. He swung the whip upward, seeing it coil around a beam, then he tugged on the whip and tested it for strength.

Satipo shook his head. 'No. You're crazy.'

'Can you think of a better way, friend?'

'The whip will not hold us. The beam will snap.'

'Save me from pessimists,' Indy said. 'Save me from disbelievers. Just trust me. Just do what I do, okay?'

Indy curled both hands around the whip, pulled on it again to test it, then swung himself slowly through the air, conscious all the time of the illusory floor underneath him, of the darkness of the pit that lay deep below the layers of cobwebs and dust, aware of the possibility that the beam might snap, the whip work itself loose, and then . . . but he didn't have time to consider these bleak things. He swung, clutching the whip, feeling air rush against him. He swung until he was sure he was beyond the margins of the pit and then he lowered himself, coming down on solid ground. He pushed the whip back across to the Peruvian, who muttered something in Spanish under his breath, something Indy was sure had religious significance. He wondered idly if there might exist, somewhere in the vaults of the Vatican, a patron saint for those who had occasion to travel by whip.

He watched the Peruvian land beside him.

'Told you, didn't I? Beats travelling by bus.'

Satipo said nothing. Even in the dim light, Indy could see his face was pale. Indy now wedged the handle of the bullwhip against the wall. 'For the return trip,' he said. 'I never go anywhere one way, Satipo.'

The Peruvian shrugged as they moved through the sunlit doorway into a large domed room, the ceiling of which had skylights that sent bands of sunlight down on the black-and-white tiled floor. And then Indy noticed something on the other side of the chamber, something that took his breath away, filled him with awe, with a pleasure he could barely define.

The Idol.

Set on some kind of altar, looking both fierce and lovely, its gold shape glittering in the flames of the torch, shining in the sunlight that slipped through the roof – *the Idol.*

The Idol of the Chachapoyan Warriors.

What he felt then was the excitement of an overpowering lust, the desire to race across the room and touch its beauty – a beauty surrounded by obstacles and traps. And what kind of booby trap was saved for last? What kind of trap surrounded the Idol itself?

'I'm going in,' he said.

The Peruvian now also saw the Idol and said nothing. He stared at the figurine with an expression of avarice that suggested he was suddenly so possessed by greed that nothing else mattered except getting his hands on it. Indy watched him a moment, thinking, *He's seen it. He's seen its beauty. He can't be trusted.* Satipo was about to step beyond the threshold when Indy stopped him.

'Remember Forrestal?' Indy said.

'I remember.'

He stared across the intricate pattern of black-and-white tiles, wondering about the precision of the arrangement, about the design. Beside the doorway there were two ancient torches in rusted metal holders. He reached up, removed one, trying to imagine the face of the last person who might have held this very torch; the span of time – it never failed to amaze him that the least important of objects endured through centuries. He lit it, glanced at Satipo, then bent down and pressed the unlit end against one of the white tiles. He tapped it. Solid. No echo, no resonance. Very solid. He next tapped one of the black tiles.

It happened before he could move his hand away. A noise, the sound of something slamming through the air, something whistling with the speed of its movement, and a small dart drove itself into the shaft of his torch. He pulled his hand away. Satipo exhaled quietly, then pointed inside the room.

'It came from there,' he said. 'You see that hole? The dart came from there.'

'I also see hundreds of other holes,' Indy said. The place, the whole place, was honeycombed with shadowy recesses, each of which would contain a dart, each of which would release its missile whenever there was pressure on a black tile.

'Stay here, Satipo.'

Slowly, the Peruvian turned his face. 'If you insist.'

Indy, holding the lit torch, moved cautiously into the chamber, avoiding the black tiles, stepping over them to reach the safe white ones. He was conscious of his shadow thrown against the walls of the room by the light of the torch, conscious of the wicked holes, seen now in half-light, that held the darts. Mainly, though, it was the idol that demanded his attention, the sheer beauty of it that became more apparent the closer he got to it, the hypnotic glitter, the enigmatic expression on the face. Strange, he thought: six inches high, two thousand years old, a lump of gold whose face could hardly be called lovely – strange that men would lose their minds for this, kill for this. And yet it mesmerized him and he had to look away. Concentrate on the tiles, he told himself. Only the tiles. Nothing else. Don't lose the fine edge of your instinct here.

Underfoot, sprawled on a white tile and riddled with darts, lay a small dead bird. He stared at it, sickened for a moment, seized by the realization that whoever had built this Temple, whoever had planned the traps, would have been too cunning to booby trap only the black tiles: like a wild card in a deck, at least one white tile would have been poisoned.

At least one.

What if there were others?

He hesitated, sweating now, feeling the sunlight from above, feeling the heat of the torch flame on his

face. Carefully, he stepped around the dead bird and looked at the white tiles that lay between himself and the Idol as if each were a possible enemy. Sometimes, he thought, caution alone doesn't carry the day. Sometimes you don't get the prize by being hesitant, by failing to take the final risk. Caution has to be married with chance – but then, you need to know in some way the odds are on your side. The sight of the Idol drew him again. It magnetized him. And he was aware of Satipo behind him, watching from the doorway, no doubt planning his own treachery.

Do it, he said to himself. What the hell. Do it and caution be damned.

He moved with the grace of a dancer. He moved with the strange elegance of a man weaving between razor blades. Every tile now was a possible land mine, a depth charge.

He edged forward and stepped over the black squares, waiting for the pressure of his weight to trigger the mechanism that would make the air scream with darts. And then he was closer to the altarpiece, closer to the idol. The prize. The Triumph. And the last trap of all.

He paused again. His heart ran wildly, his pulses thudded, the blood burned in his veins. Sweat fell from his forehead and slicked across his eyelids, blinding him. He wiped at it with the back of his hand. A few more feet, he thought. A few more feet.

And a few more tiles.

He moved again, raising his legs and then gently lowering them. If he ever needed balance, it was now. The idol seemed to wink at him, to entice him.

Another step.

Another step.

He put his right leg forward, touching the last white tile before the altar.

He'd made it. He'd done it. He pulled a liquor flask from his pocket, uncapped it, drank hard from it. This one you deserve, he thought. Then he stuck the flask away and stared at the idol. The last trap, he wondered. What could the last trap be? The final hazard of all.

He thought for a long time, tried to imagine himself into the minds of the people who'd created this place, who'd constructed these defenses. Okay, somebody comes to take the idol away, which means it has to be lifted, it has to be removed from the slab of polished stone, it has to be *physically* taken.

Then what?

Some kind of mechanism under the idol detects the absence of the thing's weight, and that triggers – what? More darts? No, it would be something even more destructive than that. Something more deadly. He thought again; his mind sped, his nerves pulsated. He bent down and stared around the base of the altar. There were chips of stone, dirt, grit, the accumulation of centuries. Maybe, he thought. Just maybe. He took a small drawstring bag from his pocket, opened it, emptied out the coins it contained, then began to fill the bag with dirt and stones. He weighed it in the palm of his hand for a while. Maybe, he thought again. If you could do it quickly enough. You could do it with the kind of speed that might defeat the mechanism. If that was indeed the kind of trap involved here.

If if if. Too many hypotheticals.

Under other circumstances he knew he would walk away, avoid the consequences of so many intangibles. But not now, not here. He stood upright, weighed the bag again, wondered if it was the same weight as the idol, hoped that it was. Then he moved quickly, picking up the idol and setting the bag down in its place, setting it down on the polished stone.

Nothing. For a long moment, nothing.

He stared at the bag, then at the idol in his hand, and then he was aware of a strange, distant noise, a rumbling like that of a great machine set in motion, a sound of things waking up from a long sleep, roaring and tearing and creaking through the spaces of the Temple. The polished stone pedestal suddenly dropped – five inches, six. And then the noise was greater, deafening, and everything began to shake, tremble, as if the very foundations of the place were coming apart, splitting, opening, bricks and wood splintering and cracking.

He turned and moved quickly back across the tiles, moving as fast as he could toward the doorway. And still the noise, like desperate thunder, grew and rolled and echoed through the old hallways and passages and chambers. He moved toward Satipo, who was standing in the doorway with a look of absolute terror on his face.

Now everything was shaking, everything moving, bricks collapsing, walls toppling, everything. When he reached the doorway he turned to see a rock fall across the tiled floor, setting off the darts, which flew pointlessly in their thousands through the disintegrating chamber.

Satipo, breathing hard, had moved toward the whip and was swinging himself across the pit. When he reached the other side he regarded Indy a moment.

I knew it was coming, Indy thought.

I felt it, I knew it, and now that it's about to happen, what can I do? He watched Satipo haul the whip from the beam and gather it in his hand.

'A bargain, Señor. An exchange. The idol for the whip. You throw me the idol, I throw you the whip.'

Indy listened to the destruction behind him and watched Satipo.

'What choices do you have, Señor Jones?' Satipo asked.

'Suppose I drop the Idol into the pit, my friend? All you've got for your troubles is a bullwhip, right?'

'And what exactly have *you* got for *your* troubles, Señor?'

Indy shrugged. The noise behind him was growing; he could feel the Temple tremble, the floor begin to sway. The idol, he thought – he couldn't just let the thing fall into the abyss like that.

'Okay, Satipo. The idol for the whip.' And he tossed the idol toward the Peruvian. He watched as Satipo seized the relic, stuffed it in his pocket and then dropped the whip on the floor.

Satipo smiled. 'I am genuinely sorry, Señor Jones.

Adios. And good luck.'

'You're no more sorry than me,' Indy shouted as he watched the Peruvian disappear down the passageway. The whole structure, like some vengeful deity of the jungle, shook even more.

He heard the sound of more stones falling, pillars toppling. *The curse of the idol*, he thought. It was a matinee movie, it was the kind of thing kids watched wild-eyed on Saturday afternoons in dark cinemas. There was only one thing to do – one thing, no alternative. You have to jump, he realized. You have to take your chances and jump across the pit and hope that gravity is on your side. All hell is breaking loose behind you and there's a godawful abyss just in front of you. So you jump, you wing it into darkness and keep your fingers crossed.

Jump!

He took a deep breath, swung himself out into the air above the pit, swung himself hard as he could, listened to the *swish* of the air around him as he moved. He would have prayed if he were the praying kind, prayed he didn't get swallowed up by the dark nothingness below.

He was dropping now. The impetus was gone from his leap. He was falling. He hoped he was falling on the other side of the pit.

But he wasn't.

He could feel the darkness, dank smelling and damp, rush upward from below, and he threw his hands out, looking for something to grip, some edge, anything to hold on to. He felt his fingertips dig into the edge of the pit, the crumbling edge, and he tried to drag himself upward while the edge yielded and gave way and loose stones dropped into the chasm. He swung his legs, clawed with his hands, struggled like a beached fish to get up, get out, reach whatever might pass now for safety. Straining, groaning, thrashing with his legs against the inside wall of the pit, he struggled to raise himself. He couldn't let the treacherous Peruvian get away with the idol. He swung his legs again, kicked, looked for some kind of leverage that would help him climb up from the pit, something, anything, it didn't matter what. And still the Temple was falling apart like a pathetic straw hut in a hurricane. He grunted, dug his fingers into the ledge above, strained until he thought his muscles might pop, his blood vessels burst, hauled himself up even as he heard the sound of his fingernails breaking with the weight of his body.

Harder, he thought.

Try harder.

He pushed, sweat blinded him, his nerves began to tremble. Something's going to snap, he thought. Something's going to give and then you'll find out exactly what lies at the bottom of this pit. He paused, tried to regroup his strength, rearrange his waning energies, then he hauled himself up again through laborious and wearisome inches.

At last he was able to swing his leg over the top, to slither over the edge to the relative safety of the floor – a floor that was shaking, threatening to split apart at any moment.

He raised himself shakily to a standing position and looked down the hallway in the direction Satipo had taken. He had gone toward the room where Forrestal's remains had been found. The room of spikes. The torture chamber. And suddenly Indy knew what would happen to the Peruvian, suddenly he knew the man's fate even before he heard the terrible clang of the spikes, even before he heard the Peruvian's awful scream echo along the passageway. He listened, reached down for his whip, then ran

toward the chamber. Satipo hung to one side, impaled like a grotesquely large butterfly in some madman's collection.

'Adios, Satipo,' Indy said, then slipped the idol from the dead man's pocket, edged his way past the spikes and raced into the passageway beyond.

Ahead, he saw the exit, the opening of light, the stand of thick trees beyond. And still the rolling sound increased, filling his ears, vibrating through his body. He turned, astounded to see a vast boulder roll down the passageway toward him, gathering speed as it coursed forward. *The last booby trap*, he thought. They wanted to make sure that even if you got inside the Temple, even if you avoided everything the place could throw at you, then you weren't going to get out alive. He raced. He sprinted insanely toward the exit as the great stone crushed along the passageway behind him. He threw himself forward toward the opening of light and hit the thick grass outside just before the boulder slammed against the exit, sealing the Temple shut forever.

THE ADVENTURE OF THE SPECTACLED ROADMAN

John Buchan

In the dark days before World War I, Richard Hannay has stumbled on to a mysterious plot that threatens Britain's security. Wrongly suspected of murder and pursued by foreign agents, he finds himself on the run in the highlands of Scotland . . .

I sat down on the very crest of the pass and took stock of my position.

Behind me was the road climbing through a long cleft in the hills, which was the upper glen of some notable river. In front was a flat space of maybe a mile, all pitted with bog-holes and rough with tussocks, and then beyond it the road fell steeply down another glen to a plain whose blue dimness melted into the distance. To left and right were round-shouldered green hills as smooth as pancakes, but to the south – that is, the left hand – there was a glimpse of high heathery mountains, which I remembered from the map as the big knot of hill which I had chosen for my sanctuary. I was on the central boss of a huge upland country, and could see everything moving for miles. In the meadows below the road half a mile back a cottage smoked, but it was the only sign of human life. Otherwise there was only the calling of plovers and the tinkling of little streams.

It was now about seven o'clock, and as I waited I heard once again that ominous beat in the air. Then I realised that my vantage-ground might be in reality a trap. There was no cover for a tomtit in those bald green places.

I sat quite still and hopeless while the beat grew louder. Then I saw an aeroplane coming up from the east. It was flying high, but as I looked it dropped several hundred feet and began to circle round the knot of hill in narrowing circles, just as a hawk wheels before it pounces. Now it was flying very low, and now the observer on board caught sight of me. I could see one of the two occupants examining me through glasses.

Suddenly it began to rise in swift whorls, and the next I knew it was speeding eastward again till it became a speck in the blue morning.

That made me do some savage thinking. My enemies had located me, and the next thing would be a cordon round me. I didn't know what force they could command, but I was certain it would be sufficient. The aeroplane had seen my bicycle, and would conclude that I would try to escape by the road. In that case there might be a chance on the moors to the right or left. I wheeled the machine a hundred yards from the highway, and plunged it into a moss-hole, where it sank among pond-weed and water buttercups. Then I climbed to a knoll which gave me a view of the two valleys. Nothing was stirring on the long white ribbon that threaded them.

I have said there was not cover in the whole place to hide a rat. As the day advanced it was flooded with soft fresh light till it had the fragrant sunniness of the South African veld. At other times I would have liked the place, but now it seemed to suffocate me. The free moorlands were prison walls, and the keen hill air was the breath of a dungeon.

I tossed a coin – heads right, tails left – and it fell heads, so I turned to the north. In a little I came to the brow of the ridge which was the containing wall of the pass. I saw the highroad for maybe ten miles, and far down it something that was moving, and that I took to be a motor-car. Beyond the ridge I looked on a rolling green moor, which fell away into wooded glens.

Now my life on the veld has given me the eyes of a kite, and I can see things for which most men need a telescope . . . Away down the slope, a couple of miles away, several men were advancing like a row of beaters at a shoot . . .

I dropped out of sight behind the skyline. That way was shut to me, and I must try the bigger hills to the south beyond the highway. The car I had noticed was getting nearer, but it was still a long way off with some very steep gradients before it. I ran hard, crouching low except in the hollows, and as I ran I kept scanning the brow of the hill before me. Was it imagination, or did I see figures – one, two, perhaps more – moving in a glen beyond the stream?

If you are hemmed in on all sides in a patch of land there is only one chance of escape. You must stay in the patch, and let your enemies search it and not find you. That was good sense, but how on earth was I to escape notice in that table-cloth of a place? I would have buried myself to the neck in mud or lain below water or climbed the tallest tree. But there was not a stick of wood, the bog-holes were little puddles, the stream was a slender trickle. There was nothing but short heather, and bare hill bent, and the white highway.

Then in a tiny bight of road, beside a heap of

stones, I found the roadman.

He had just arrived, and was wearily flinging down his hammer. He looked at me with a fishy eye and yawned.

'Confound the day I ever left the herdin'!' he said, as if to the world at large. 'There I was my ain maister. Now I'm a slave to the Government, tethered to the roadside, wi' sair een, and a back like a suckle.'

He took up the hammer, struck a stone, dropped the implement with an oath, and put both hands to his ears. 'Mercy on me! My heid's burstin'!' he cried.

He was a wild figure, about my own size but much bent, with a week's beard on his chin, and a pair of big horn spectacles.

'I canna dae't,' he cried again. 'The Surveyor maun just report me. I'm for my bed.'

I asked him what was the trouble, though indeed that was clear enough.

'The trouble is that I'm no sober. Last nicht my dochter Merran was waddit, and they danced till fower in the byre. Me and some ither chiels sat down to the drinkin', and here I am. Peety that I ever lookit on the wine when it was red!'

I agreed with him about bed.

'It's easy speakin',' he moaned. 'But I got a post-caird yestreen sayin' that the new Road Surveyor would be round the day. He'll come and he'll no find me, or else he'll find me fou, and either way I'm a done man. I'll awa' back to my bed and say I'm no weel, but I doot that'll no help me, for they ken my kind o' no-weel-ness.'

Then I had an inspiration. 'Does the new Surveyor know you?' I asked.

'No him. He's just been a week at the job. He rins about in a wee motor-cawr, and wad speir the inside oot o' a whelk.'

'Where's your house?' I asked, and was directed by a wavering finger to the cottage by the stream.

'Well, back to your bed,' I said, 'and sleep in peace. I'll take on your job for a bit and see the Surveyor.'

He stared at me blankly; then, as the notion dawned on his fuddled brain, his face broke into a vacant drunkard's smile.

'You're the billy,' he cried. 'It'll be easy eneuch managed. I've finished that bing o' stanes, so you needna chap ony mair this forenoon. Just take the barry, and wheel eneuch metal frae yon quarry doon the road to mak anither bing the morn. My name's Alexander Turnbull, and I've been seeven year at the trade, and twenty afore that herdin' on Leithen Water. My freens ca' me Ecky, and whiles Specky, for I wear glesses, being weak i' the sicht. Just you speak the Surveyor fair, and ca' him Sir, and he'll be fell pleased. I'll be back or midday.'

I borrowed his spectacles and filthy old hat; stripped off coat, waistcoat, and collar, and gave him them to carry home; borrowed, too, the foul stump of a clay pipe as an extra property. He indicated my simple tasks, and without more ado set off at an amble bedwards. Bed may have been his chief object, but I think there was also something left in the foot of a bottle. I prayed that he might be safe under cover before my friends arrived on the scene.

Then I set to work to dress for the part. I opened the collar of my shirt – it was a vulgar blue-and-white check such as ploughmen wear – and revealed a neck as brown as any tinker's. I rolled up my sleeves, and there was a forearm which might have been a blacksmith's, sunburnt and rough with old scars. I got my boots and trouser-legs all white from the dust of the road, and hitched up my trousers, tying them with string below the knee. Then I set to work on my face. With a handful of dust I made a water-mark round my neck, the place where Mr Turnbull's Sunday ablutions might be expected to stop. I rubbed a good deal of dirt also into the sunburn off my cheeks. A roadman's eyes would no doubt be a little inflamed, so I contrived to get some dust in both of mine, and by dint of vigorous rubbing produced a bleary effect.

The sandwiches Sir Harry had given me had gone off with my coat, but the roadman's lunch, tied up in a red handkerchief, was at my disposal. I ate with great relish several of the thick slabs of scone and cheese and drank a little of the cold tea. In the handkerchief was a local paper tied with string and addressed to Mr Turnbull – obviously meant to solace his midday leisure. I did up the bundle again, and put the paper conspicuously beside it.

My boots did not satisfy me, but by dint of kicking among the stones I reduced them to the granite-like surface which marks a roadman's foot-gear. Then I bit and scraped my finger-nails till the edges were all cracked and uneven. The men I was matched against would miss no detail. I broke one of the bootlaces and retied it in a clumsy knot, and loosed the other so that my thick grey socks bulged over the uppers. Still no sign of anything on the road. The motor I had observed half an hour ago must have gone home.

My toilet complete, I took up the barrow and began my journeys to and from the quarry a hundred yards off.

I remember an old scout in Rhodesia, who had done many queer things in his day, once telling me that the secret of playing a part was to think yourself into it. You could never keep it up, he said, unless you could manage to convince yourself that you were

it. So I shut off all other thoughts and switched them
on to the road-mending. I thought of the little white
cottage as my home, I recalled the years I had spent
herding on Leithen Water, I made my mind dwell
lovingly on sleep in a box-bed and a bottle of cheap
whisky. Still nothing appeared on that long white
road.

Now and then a sheep wandered off the heather to
stare at me. A heron flopped down to a pool in the
stream and started to fish, taking no more notice of
me than if I had been a milestone. On I went,
trundling my loads of stone, with the heavy step of
the professional. Soon I grew warm, and the dust on
my face changed into solid and abiding grit. I was
already counting the hours till evening should put a
limit to Mr Turnbull's monotonous toil.

Suddenly a crisp voice from the road, and looking
up I saw a little Ford two-seater, and a round-faced
young man in a bowler hat.

'Are you Alexander Turnbull?' he asked. 'I am the
new County Road Surveyor. You live at Black-
hopefoot, and have charge of the section from
Laidlawbyres to the Riggs? Good! A fair bit of road,
Turnbull, and not badly engineered. A little soft
about a mile off, and the edges want cleaning. See
you look after that. Good morning. You'll know me
the next time you see me.'

Clearly my get-up was good enough for the
dreaded Surveyor. I went on with my work, and as
the morning grew towards noon I was cheered by a
little traffic. A baker's van breasted the hill, and sold
me a bag of ginger biscuits which I stowed in my
trouser pockets against emergencies. Then a herd
passed with sheep, and disturbed me somewhat by
asking loudly, 'What had become o' Specky?'

'In bed wi' the colic,' I replied, and the herd

passed on . . .

Just about midday a big car stole down the hill, glided past and drew up a hundred yards beyond. Its three occupants descended as if to stretch their legs, and sauntered towards me.

Two of the men I had seen before from the window of the Galloway inn – one lean, sharp, and dark, the other comfortable and smiling. The third had the look of a countryman – a vet, perhaps, or a small farmer. He was dressed in ill-cut knickerbockers, and the eye in his head was as bright and wary as a hen's.

''Morning,' said the last. 'That's a fine easy job o' yours.'

I had not looked up on their approach, and now, when accosted, I slowly and painfully straightened my back, after the manner of roadmen; spat vigorously, after the manner of the low Scot; and regarded them steadily before replying. I confronted three pairs of eyes that missed nothing.

'There's waur jobs and there's better,' I said sententiously. 'I wad rather hae yours, sittin' a' day on your hinderlands on thae cushions. It's you and your muckle cawrs that wreck my roads! If we a' had oor richts, ye sud be made to mend what ye break.'

The bright-eyed man was looking at the newspaper lying beside Turnbull's bundle.

'I see you get your papers in good time,' he said.

I glanced at it casually. 'Aye, in gude time. Seein' that that paper cam' out last Setterday I'm just sax days late.'

He picked it up, glanced at the superscription, and laid it down again. One of the others had been looking at my boots, and a word in German called the speaker's attention to them.

'You've a fine taste in boots,' he said. 'These were never made by a country shoemaker.'

'They were not,' I said readily. 'They were made in London. I got them frae the gentleman that was here last year for the shootin'. What was his name now?' And I scratched a forgetful head.

Again the sleek one spoke in German. 'Let us get on,' he said. 'This fellow is all right.'

They asked one last question.

'Did you see anyone pass early this morning? He might be on a bicycle or he might be on foot?'

I very nearly fell into the trap and told a story of a bicyclist hurrying past in the grey dawn. But I had the sense to see my danger. I pretended to consider very deeply.

'I wasna up very early,' I said. 'Ye see, my dochter was merrit last nicht, and we keepit it up late. I opened the house door about seeven and there was naebody on the road then. Since I cam' up here there has just been the baker and the Ruchill herd, besides you gentlemen.'

One of them gave me a cigar, which I smelt gingerly and stuck in Turnbull's bundle. They got into their car and were out of sight in three minutes.

My heart leaped with an enormous relief, but I went on wheeling my stones. It was as well, for ten minutes later the car returned, one of the occupants waving a hand to me. Those gentry left nothing to chance.

I finished Turnbull's bread and cheese, and pretty soon I had finished the stones. The next step was what puzzled me. I could not keep up this road-making business for long. A merciful Providence had kept Mr Turnbull indoors, but if he appeared on the scene there would be trouble. I had a notion that the cordon was still tight round the glen, and that if I walked in any direction I should meet with question-ers. But get out I must. No man's nerve could stand more than a day of being spied on.

I stayed at my post till about five o'clock. By that time I had resolved to go down to Turnbull's cottage at nightfall and take my chance at getting over the hills in the darkness. But suddenly a new car came up the road, and slowed down a yard or two from me. A fresh wind had risen, and the occupant wanted to light a cigarette.

It was a touring car, with the tonneau full of an assortment of baggage. One man sat in it, and by an amazing chance I knew him. His name was Marma-duke Jopley, and he was an offence to creation. He was a sort of blood stockbroker, who did his business by toadying eldest sons and rich young peers and foolish old ladies. 'Marmie' was a familiar figure, I understood, at balls and polo-weeks and country houses. He was an adroit scandal-monger, and would crawl a mile on his belly to anything that

had a title or a million. I had a business introduction
to his firm when I came to London, and he was good
enough to ask me to dinner at his club. There he
showed off at a great rate, and pattered about his
duchesses till the snobbery of the creature turned me
sick. I asked a man afterwards why nobody kicked
him, and was told that Englishmen reverenced the
weaker sex.

Anyhow there he was now, nattily dressed, in a
fine new car, obviously on his way to visit some of
his smart friends. A sudden daftness took me, and in
a second I had jumped into the tonneau and had him
by the shoulder.

'Hullo, Jopley,' I sang out. 'Well met, my lad!' He
got a horrid fright. His chin dropped as he stared at
me. 'Who in the devil are you?' he gasped.

'My name's Hannay,' I said 'From Rhodesia, you
remember.'

'Good God, the murderer!' he choked.

'Just so. And there'll be a second murder, my dear,
if you don't do as I tell you. Give me that coat of
yours. That cap, too.'

He did as bid, for he was blind with terror. Over
my dirty trousers and vulgar shirt I put on his smart
driving-coat, which buttoned high at the top and
thereby hid the deficiencies of my collar. I stuck the
cap on my head, and added his gloves to my get-up.
The dusty roadman in a minute was transformed into
one of the neatest motorists in Scotland. On Mr
Jopley's head I clapped Turnbull's unspeakable hat,
and told him to keep it there.

Then with some difficulty I turned the car. My plan
was to go back the road he had come, for the
watchers, having seen it before, would probably let it
pass unremarked, and Marmie's figure was in no
way like mine.

'Now, my child,' I said, 'sit quite still and be a good boy. I mean you no harm. I'm only borrowing your car for an hour or two. But if you play me any tricks, and above all if you open your mouth, as sure as there's a God above me I'll wring your neck. *Savez?*'

I enjoyed that evening's ride. We ran eight miles down the valley, through a village or two, and I could not help noticing several strange-looking folk lounging by the roadside. These were the watchers who would have had much to say to me if I had come in other garb or company. As it was, they looked incuriously on. One touched his cap in salute, and I responded graciously.

As the dark fell I turned up a side glen which, as I remembered from the map, led into an unfrequented corner of the hills. Soon the villages were left behind, then the farms, and then even the wayside cottage. Presently we came to a lonely moor where the night was blackening the sunset gleam in the bog pools. Here we stopped, and I obligingly reversed the car and restored to Mr Jopley his belongings.

'A thousand thanks,' I said. 'There's more use in you than I thought. Now be off and find the police.'

As I sat on the hillside, watching the tail-light dwindle, I reflected on the various kinds of crime I had now sampled. Contrary to general belief, I was not a murderer, but I had become an unholy liar, a shameless impostor, and a highwayman with a marked taste for expensive motor-cars.

SAMPAN IN THE RIVER

Meindert DeJong

Desperate to escape the Japanese invasion of China during World War II, little Tien Pao and his family have fled in their river boat, or sampan, to the city of Hengyang. Tien Pao's parents find work on an American airfield, and every day they leave Tien Pao all alone to look after the boat. . .

Early the next morning Tien Pao again watched his father and his mother, with the baby sister strapped to her back, clamber through the rain up the long, steep river bank. Tien Pao stood in the opening of the sampan. 'Remember now, you promised. Tomorrow I'm going with you to the great field for aeroplanes.'

They did not hear him in the heavy rain. The sky was black with rain. It almost seemed as if the black sky were in the black river, and there was no sign of dawn. Tien Pao sighed, and shut himself up in the sampan behind the matting in the dreary, clammy dark. He looked wistfully towards the altar and the saucer lamp, but his mother had warned him not to waste oil in the long week before the Americans paid them for their work at the airfield.

The little pig was sleeping. The ducklings sat huddled in the bottom of their dry dishpan. Tien Pao lifted out the ducklings and went outside and scooped water out of the river into the dishpan. Maybe if the ducklings had water they'd start to swim and whisper their soft little peeps. It was so quiet. And if nothing moved, the long day would never move on.

Long before a little daylight came creeping over the river, Tien Pao had dragged out the rice mill, and had begun grinding some rice for the baby sister's evening meal. The dreary grinding at the stone mill seemed to make the time pass even slower, but it was something to do. Tien Pao went to fetch another handful of rice, later he fetched still another handful. He had to stop himself – if he ground anymore, they'd all have to eat babyfood for supper.

Now there was nothing left to do. Tien Pao was regretfully shoving the rice mill under the bench when a mighty thump sent the sampan crashing into the row of sampans. It knocked Tien Pao flat on his back. One of the ducklings spilled out of the dishpan with the splash of water that went over the side. The little pig jumped high and squealed in alarm.

Tien Pao scrambled to his feet. There were strange snortings right beside the sampan. Water gurgled and bubbled. Again there was a crash. Tien Pao clung to the bench with both hands. The other two ducklings splashed over the side in the new tidal wave in the dishpan. Tien Pao could not imagine what was happening. On hands and knees he crawled through the rocking boat, and pulled the mat out of the doorway. What he saw made him laugh. Five water buffaloes had come down the bank to wallow in the swollen river. Only their stretched, snorting noses and long flat horns were above the water. They were playing some kind of stupid cow game – pushing and ramming each other in the water.

Now again a rammed buffalo blundered backwards into the sampan. The sampan rocked wildly on the water. They'd knock it loose from its moorings! Tien Pao reached back into the sampan, grabbed the dishpan, just letting the water splash. He waited for the first hard, bony rump to get within his reach. Then, yelling like mad, he crashed the empty pan down on a buffalo. The dishpan bonged like a temple gong. Five scared buffaloes reared up out of the water; they shoved each other out of the river and up the slippery bank with great alarmed snorts. They clambered clumsily, then the lead buffalo slipped and slid down the bank, bringing the others down. They piled up, heaved themselves to their feet again.

Dishpan in hand, Tien Pao stood laughing at the silly sight. He was still chuckling when he went back into the sampan, after having once more filled the dishpan with water from the river. He set the ducklings in the dishpan, replaced the mat in the doorway. He did not see that the stake by which the sampan was tied to the bank was lying on top of the rain-soaked ground. One of the buffaloes had blundered under the rope, had scraped it over his bony back, and had ripped the stake out of the soggy ground. The rope with the stake lay loose on the watery mud. Nothing held the sampan to the bank. Inside the sampan Tien Pao still sat chuckling. He had not seen it.

Tien Pao sat thinking out just how he'd tell the story of the buffaloes to his father and mother when they came home at night. It had been fun. He was almost sorry that he had scared the buffaloes away so soon. Now the long day loomed before him again.

Tien Pao sat awhile, then he imagined himself hungry. Sure, he felt a little hungry. It couldn't possibly be noon, but it was something to do. He took down the bowl of cold rice his mother had prepared the day before and sat down with it on the floor. To make the simple meal last, he invented a game. He took the ducklings out of the dishpan and placed them around his rice bowl. The ducklings immediately began dipping their little flat bills into the rice. The faster Tien Pao dug with his chopsticks, the faster the ducklings pecked and gobbled. It became a race, but the rice was going too fast that way. The meal had to last.

Tien Pao had another idea. He tried to feed the ducklings with his chopsticks. He tried each duckling in turn, but it didn't work too well, and as he was absorbed with his chopsticks, the little pig unexpectedly rushed in and spoiled the whole game. The pig grabbed the lump of rice between the chopsticks, chopsticks and all. Tien Pao had to work to get the chopsticks from between his teeth. Then, with Tien Pao busy bending the chopsticks back into shape, the little pig pushed his snout into the rice bowl and snatched a big, greedy mouthful. In disgust Tien Pao elbowed the pig away, but there was nothing left in the bowl but a few crumbs. Tien Pao scattered the crumbs on the floor for the ducklings. For punishment he held the little pig over the crumbs, but just out of reach of the scattered rice. The little pig grunted in disgust and greed.

The miserable pig had ended the meal in one blow. Now there was absolutely nothing to do. The ducklings, back in their dishpan, already drifted in their huddled sleep. The pig lay stretched out on his side on the floor. Tien Pao decided he might as well sleep, too. What else was there to do? Using the pig for a pillow, he, too, stretched out on the floor.

He couldn't sleep. At least tomorrow he was going

to the great field for aeroplanes. Tomorrow he'd at last see it, too. The thought made him restless, kept him awake. He tried to imagine from what he'd heard his father and mother say just what an airfield would be like. It seemed a bit odd – a big, grassy field for aeroplanes, as if they were horses or grazing goats. Tien Pao laughed too hard at the silly thought. It wasn't that funny. He began pestering the pig, tickling him on his undersides until the little pig could stand no more. With an annoyed squeal the pig jumped up. Tien Pao's head hit the floor.

In revenge for getting his head thumped, Tien Pao made a wild grab for the pig's hind leg. The little pig squealed wildly, managed to jerk away. He raced through the sampan. Now he seemed to want Tien Pao to chase him – he must be bored, too. But Tien Pao made believe he was sound asleep.

At last the impatient little pig edged back to Tien Pao, nudged him with his snout. Tien Pao reared up and let out such a crazy yell, the startled little animal almost fell over backwards. A wild game began. They raced around the narrow sampan, Tien Pao yelling, the little pig squealing. The sampan rocked on the water with the commotion. It rocked, it inched forward, slid a little away from the bank. The galloping, yelling game went on inside the sampan, and the sampan pulled from under its gangplank. The plank fell on the water with a hard, flat slap, but the yelling Tien Pao did not hear it.

At last the little pig could run no more. His sides heaved, he held his mouth wide open for breath. He threw himself down and lay where he fell. Tien Pao himself lay down, panting. He had to rest for a while.

Under the drumming of the rain on the matting there was not another sound anywhere. In all the sampans people seemed to have gone to sleep in the

long, dull, rainy afternoon. Tien Pao fell asleep.

Quietly the shore end of the gangplank loosed itself from the slippery mud underneath the riverbank as the swollen river rose still higher with the rain. The plank scraped along the sampan; it edged out into the river, shot away as the river current caught it.

Almost as if the sampan had seen its gangplank race away and wanted to go after it, the sampan, too, loosed itself from the watery mud at the river's edge. First it drifted slowly, slowly it twirled. Slowly and quietly it edged along the row of sampans with the rope and stake dangling behind it. Then, like the plank, it was grabbed by the current. It shot away. It was swifter than the plank. It swept under a high, arched bridge. Under the bridge it passed the swiftly riding plank.

An old man under a silk umbrella stepped on to the bridge. In the rain darkness he saw a lone sampan sweeping away downriver. But the wind over the high bridge caught his umbrella. He pulled it down in front of his face and shuffled across the long bridge. When he looked again at the far end of the bridge, the sampan had disappeared. The old man looked at the racing river. He muttered to himself.

In the sampan Tien Pao woke up, but he was still too fuzzy with sleep to get up. From where he lay he idly tried to peer through a crack in the matting at the riverbank to see if it was nearly dark and if it was almost time for his father and mother to come. It felt as if he'd slept long.

He rubbed his eyes. But it was dark! Darker than rain dark. A rushing sound was in his ears! There wasn't any matting at the back of the sampan. The wind had ripped the matting away. There wasn't any riverbank! This was the night! This was the river! This was the sampan rushing headlong down the roaring river in the night!

Tien Pao jumped up. He clutched the side of the racing sampan.

'Mother!'

The wind caught up his shriek, but lost it in the rain.

'Mother!'

Tien Pao began to cry. Then he hopelessly still yelled out one word:

'Father!'

He suddenly was still. Hopeless, numb with fear, he sank to the bottom of the sampan. He did not dare shout again. It was no use. His mother and father couldn't possibly hear. But the Japanese could hear! The river was taking him back – back to the Japanese. With a terrified whimper Tien Pao caught the little pig to him. He shook the pig awake – shook him hard. Then he held him so hard the little pig groaned.

Outside there were only the night and roaring river and rain. Wide-eyed and unseeing, Tien Pao stared into the darkness, clutching his pig. He hugged the little pig until his arms ached. The ache in his throat stayed but he could not cry. He whispered something to the pig. The words made no sense, they had no meaning, but it made him feel a little better to whisper to someone. He did it again. He said: 'Beauty-of-the-Republic.' He whispered it once more as a hard, hurting sob came breaking out of his throat. Tien Pao heard his own whispered words, he wondered at himself for a brief, fleeting moment. He'd said: 'Beauty-of-the-Republic.' He'd called the pig by the name of his baby sister. It was silly, babyish, naming a pig that. No, it wasn't! It felt safer being with something that had a name. He said it aloud: 'Beauty-of-the-Republic.' And somehow it felt safer.

But the little pig, tired of his odd position, wriggled out of Tien Pao's arms, jumped to the floor, scampered to the back of the sampan. 'Beauty-of-the-Republic!' Tien Pao screamed as he lunged after him. He grabbed him by a hind leg, dragged him back. The little pig let out a long, loud squeal. It scared Tien Pao. He caught the pig's snout, held it so fiercely, the little pig had to struggle and scratch and fight to get breath.

'I mustn't yell, and you musn't scream,' Tien Pao whispered in his ear. 'And you can't jump to the bank – there isn't any bank.' With the pig under his arm he crawled to the back of the sampan and pulled in the rope. He crawled back. He kept the little pig pinched between his legs while he unknotted the rope and removed the stake. He doubled the rope, tied one end to the pig's front leg and the other end around his own wrist.

'We have to stay together,' he earnestly whispered. 'We might hit something and smash. We've got to stay together.' He reached back into the sampan,

found the dishpan in the dark, and pulled it tightly against him. He and the pig and ducklings sat in a tight huddle in the centre of the sampan.

The little pig began grunting sleepily. Tien Pao could not let him sleep. He shook him fiercely, but then in regret held him snug in his arms again. 'Beauty-of-the-Republic,' he pleaded. He looked fondly down at the little pig. Somehow calling him that and holding him made it feel a little bit as if he still had a family. And now it didn't sound crazy or silly. But he shouldn't call a pig by his own little sister's name. 'I'll call you – Glory-of-the-Republic,' Tien Pao decided. He peered at the ducklings peeping sleepily in their dishpan. Glory-of-the-Republic and the ducklings – they were his family. It was better, much better than being alone, storming down the river in the pitch-black sampan. 'Glory-of-the-Republic, we've got to stay together,' Tien Pao said tenderly. In the dark he tested the knots in the rope.

The wind began to blow. The wind rushed in with the rain, swept it through the sampan from one end to the other. Tien Pao turned his back to the lashing

rain, bowed his head. Dimly he could see the little mirror in the altar to the river god. His lips moved. 'River god – good river god, the wind. The wind! Make it push the sampan to shore.'

Later the wind on the river must have changed, as the sampan seemed to rush in a great, sweeping curve. Tien Pao was almost sure that now the sampan was racing into another river. But in the new river the wind fell down from the mountains, crashed down on the sampan in one shrieking blow. In one blow it tore the arched roof of mats off the sampan, flung them up, flung them down into the river. The mirror of the altar to the river god smashed to bits on the floor. The sampan rushed along wide open to the sky and slashing rain and wind. Rain hurled against the wooden floor.

Down from the mountains the rain came in sheets, in torrents. In one moment Tien Pao was soaked. He crawled under the bench – there was no other place to crawl for shelter. He crouched under the bench on hands and knees and pulled Glory-of-the-Republic under him to shelter him from the hard, beating rain. He pulled the dishpan before him, kept his hands clenched around the rim.

The rain water rose fast in the open sampan. Under him Glory-of-the-Republic uttered distressed little grunts, but the numbed Tien Pao kept the rope short, kept him where he was. He felt the water flowing over his hands clenched around the dishpan, crawling up his wrists. Now the three ducklings flowed out of the dishpan with the rising rain water. They swam about happily in their new big pool. One behind the other they swam in excited whispering circles through the sampan. Suddenly their peeping stopped, they became very busy. They dived and dipped. Tien Pao could hear the tiny clatter of their bills along the floor under the water.

At first he paid no attention. Suddenly he pushed the pig out of his way. The ducklings were diving for rice! The water had reached the little shelf under the bench and was washing all the ground rice away. All the rice was lost! His only food! But if the water had reached the shelf, it could sink the sampan. Tien Pao grabbed the dishpan and wildly started bailing the rain water overboard. He had a scare when he almost scooped a diving duckling overboard with the water. He went at it more quietly, forced himself to make no loud scraping sounds.

When at last the dishpan began touching the bottom, Tien Pao tried to save some of the gritty rice that had settled to the floor. He found his rice bowl. He drained the watery rice through his fingers, feeling carefully for any glass splinters from the shattered mirror. Crumb by pasty crumb he gathered a half-bowlful of wet rice.

And while Tien Pao worked like that, the rain stopped and light came – morning came to the river.

In the first glimmer of the dawn Tien Pao saw the dim, far banks. It was a wide river. It was three times wider than the river at Hengyang. But when Tien Pao peered ahead under the morning mists floating up from the river, the great river swept into a still wider river. Rivers, Tien Pao knew, widen as they near the sea. And near the sea were the Japanese. Tien Pao's scalp crawled with horror.

Where the two rivers finally met, Tien Pao saw a village loom up in the misty dawn. His own village had been at the corner of two rivers! His mouth dry with fear, Tien Pao stared at the distant village. It couldn't be his village! The Japanese had burned his village to the ground, but in this village the houses still stood.

The sampan swung into the new river. The village came closer. But this wasn't a living village! The houses weren't houses. They were empty, blackened, roofless walls. His village! And there, pacing slowly back and forth along the riverbank, was a Japanese soldier. Behind the sentry lay the gutted village.

Tien Pao crouched low in the sampan, but he couldn't keep himself from peering fearfully over the edge. The soldier stopped, stood looking up the river. He took his rifle down. To Tien Pao, crouched in the approaching sampan, it seemed that the soldier was looking right at him – that a shot must come. He couldn't take his horrified eyes off the soldier. But the sentry merely shifted his rifle to the other shoulder and began pacing again.

It broke the horror spell, and as the sentry shifted the gun, Tien Pao made his move. He slid himself flat in the watery bottom of the sampan. He mustn't crouch, mustn't stare over the edge. He kept one arm tightly over the pig so he wouldn't move. Nothing must move. It must be that the rain mists sifting over the river towards the shore had hidden the flat, roofless sampan from the staring sentry, but the rain was over, the mist was lifting, clear bright light was coming to the river. Nothing must move.

As he lay there motionless, his back exposed to the open sky went rigid with dread. It was again as if he heard the aeroplanes screaming over the treetops, the stutter of bullets, the whining, biting of bullets in the water. He fought an almost insane urge to keep his eyes on the sentry. He hid his face in the crook of his arm, and lay still again.

It seemed hours before Tien Pao at last allowed himself to lift his head and fearfully look back. The village was gone. This was new country completely unknown to him. Tien Pao looked ahead. The river had become fearfully wide – wide and straight. It must be going straight to the sea now. With the wideness of the river the current had spread, the sampan seemed to move more slowly. Straight ahead was a deep bay in the bank of the river – there the water seemed almost quiet. Tien Pao grabbed the dishpan. Stretching flat on his face in the back of the sampan, he held the dishpan at a sharp angle down in the water. With the dishpan as a rudder, the sampan slowly began to respond. Slowly, in a seemingly endless curve, it turned towards the quiet bay. At last the sampan rode into the wide, shallow bay. There was a scraping of sand and gravel as it ground to a stop near the shore.

Tien Pao scooped up the swimming ducklings and set them in the dishpan in the river. He grabbed the little pig, the bowl of watery rice, and jumped into the shallow water. With the rice bowl in one hand, pushing the dishpan ahead of him with the other hand, and tugging Glory-of-the-Republic, splashing snout-deep, behind him, Tien Pao hurried to the silent shore.

The ducklings in the dishpan peered up at Tien Pao with their black beads of eyes; they peeped excited little whispers up at him. Tien Pao stopped. But he couldn't carry a dishpan and ducklings over the mountains! Ducklings were food. If he wrung their necks, he could sling them over his shoulder, and he'd have food for days.

The thought of the three ducklings hanging limp over his shoulder was all of a sudden too much for Tien Pao. He looked at the ducklings, then he shut his eyes tight and gave the dishpan a hard shove back into the bay. Without looking back, Tien Pao climbed up from the river and up the first rocky cliff.

TRAPPED IN HAZELL'S WOOD

Roald Dahl

anny loves to help his father in the garage which his father owns. One evening, after cleaning up an old Baby Austin, Danny's father goes off poaching in Hazell's Wood. In the caravan where they live, Danny waits anxiously for his father's return. . .

Inside the caravan I stood on a chair and lit the oil lamp in the ceiling. I had some weekend homework to do and this was as good a time as any to do it. I laid my books out on the table and sat down. But I found it impossible to keep my mind on my work.

The clock said half-past seven. This was the twilight time. He would be there now. I pictured him in his old navy-blue sweater and peaked cap walking soft-footed up the track towards the wood. He told me he wore the sweater because navy-blue hardly showed up at all in the dark. Black was even better, he said. But he didn't have a black one and navy-blue was next best. The peaked cap was important too, he explained, because the peak cast a shadow over one's face. Just about now he would be wriggling through the hedge and entering the wood. Inside the wood I could see him treading carefully over the leafy ground, stopping, listening, going on again, and all the time searching and searching for the keeper who would somewhere be standing still as a post beside a big tree with a gun under his arm. Keepers hardly move at all when they are in a wood watching for poachers, he had told me. They stand dead still right up against the trunk of a tree and it's not easy to spot a motionless man in that position at twilight when the shadows are as dark as a wolf's mouth.

I closed my books. It was no good trying to work. I decided to go to bed instead. I undressed and put on my pyjamas and climbed into my bunk. I left the lamp burning. Soon I fell asleep.

When I opened my eyes again, the oil-lamp was still glowing and the clock on the wall said ten minutes past two.

Ten minutes past two!

I jumped out of my bunk and looked into the bunk above mine. It was empty.

He had promised he would be home by ten-thirty at the latest, and he never broke promises.

He was nearly four hours overdue!

At that moment, a frightful sense of doom came over me. Something really had happened to him this time. I felt quite certain of it.

Hold it, I told myself. Don't get panicky. Last week you got all panicky and you made a bit of a fool of yourself.

Yes, but last week was a different thing altogether. He had made no promises to me last week. This time he had said, 'I promise I'll be back by ten-thirty.' Those were his exact words. And he never, absolutely never, broke a promise.

I looked again at the clock. He had left the caravan at six, which meant *he had been gone over eight hours!*

It took me two seconds to decide what I should do.

Very quickly I stripped off my pyjamas and put on my shirt and my jeans. Perhaps the keepers had shot him up so badly he couldn't walk. I pulled my sweater over my head. It was neither navy-blue nor black. It was a sort of pale brown. It would have to do. Perhaps he was lying in the wood bleeding to death. My sneakers were the wrong colour too. They were white. But they were also dirty and that took a lot of the whiteness away. How long would it take me to get to the wood? An hour and a half. Less if I ran most of the way, but not much less. As I bent down to tie the laces, I noticed my hands were shaking. And my stomach had that awful prickly feeling as though it were full of small needles.

I ran down the steps of the caravan and across to the workshop to get the torch. A torch is a good companion when you are alone outdoors at night and I wanted it with me. I grabbed the torch and went out of the workshop. I paused for a moment beside the pumps. The moon had long since disappeared but the sky was clear and a great mass of stars was wheeling above my head. There was no wind at all, no sound of any kind. To my right, going away into the blackness of the countryside, lay the lonely road that led to the dangerous wood.

Six-and-a-half miles.

Thank heavens I knew the way.

But it was going to be a long hard slog. I must try to keep a good steady pace and not run myself to a standstill in the first mile.

At that point a wild and marvellous idea came to me.

Why shouldn't I go in the Baby Austin? I really did know how to drive. My father had always allowed me to move the cars around when they came in for repair. He let me drive them into the workshop and back them out again afterwards. And sometimes I drove one of them slowly around the pumps in first gear. I loved doing it. And I would get there much quicker if I went by car. This was an emergency. If he was wounded and bleeding badly, then every minute counted. I had never driven on the road, but I would surely not meet any other cars at this time of night. I would go very slowly and keep close to the hedge on the proper side.

I went back to the workshop and switched on the light. I opened the double doors. I got into the driver's seat of the Baby Austin. I turned on the ignition key. I pulled out the choke. I found the starter-button and pressed it. The motor coughed once, then started.

Now for the lights. There was a pointed switch on the dash-board and I turned it to S for sidelights only. The sidelights came on. I felt for the clutch pedal with my toe. I was just able to reach it, but I had to point my toe if I wanted to press it all the way down. I pressed it down. Then I slipped the gear-lever into reverse. Slowly I backed the car out of the workshop.

I left her ticking over and went back to switch off the workshop light. It was better to keep everything looking as normal as possible. The filling-station was in darkness now except for a dim light coming from the caravan where the little oil-lamp was still burning. I decided to leave that on.

I got back into the car. I closed the door. The sidelights were so dim I hardly knew they were there. I switched on the headlamps. That was better. I searched for the dipper with my foot. I found it. I tried it and it worked. I put the headlamps on full. If I met another car, I must remember to dip them, although actually they weren't bright enough to dazzle a cockroach. They didn't give any more light than a couple of good torches.

I pressed down the clutch pedal again and pushed the gear-lever into first. This was it. My heart was thumping away so fiercely I could hear it in my throat. Ten yards away lay the main road. It was as dark as doomsday. I released the clutch very slowly. At the same time, I pressed down just a fraction of an inch on the accelerator with my right toe, and stealthily, oh most wonderfully, the little car began to lean forward and steal into motion. I pressed a shade harder on the accelerator. We crept out of the filling-station on to the dark deserted road.

I will not pretend I wasn't petrified. I was. But mixed in with the awful fear was a glorious feeling of excitement. Most of the really exciting things we do in our lives scare us to death. They wouldn't be exciting if they didn't. I sat very stiff and upright in my seat, gripping the steering-wheel tight with both hands. My eyes were about level with the top of the steering-wheel. I could have done with a cushion to raise me up higher, but it was too late for that.

The road seemed awfully narrow in the dark. I knew there was room enough for two cars to pass each other. I had seen them from the filling-station doing it a million times. But it didn't look that way to me from where I was. At any moment something with blazing headlamps might come roaring towards me at sixty miles an hour, a heavy lorry or one of those big long-distance buses that travel through the night full of passengers. Was I too much in the middle of the road? Yes, I was. But I didn't want to pull in closer for fear of hitting the bank. If I hit the bank and bust the front axle, then all would be lost and I would never get my father home.

The motor was beginning to rattle and shake. I was still in first gear. It was vital to change up into second otherwise the engine would get too hot. I knew how the change was done but I had never actually tried doing it. Around the filling-station I had always

stayed in first gear.

Well, here goes.

I eased my foot off the accelerator. I pressed the clutch down and held it there. I found the gear-lever and pulled it straight back, from first into second. I released the clutch and pressed on the accelerator. The little car leaped forward as though it had been stung. We were in second gear.

What speed were we going? I glanced at the speedometer. It was lit up very faintly, but I was able to read it. It said fifteen miles an hour. Good. That was quite fast enough. I would stay in second gear. I started figuring out how long it would take me to do six miles travelling at fifteen miles an hour.

At sixty miles an hour, six miles would take six minutes.

At thirty, it would take twice as long, twelve minutes.

At fifteen, it would take twice as long again, twenty-four minutes.

I kept going. I knew every bit of the road, every curve and every little rise and dip. Once a fox flashed out of the hedge in front of me and ran across the road with his long bushy tail streaming out behind him. I saw him clearly in the glow of my headlamps. His fur was red-brown and he had a white muzzle. It was a thrilling sight. I began to worry about the motor. I knew very well it would be certain to overheat if I drove for long in either first or second gear. I was in second. I must now change up into third. I took a deep breath and grasped the gear-lever again. Foot off the accelerator. Clutch in. Gear-lever up and across and up again. Clutch out. I had done it! I pressed down on the accelerator. The speedometer crept up to thirty. I gripped the wheel very tight with both hands and stayed in the middle of the road. At this rate I would soon be there.

Hazell's Wood was not on the main road. To reach it you had to turn left through a gap in the hedge and go uphill over a bumpy track for about a quarter of a mile. If the ground had been wet, there would have been no hope of getting there in a car. But there hadn't been any rain for a week and the ground would surely be hard and dry. I figured I must be getting pretty close to the turning place now. I must watch out for it carefully. It would be easy to miss it. There was no gate or anything else to indicate where it was. It was simply a small gap in the hedge just wide enough to allow farm tractors to go through.

Suddenly, far ahead of me, just below the rim of the night sky, I saw a splash of yellow light. I watched it, trembling. This was something I had been dreading all along. Very quickly the light got brighter and brighter, and nearer and nearer, and in a few seconds it took shape and became the long white beam of headlamps from a car rushing towards me.

My turning place must be very close now. I was desperate to reach it and swing off the road before that monster reached me. I pressed my foot hard down for more speed. The little engine roared. The speedometer needle went from thirty to thirty-five and then to forty. But the other car was closing fast. Its headlamps were like two dazzling white eyes. They grew bigger and bigger and suddenly the whole road in front of me was lit up as clear as daylight, and *swish!* the thing went past me like a bullet. It was so close I felt the wind of it through my open window. And in that tiny fraction of a second when the two of us were alongside one another, I caught a glimpse of its white-painted body and I knew it was the police.

I didn't dare look round to see if they were stopping and coming back after me. I was certain they would stop. Any policeman in the world would stop if he suddenly passed a small boy in a tiny car chugging along a lonely road at half-past two in the morning. My only thought was to get away, to escape, to vanish, though heaven knows how I was going to do that. I pressed my foot harder still on the accelerator. Then all at once I saw in my own dim headlamps the tiny gap in the hedge on my left-hand side. There wasn't time to brake or slow down, so I just yanked the wheel hard over and prayed. The little car swerved violently off the road, leaped through the gap, hit the rising ground, bounced high in the air, then skidded round sideways behind the hedge and stopped.

The first thing I did was to switch off all my lights. I am not quite sure what made me do this except that I knew I must hide and I knew that if you are hiding from someone in the dark you don't shine lights all over the place to show where you are. I sat very still in my dark car. The hedge was a thick one and I couldn't see through it. The car had bounced and skidded sideways in such a way that it was now right off the track. It was behind the hedge and in a sort of field. It was facing back towards the filling-station, tucked in very close to the hedge. I could hear the police car. It had pulled up about fifty yards down the road, and now it was backing and turning. The road was far too narrow for it to turn round in one go. Then the roar from the motor got louder and he came back fast with engine revving and headlamps blazing. He flashed past the place where I was hiding and raced away into the night.

That meant the policeman had not seen me swing off the road.

But he was certain to come back again looking for me. And if he came back slowly enough he would probably see the gap. He would stop and get out of his car. He would walk through the gap and look behind the hedge, and then . . . then his torch would shine in my face and he would say, 'What's going on, sonny? What's the big idea? Where do you think you're going? Whose car is this? Where do you live? Where are your parents?' He would make me go with him to the police-station, and in the end they would get the whole story out of me, and my father would be ruined.

I sat quiet as a mouse and waited. I waited for a long time. Then I heard the sound of the motor coming back again in my direction. It was making a terrific noise. He was going flat out. He whizzed past me like a rocket. The way he was gunning that motor told me he was a very angry man. He must have been a very puzzled man, too. Perhaps he was thinking he had seen a ghost. A ghost boy driving a ghost car.

I waited to see if he would come back again.

He didn't come.

I switched on my lights.

I pressed the starter. She started at once.

But what about the wheels and the chassis? I felt sure something must have got broken when she jumped off the road on to the cart-track.

I put her into gear and very gently began to ease her forward. I listened carefully for horrid noises. There were none. I managed to get her off the grass and back on to the track.

I drove very slowly now. The track was extremely rough and rutted, and the slope was pretty steep. The little car bounced and bumped all over the place, but she kept going. Then at last, ahead of me and over to the right, looking like some gigantic black creature crouching on the crest of the hill, I saw Hazell's Wood.

Soon I was there. Immense trees rose up towards the sky all along the right-hand side of the track. I stopped the car. I switched off the motor and the lights. I got out, taking the torch with me.

There was the usual hedge dividing the wood from the track. I squeezed my way through it and suddenly I was right inside the wood. When I looked up the trees had closed in above my head like a prison roof and I couldn't see the smallest patch of sky or a single star. I couldn't see anything at all. The darkness was so solid around me I could almost touch it.

'Dad!' I called out. 'Dad, are you there?'

My small high voice echoed through the forest and faded away. I listened for an answer, but none came.

I cannot possibly describe to you what it felt like to be standing alone in the pitchy blackness of that

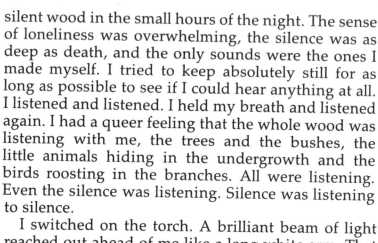

silent wood in the small hours of the night. The sense of loneliness was overwhelming, the silence was as deep as death, and the only sounds were the ones I made myself. I tried to keep absolutely still for as long as possible to see if I could hear anything at all. I listened and listened. I held my breath and listened again. I had a queer feeling that the whole wood was listening with me, the trees and the bushes, the little animals hiding in the undergrowth and the birds roosting in the branches. All were listening. Even the silence was listening. Silence was listening to silence.

I switched on the torch. A brilliant beam of light reached out ahead of me like a long white arm. That was better. Now at any rate I could see where I was going.

The keepers would also see. But I didn't care about the keepers any more. The only person I cared about was my father. I wanted him back.

I kept the torch on and went deeper into the wood.

'Dad!' I shouted. 'Dad! It's Danny! Are you there?'

I didn't know which direction I was going in. I just went on walking and calling out, walking and calling; and each time I called, I would stop and listen. But no answer came.

After a time, my voice began to go all trembly. I started to say silly things like, 'Oh Dad, please tell me where you are! Please answer me! Please, oh please...' And I knew that if I wasn't careful, the sheer hopelessness of it all would get the better of me and I would simply give up and lie down under the trees.

'Are you there, Dad? Are you there?' I shouted. 'It's Danny!'

I stood still, listening, listening, listening, and in the silence that followed, I heard or thought I heard the faint, but oh so faint, sound of a human voice.

I froze and kept listening.

Yes, there it was again.

I ran towards the sound. 'Dad!' I shouted. 'It's Danny! Where are you?'

I stopped again and listened.

This time the answer came just loud enough for me to hear the words. 'I'm here!' the voice called out. 'Over here!'

It was him!

I was so excited my legs began to get all shaky.

'Where are you, Danny?' my father called out.

'I'm here, Dad! I'm coming.'

With the beam of the torch shining ahead of me, I ran towards the voice. The trees were bigger here and spaced farther apart. The ground was a carpet of brown leaves from last year and was good to run on. I didn't call out any more after that. I simply dashed ahead.

And all at once, his voice was right in front of me. 'Stop, Danny, stop!' he shouted.

I stopped dead. I shone the torch over the ground. I couldn't see him.

'Where are you, Dad?'

'I'm down here. Come forward slowly. But be careful. Don't fall in.'

I crept forward. Then I saw the pit. I went to the edge of it and shone the light downward and there was my father. He was sitting on the floor of the pit and he looked up into the light and said, 'Hello, my marvellous darling. Thank you for coming.'

'Are you all right, Dad?'

'My ankle seems to be broken,' he said. 'It happened when I fell in.'

The pit had been dug in the shape of a square, with each side about six feet long. But it was the

depth of it that was so awful. It was at least twelve feet deep. The sides had been cut straight down into the earth, presumably with a mechanical shovel, and no man could have climbed out of it without help.

'Does it hurt?' I asked.

'Yes,' he said. 'It hurts a lot. But don't worry about that. The point is, *I've got to get out of here before morning.* The keepers know I'm here and they're coming back for me as soon as it gets light.'

'Did they dig the hole to catch people?' I asked.

'Yes,' he said.

I shone my light around the top of the pit and saw how the keepers had covered it over with sticks and leaves and how the whole thing had collapsed when my father stepped on it. It was the kind of trap hunters in Africa dig to catch wild animals.

'Do the keepers know who you are?' I asked.

'No,' he said. 'Two of them came and shone a light down on me but I covered my face with my arms and they couldn't recognise me. I heard them trying to guess. They were guessing all sorts of names but they didn't mention mine. Then one of them shouted, "We'll find out who you are all right in the morning, my lad. And guess who's coming with us to fish you out?" I didn't answer. I didn't want them to hear my voice. "We'll tell you who's coming," he said. "Mr Victor Hazell himself is coming with us to say hello to you!" And the other one said, "Boy, I hate to think what he's going to do when he gets his hands on you!" They both laughed and then they went away. Ouch! My poor ankle!'

'Have the keepers gone, Dad?'

'Yes,' he said. 'They've gone for the night.'

I was kneeling on the edge of the pit. I wanted so badly to go down and comfort him, but that would have been madness.

'What time is it?' he said. 'Shine the light down so I can see.' I did as he asked. 'It's ten to three,' he said. 'I must be out of here before sunrise.'

'Dad,' I said.

'Yes?'

'I brought the car. I came in the Baby Austin.'

'You *what*?' he cried.

'I wanted to get here quickly so I just drove it out of the workshop and came straight here.'

He sat there staring at me. I kept the torch pointed to one side of him so as not to dazzle his eyes.

'You mean you actually drove here in the Baby Austin?'

'Yes.'

'You're crazy,' he said. 'You're absolutely plumb crazy.'

'It wasn't difficult,' I said.

'You could have been killed,' he said. 'If anything had hit you in that little thing, you'd have been smashed to smithereens.'

'It went fine, Dad.'

'Where is it now?'

'Just outside the wood on the bumpy track.'

His face was all puckered up with pain and as white as a sheet of paper. 'Are you all right?' I asked.

'Yes,' he said. 'I'm fine.' He was shivering all over though it was a warm night.

'If we could get you out, I'm sure I could help you to the car,' I said. 'You could lean on me and hop on one leg.'

'I'll never get out of here without a ladder,' he said.

'Wouldn't a rope do?' I asked.

'A rope!' he said. 'Yes, of course! A rope would do it! There's one in the Baby Austin! It's under the back seat! Mr Pratchett always carries a tow-rope in case of a breakdown.'

'I'll get it,' I said. 'Wait there, Dad.'

I left him and ran back the way I had come, shining the torch ahead of me. I found the car. I lifted up the back seat. The tow-rope was there, tangled up with the jack and the wheel-brace. I got it out and slung it over my shoulder. I wriggled through the hedge and ran back into the wood.

'Where are you, Dad?' I called out.

'Over here,' he answered.

With his voice to guide me, I had no trouble finding him this time. 'I've got the rope,' I said.

'Good. Now tie one end of it to the nearest tree.'

Using the torch all the time, I tied one end of the rope round the nearest tree. I lowered the other end down to my father in the pit. He grasped it with both hands and hauled himself up into a standing position. He stood only on his right leg. He kept his left foot off the ground by bending his knee.

'Jeepers,' he said. 'This hurts.'

'Do you think you can make it, Dad?'

'I've got to make it,' he said. 'Is the rope tied properly?'

'Yes.'

I lay on my stomach with my hands dangling down into the pit. I wanted to help pull him up as soon as he came within reach. I kept the torch on him all the time.

'I've got to climb this with hands only,' he said.

'You can do it,' I told him.

I saw his knuckles tighten as he gripped the rope. Then he came up, hand over hand, and as soon as he was within reach I got hold of one of his arms and pulled for all I was worth. He came over the top edge of the pit sliding on his chest and stomach, him pulling on the rope and me pulling on his arm. He lay on the ground, breathing fast and loud.

'You've done it!' I said.

'Let me rest a moment.'

I waited, kneeling beside him.

'All right,' he said. 'Now for the next bit. Give me a hand, Danny. You'll have to do most of the work from now on.'

I helped him to keep his balance as he got up on to his one good foot. 'Which side do you want me on?' I asked.

'On my right,' he said. 'Otherwise you'll keep knocking against my bad ankle.'

I moved up close to his right side and he put both his hands on my shoulders.

'Go on, Dad,' I said. 'You can lean harder than that.'

'Shine the light forward so we can see where we're going,' he said.

I did as he asked.

He tried a couple of hops on his right foot.

'All right?' I asked him.

'Yes,' he said. 'Let's go.'

Holding his left foot just clear of the ground and leaning on me with both hands, he began to hop forward on one leg. I shuffled along beside him, trying to go exactly the speed he wanted.

'Say when you want a rest.'

'Now,' he said. We stopped. 'I've got to sit down,' he said. I helped him to lower himself to the ground. His left foot dangled helplessly on its broken ankle, and every time it touched the ground he jumped with pain. I sat beside him on the brown leaves that covered the floor of the wood. The sweat was pouring down his face.

'Does it hurt terribly, Dad?'

'It does when I hop.' he said. 'Each time I hop, it jars it.'

He sat on the ground resting for several minutes.

'Let's try again,' he said.

I helped him up and off we went. This time I put an arm round his waist to give him extra support. He put his right arm round my shoulders and leaned on me hard. It went better that way. But boy, was he heavy. My legs kept bending and buckling with each hop.

Hop . . .

Hop . . .

Hop . . .

'Keep going,' he gasped. 'Come on. We can make it.'

'There's the hedge,' I said, waving the torch. 'We're nearly there.'

Hop . . .

Hop . . .

Hop . . .

When we reached the hedge, my legs gave way and we both crashed to the ground.

'I'm sorry,' I said.

'It's O.K. Can you help me get through the hedge?'

I'm not quite sure how he and I got through that hedge. He crawled a bit and I pulled a bit, and little by little we squeezed through and out the other side on to the track. The tiny car was only ten yards away.

We sat on the grassy bank under the hedge to get a breather. His watch said it was nearly four o'clock in the morning. The sun would not be up for another two hours, so we had plenty of time.

'Shall I drive?' I asked.

'You'll have to,' he said. 'I've only got one foot.'

I helped him to hop over to the car, and after a bit of a struggle he managed to get in. His left leg was doubled up underneath his right leg and the whole thing must have been agony for him. I got into the driver's seat beside him.

'The rope,' I said. 'We left it behind.'

'Forget it,' he said. 'It doesn't matter.'

I started the motor and switched on the head-lamps. I backed the car and turned it round and soon we were heading downhill on the bumpy track.

DOLPHIN TO THE RESCUE

Jill Paton Walsh

 t is 1940, and the British army has been forced to retreat across France to the port of Dunkirk. John Aston, too young to fight in the war, is determined to help rescue the stranded soldiers. Taking the family boat, the *Dolphin*, he and his friend Pat have sailed together from Kent across the grey waters of the English Channel . . .

The coast of France started as a thin line of mist on the horizon. It was mid-morning when it became clear in the circle of John's binoculars. The country behind the coastline was flat, for there were no hills to be seen, but there were a lot of rolling dunes and wide beaches, stretching for miles. Scanning this alien shore John saw a group of houses on the beach; the sea-side end of a small town.

They were still following the route of many companion ships and boats. They had come much farther north than John had expected, going round the Goodwin sands, and then striking southeast towards France. John supposed that the German guns at Calais had closed the more direct route. Now they were moving in southwards, and a great cloud of black smoke a few miles to the right must mask the town and port at Dunkirk.

The sun was shining. The whole scene looked like one of those great paintings of sea-battles, with modern ships instead of galleons. All around them, up and down the coast as far as they could see, there were ships of all sizes. Big naval ships painted silver-grey were standing offshore, and among them a motley collection of cargo and passenger ships. Beyond them was a stretch of patchy water, blue and indigo, and green in the warm light. And across these wide shallows hundreds of little ships were swarming. There were wrecks too; small boats capsized and drifting, and larger ones grounded and smashed. They sailed through a great patch of floating oil, which stuck to *Dolphin's* paint. And there seemed to be a lot of oil washed up on the beaches; irregular dark shiny patches spreading over the sands to the water's edge. The beach was littered with abandoned lorries and tanks. It all looked very confused.

But it was clear enough what the small boats were doing; they were ferrying to and fro between the shore and the big destroyers and great ships which could not get farther in.

They took *Dolphin* close under the bows of a great destroyer riding at anchor in the sea lanes, and moved towards the shore. Then they saw that the dark patches on the beaches were moving; flowing slowly like spilt water on a flat plate. It wasn't oil; it was great crowds of men. They stood in wide masses on the sands, and the sun struck a dull metallic glint off their steel helmets. Great groups of them moved slowly down towards the water's edge. Long lines of them snaked from behind the dunes, and the head of some of the lines stretched out into the water. They had waded out shoulder deep, and they stood there, looking all one way – seawards.

John took *Dolphin* in towards one of these lines of men. They could hear the distant noise of guns – a low rumble and now and then a big bang, muffled by distance. But somewhere overhead there was also a droning sound. It got louder and nearer. Looking up, John saw a great swarm of black planes coming from the landward sky. On the beaches men were running for shelter among the dunes, or flinging themselves on their faces in the sand. The planes swooped down, diving low, and flying along the line of the beaches. John saw the black bombs falling in diagonal formation from the swiftly moving planes. A line of fountain-like upward spurts of sand ran along the beach, among the groups of helpless men. From the heart of each jet of sand came a flash of fire, and clouds of thick black smoke. A man with his body stiffly spreadeagled was thrown high in the air, and shot backwards twenty yards from one of them. Then the noise of the explosions crashed round *Dolphin*, wiping all other sounds out entirely, and the beach they were heading for disappeared behind a thick blanket of smoke, which rolled across the water to meet them. A great blast of air smote *Dolphin*, and rocked her violently, and then they were wrapped in blinding, choking smoke.

They coughed and rubbed their eyes. Pat was saying something, but there was only a deafening ringing noise in John's ears. Helplessly he watched Pat's lips moving. The smoke rolled over them and away. They could see to the left now flashes of fire from the muzzles of skyward guns behind the long mole of Dunkirk harbour. A long mole extended seawards on the near side of the harbour, and large ships were tied up there. From the decks of these great ships avenging guns stammered angry retorts into the sky.

On the beaches men were getting to their feet again, and stumbling back into formation. From among them a number of pairs of men were tramping wearily up the beach towards the line of buildings, each pair with a limp body extended between them. The sun broke through the smoke in misty patches over them.

The planes did not go when they had dropped their bombs. They came back again and again, flying low over the beaches and the shallows, machine-gunning the soldiers and the little boats. A hissing line of bullets spattered the water just in front of *Dolphin's* prow.

John's hands were clenched on the wheel, but his arms were shaking violently from shoulder to wrist. He could hear his teeth chattering, and a hard lump had grown in his stomach, and was pressing against his ribs, so that he had to force himself to breathe. He stood at the wheel, shaking, and *Dolphin* moved steadily in towards the shore. A smoky haze blurred the whole scene. A choking, bitter smell of burning smarted in John's nostrils at every breath. Pat had gone white, and was crouched down against the bench. His pale eyes looked dark; the pupils were widened with fear. John fixed his eyes on a point on the beach ahead, and tried to steer for it, though he could scarcely make his trembling arms move his clenched fists. A lifeboat, full of soldiers, was just being pushed out into the waves ahead of him. He steered to come in beside it.

The planes were coming back again. The noise of their engines as they plunged low over the sands roared in his ears. He looked, and saw one of them coming straight towards *Dolphin*. He flung himself on the cockpit floor, and at the same moment Pat dropped down beside him, and the wave of noise and the sharp cracking of the plane's machine guns went over and past them. They were still alive. They got up.

Where the lifeboat had been there was a blazing wall of flame on the water. Someone was screaming. The flame floated towards them, and sank. John took the wheel, and brought *Dolphin* on course again. She chugged slowly through charred lumps of floating driftwood, until a gentle scrape on *Dolphin*'s keel told him she had grounded. The tide was low, and a stretch of shallow water still lay between them and the sand. John put the engine out of gear. The two boys stood and looked round. The water was full of floating bodies. They stained the froth on the waves with faintly visible red streaks. They rolled to and fro in the surf. Some of the soldiers waiting in the line on the beach had run forward, and were dragging limp wounded figures from the water.

The hard lump in John's stomach suddenly lurched up his throat. He staggered to the side, doubled up, and vomited into the water. As he hung there the body of a man with no face floated by, smelling of charred flesh. He was instantly doubled up again, retching on an empty stomach. Then Pat's hand was on his shoulder, pulling him up.

'Snap out of it, mate. Here's some poor bastards

wanting a lift out of this.' Pat's voice came from far away, sounding tight, and unduly loud.

A group of soldiers were wading out towards them, holding their guns over their heads. They came right up to *Dolphin*, and stood waiting waist deep in the sea. Pat took their guns, and John told two of them to hang on to one side, to steady *Dolphin*, while others scrambled over the other side. The water poured from their clothes on to the cockpit floor. They took eight on board, and then John thought they were low enough in the water, and turned the others away. The men who were left pushed *Dolphin* off the sand, grunting under the strain, for she was weighed down now, and turned to scramble through the waves to the beach again.

An agonized expression crossed Pat's face as they went.

'We'll come back for you!' he called to their retreating backs.

'If you don't get sent to the bottom first!' said one of the soldiers beside him.

John was getting used to the different feel of *Dolphin* with her heavy load on board. She was sluggish, and slower to respond to her wheel. Still,

when he gave her full power she roared away from the terrible beach towards the tall destroyer waiting off shore.

Over the side of the destroyer hung great swathes of coarse rope netting, draping her wall of riveted plates from stem to stern. Small boats bobbed alongside her all the way, and out of them swarms of soldiers scrambled up the netting, to be pulled over the rails to the decks. John took *Dolphin* up alongside, nosing carefully between two drifters, from whose crowded decks hundreds of climbers were slowly and jerkily heaving themselves away. *Dolphin*'s eight men clambered out of her, making her rock and sway with their movements, and merged with the throng.

Gently John backed *Dolphin* away. When he was clear he gave the wheel to Pat, and looked back at the destroyer through his binoculars. Absurdly, he caught himself trying to find the men they had just put safely on board, but of course on the thickly crowded decks he could not find them. He picked out somewhere amidships a little board with the name WAKEFUL on it in brass letters. At her bows she carried her code number, painted in huge white letters. John regarded her with satisfaction. She was big, and strong, and armed with her own guns, and the men on board her were going safely home.

As they went back towards the beach, leaving a foaming wake behind them, the attack began again. But this time it was different. John felt oddly numb, almost lightheaded. He saw the exposed position of his own body, sitting in *Dolphin*'s cockpit, as though he were outside himself, seeing the danger from a safe place a little way off. It wasn't really him being fired at; he was somebody else; somebody he didn't really care about much. Pat held the wheel quite steady, and John could hear him in the brief gaps between the deafening noise of exploding shells, cursing volubly in his everyday voice. John listened to the stream of foul language with admiration. He himself knew very few rude words.

The continued shattering noise, the confusion, and this strange feeling of being outside himself, numbed, moving in a daze, blurred John's memories of the hours that followed, so that he could remember them only in patches, and could not have said clearly exactly what they did. They did what all the others were doing; they went in to the beach, picked up a load of men, and took them to the *Wakeful*. They did it again and again, for hours on end, and John's memory would not sort one journey from another; they were all alike.

He remembered heaving wet bodies over the side into the cockpit. He remembered how they made

Dolphin take eight men; two on each bunk, two on the cabin floor, two on the benches round the cockpit. Pat kept wanting to pack men in standing up, and so take more, but John was worried about the possibility of capsizing or foundering, if they loaded her too much; as it was she hadn't been built to take eight.

He remembered the roar of the engine, and the swoosh of water as they raced out to the destroyer. Then the grey towering wall of riveted steel, the swinging nets and ladders, the dipping and rocking of *Dolphin* as tired men dragged themselves clumsily out of her and up the side of their homeward-bound ship. And then they went back for more.

Sometimes they went in sunlight, sometimes in black smoke. There were hundreds of other boats bustling along, loaded with men, standing so thick on their decks that they couldn't move without pushing one of their number into the water. The buzzing planes overhead did their best to thin them out. John remembered seeing men falling from the decks of a drifter which was getting peppered with bullets. He felt a wave of anger against the German pilots who shot down such helpless victims. Then he realized that our own pilots would do the same, if the positions of the two armies were reversed. And it struck him suddenly that it was this sort of thing which Andrew had refused to do. For the first time a glimmer of understanding of Andrew's ideas entered his head. But he had no time to think about it. The next second a crackle, a smacking splintering noise of *Dolphin*'s timbers sent him scrambling forward. There was no bad damage done, but a line of holes disfigured the foredeck. Pat made an obscene gesture at the sky. He looked extremely cheerful and quite unafraid. *There is at least as much courage in his bucket,*

John thought, *as in mine. More, probably.*

Although it was for the sake of all those soldiers that they were there at all, John remembered least of all about the boatloads of men. They were all tired, and wet and cold. Tired most of all. Not the tiredness which makes one sleepy, but a terrible weariness of body and mind, which made them slow in all their movements, and glazed their eyes, and made their faces blank. Pat was very good at managing them. He called the men 'Mate!' and the officers 'gaffer!' and he shouted 'One more inside!' and 'Hold tight!' just like the conductor of a London bus. He raised grins on tired faces, and nobody seemed to mind doing what he told them.

Of course, some of the passengers caught John's attention, and so he remembered them later. One officer said to him, 'I've got a boy about your age,' and produced a soaking wet snapshot to show him. It was of a boy in scout's uniform. There was one group who came aboard every one still carrying pack and rifle, unlike most. In charge of them was a very quiet officer, and a very fierce sergeant, with a round baby face, who yelled at them as though he had them on parade. They waded into the water in a line as straight as a ruler, and they were much more cheerful than most. They even sang as *Dolphin* took them across to safety in the *Wakeful*. The song was about the round-faced sergeant. It went to the tune of 'It's a long way to Tipperary'. The words made even Pat raise his eyebrows.

Towards evening, in one of Pat's spells at the wheel John poured some of Crossman's soup into mugs for supper. They drank soup and ate biscuit without stopping; one hand was enough to steady *Dolphin*'s wheel. They had got used to noise, and the gunshot, and the blast from bombs and shells. They didn't jump any more, they just carried on. But the evening seemed long. They were very tired now. But at last dusk crept up upon them.

And with the dusk, slowly, so that they hardly noticed it at first, the fighting died down. No more planes came over, the guns on shore fired only sporadically, and there was a lull. They went back to the beach in the unaccustomed quiet, straining their eyes in the half-light. A small motor-cruiser which had worked beside them all day was going in the same direction a little way off on the port side. Looking towards her John saw a dark round shadow bobbing in the water in front of her. The next instant she had struck it.

The explosion stunned John. He struggled to see and hear, to realize what had happened. A great wave had washed over *Dolphin*, and he was standing in a few inches of water.

'Pat!' he called. 'Pat, where are you?'

'Here,' said a voice at his feet. Pat had been knocked over by the blast. He scrambled up again, and they looked for the little cruiser. There was not the smallest trace of her. Pat was looking at John in alarm. And John realized that there was a nasty hot, wet feeling in his left arm. He looked down at it, and saw that he was pouring with blood. He felt weak and faint.

Pat did not panic. He got John lying on a bunk, and pulled his arm out of the sleeve of his sweater. He opened the first aid box Crossman had given them. There was a ragged piece of metal stuck in John's upper arm. It was bleeding profusely. Somehow Pat got the thing out. John was looking the other way, biting his lip. It didn't hurt as much as he feared; it was still numb, but the iodine Pat used to clean it up with hurt so much he could hardly stop himself crying out. Pat put a lot of bandage round his arm, and then got the brandy bottle, and insisted that John drank some.

'I'll be all right now,' said John, getting to his feet. 'Thank goodness it was my left arm, and not my right.' As he spoke they heard shouting, coming from just outside. *Dolphin* had been drifting, and had nearly run aground on the beach. And a mob of soldiers were scrambling out towards her, shouting. 'A boat! A boat!'

John grabbed the wheel, and swung it hard round. The prow turned away from the beach, bringing her sideways on the shore. A stab of pain from his shoulder stopped John's hand halfway to the switch to put the engine on. A dozen hands grabbed *Dolphin*. She tiled down towards them. A rabble of hysterical men were all trying to board her at once.

'Let go!' cried John. 'You'll capsize her!' Pat grabbed a saucepan from the galley, and laid about him like a fishwife, smashing at the knuckles of the raiders, banging them till they let go. Cries and curses rang through the growing darkness.

Suddenly a voice from the shore cried, 'Let go that boat!' A man waded out towards them. He was only a private, but he still had his gun. One of the mob had succeeded in getting aboard. The newcomer looked at him.

'You're an officer, aren't you? Where are your men?' There was no answer. Then, very slowly, the officer got over the side, and let himself down into the water. He waded away towards the beach.

'Right. One at a time now.' The private got them aboard at gun point. 'Had a rough time, this lot,' he observed to Pat, as though talking about the weather. But now they were aboard they seemed just like the rest; tired, silent, wet, with that expression half-way

between blankness and patience on their faces.

John put *Dolphin* full speed ahead, and made for *Wakeful* again.

'You all right?' asked Pat anxiously.

'Fine,' said John. But his arm hurt, and he let Pat take the wheel. Pat managed it well, even the tricky manoeuvre edging up to the side of the destroyer.

'Don't take long to learn to drive these things,' he observed.

John grinned. 'Wait till you meet some real weather!' he said.

When they reached *Wakeful*, her officers were leaning over the rail. 'Last few now,' they were calling down. 'We can't take any more. We'll be back tomorrow, God willing!'

Pat helped their passengers on to the ladders. Looking up to see them go, John saw stars pricking the wide black sky. His legs felt soft and bendy. He sat down. Under his instructions Pat took *Dolphin* out half a mile, to the sand-bar which bounded the sea-road along the shore. Here the water was shallow, and they let out the sea anchor among a group of drifters and tugs, whose crews were also taking a brief rest, under cover of the welcome night.

They drank some more of Crossman's soup, and ate plenty of the funny coarse biscuit with guava jam. It all tasted very odd, but it was filling. Then they lay down on the bunks to get some sleep. The bedding was soaking wet from having been sat on by all those wet soldiers, but John was too exhausted to care. He was asleep almost as soon as he lay down.

John dreamed that they were surrounded by frantic men trying to climb on board; one of them had him by the arm, and was dragging at him, trying to pull himself up. The boat seemed already to be full of water; he felt wet and cold. Then he opened his eyes. Above him was the roof strut of *Dolphin's* cabin. He felt himself floating gently. *Dolphin* was almost still, quietly riding on tranquil water, but the slight, smooth movements of her hull gave him the sensation of floating. The water he felt must be in the cabin. He woke abruptly, and sat up. She was sinking.

He looked at the dry floor boards of the cabin for several seconds before he realized that it was only the bedding in the bunk he lay in which was wet. The damp had soaked through his own clothes to his skin, and he was shivering in his clammy garb.

He got out of the bunk. But the sense of danger had not left him; hadn't there been boarders? No; the dragging at his arm was only the tightness of the bandages on the sore wound. The noise of the scrabbling, grasping hands was only a light scratching tapping noise on the side of the hull. Suddenly he remembered the mine which had blown up the motor boat yesterday. His heart was pounding and his tongue had gone dry. He went to look what it was.

A thin grey light filtered through the cabin door. Outside, it was light, but a white mist hung over the sea, shutting everything out of sight. None of the ships that had been anchored around them the night before was visible. The noise on the side of the boat was made by a drowned man, washing gently against her. He floated face upwards, and the water lapped into his staring eyes. John felt a surge of relief, but the glint in the man's eyes made him turn away shuddering. He fended him off with the boat hook.

Back in the cabin Pat was still sleeping soundly. John opened the flask of coffee Crossman had given to him. What remained in it was cold and horrid. He slopped it out of the porthole, and put a kettle on the stove. There was a small locker in the galley, where food was kept when the family took *Dolphin* sailing. John found three old, battered tea-bags, and some lump sugar lying in it. He made tea in a big saucepan, refilled the flask and poured two cups from the pan. He worked clumsily, using only one hand; his hurt arm was now very stiff. And the quietness quickly got on his nerves, so that he was glad when the tea was made, and he had an excuse to wake Pat.

'Did you hear that bang in the night?' Pat asked as they drank tea, and chewed more biscuit.

'What bang?'

'Cor, if you had heard it, you wouldn't need to ask. One helluva bang, there was. You must have been out like a light; it would have woken you otherwise.'

'A big bomb, I suppose.'

'Came from out at sea somewhere.'

'Oh.' John couldn't summon much interest in it.

'You reckon we ought to scarper off home?' asked Pat.

'No, not yet. Unless you've had enough, Pat. I wouldn't blame you. Don't be afraid to say.'

'Not me. And there are a hell of a lot of soldiers still on that beach. I'd bet *they've* had enough. I was thinking of your arm, mate.'

'I'm OK. But you'll have to manage the boat most of the time. I don't think I can handle the wheel much. My arm's very stiff this morning.'

'That's all right. I can steer your boat easy enough.'

'*If we have another calm day* . . .' thought John to himself.

There was still nothing but mist outside. They had to use the compass to work out which way to head for the beach, although when they looked up they could see a pale blue sky with some clouds in it. The mist was only a few yards thick; only a haze on the surface of the water.

'It's good cover, anyway,' said Pat.

It muffled sound as well as sight. They were quite near in before they heard the gunfire rolling from the hinterland behind the beaches. But they had not heard it for many minutes before they knew that it was nearer than it had been yesterday; the rearguard had given a few miles. It proved impossible to work as they had done yesterday, because there were no big ships there to take on men. With Pat at the wheel *Dolphin* nosed up and down the coastline a mile or so both ways, but there was no doubt about it; there were no big ships about.

'They've all gone off home, and haven't got back yet,' said Pat. 'What do we do now, skipper?'

'We could hang around for a bit, and see if one turns up. I suppose it would be worth waiting till noon; but we have to start back early in the afternoon; we mustn't risk running out of petrol in mid-Channel.'

Hanging around wasn't much fun. They couldn't see far in the wreathing sea-mist, and they decided to save petrol by switching the engine off, and just letting her drift gently. Pat smoked a lot of the cigarettes Crossman had given them. John just sat. It was very nasty, being so close to danger, and having nothing to do to take one's mind off it. But they didn't have to wait till noon; long before then a filthy battered coal-carrying tramp ship arrived in the sea lanes, and appearing miraculously out of the dissolving mist, a handful of little boats began to ply between her and the shore.

John turned on *Dolphin*'s engine, and Pat took her towards the beach at random. They were both immensely relieved to be able to get to work again. The mist had dissolved into hazy sunlight, and the noise of battle was growing.

They found a change in the beach. The men had built themselves a makeshift pier, by pushing a line of lorries out into the water, and making a footway of planks laid over them. Men were scrambling dryshod over this gangway, and getting into boats drawn up at the end of it. A lifeboat and a small trawler were loading up, tied to either side of the last lorry, which was so deep that the waves washed over its roof. *Dolphin* joined them. It was much easier getting men aboard from the makeshift jetty than it had been yesterday; but it was harder getting them onto the ship. The tramp ship had no nets, only ladders, up which men had to climb in single file, painfully slowly. Pat became nearly frantic with impatience

while they waited for their turn under the ladder, and then waited for their men to climb out one by one.

'Steady on, Pat,' said John to him at last. 'We are doing as well as we can. Best not to fret about it.'

'We could get another whole boatload out here in the time its taking us to get them on to that bloody ladder!'

'We won't do any better if we get worked up about it.'

'At last!' said Pat, swinging *Dolphin* away as soon as the last man got one foot on the first rung of the ladder.

'Watch it, mate!' said John protesting. 'You nearly gave him a ducking.'

'We're in a hurry!'

'Don't be a fool, Pat. We aren't in a hurry. We just take it steadily, and keep calm.'

Pat flushed. 'Oh, yea. It doesn't matter how many we leave on them flaming beaches. We just keep calm!'

'I don't know what makes you think it matters less to me than to you.' Anger made John's voice stiff and cold.

'The way you went on about them. "England needs soldiers", you said. "Save our army so they can fight again." Just push them around the country like they was toys on your map. I don't give a damn whether they can fight again; I just want to get them out of here! One of the poor bastards what has to get left behind might be my dad!'

John's anger disappeared at once. He waited a long time before answering. 'Well, can you think of anything we can do to work faster?' he asked.

'No, blast it, I can't,' said Pat. He grinned at John. His anger too had blown over.

Dolphin pulled up again at the jetty. But before anyone got on board an officer appeared, and hailed them. He was carrying despatches, and he wanted a fast boat to take him north, and land him on some beach there, quickly.

'We'll be moving into heavy fire. You're free to refuse,' he said curtly.

''Op in, codger,' returned Pat disrespectfully.

'As fast as she'll go, please,' said the officer, getting in.

'My turn at the wheel now, Pat,' said John, slightly alarmed at the thought of Pat's inexperienced hand taking *Dolphin* at full speed. He found he could use his stiff arm if he really tried. *Dolphin* sprang away, cutting a path between two walls of foam. The officer was looking from one to another of them.

'In name of heaven, how old are you?' he asked.

'Old enough to handle a boat, sir,' said John.

'You'd better put me down at once, and get home,' said the officer angrily. 'This isn't a playground!'

'Thought you was in a hurry,' said Pat. The officer looked at them again. Their faces were streaked with black from the smoke; the set of their mouths, had they but known it, showed the tiredness, and the strain.

'How long have you been here?' he asked in a changed tone of voice.

'Since yesterday morning, sir,' said John. Overhead they heard the droning noise of oncoming planes.

'Don't look up; they won't be ours,' said the officer with bitterness in his voice. 'Not a single one of our blasted air force to stop them murdering us.' Then in his normal tone. 'Nearly at La Panne now. Can you get close inshore and put me off?'

The beaches here were being heavily shelled from the shore. It was the same bedlam of smoke and noise that yesterday had been. But the protecting numbness had worn off. John was very frightened again, and Pat too was jumpy. They took the officer in to shallow water. Just before he jumped over the side he said, 'Enough's enough. You've done your bit, and more. Get home now. I hope you make it.' Then he was gone, wading towards the terrible inferno on the beach.

'He's right,' said John, looking at his watch. 'We'll have to get back now, if we're to be sure our petrol will see us safely home.'

'You mean just quit, now?'

'Well, we aren't going home empty. Take her back to that crummy jetty, and we'll pick up a load of men to take with us.' John had had as much as he could take of managing the wheel; he gave it back to Pat. They went back to Bray, where the crazy little jetty of

half submerged lorries was still crowded with men.
The coal ship however had gone, and the horizon
was empty.

On the end lorry someone was directing the line of
men. They came up in order, and scrambled down
into *Dolphin*. Pat held the wheel steady, and John,
with his good arm, took such packs and rifles as the
men still had, and told them where to sit. A little way
down the line there was some pushing and scuffing.

'Right. That's all now,' said John.

'Another bus along in a minute!' called Pat. A faint
grin appeared on some of the weary faces in the row.
Then the pushing arrived at the top of the line. It was
caused by two men carrying an officer on a stretcher.

'Can you take him?' they asked John.

'I'm sorry, no.' said John firmly. 'We're full up.'

The stretcher bearers were tired. They looked
around at the dark sea.

'He should be in hospital,' one of them said. A great silence had fallen over the waiting line of men. Nobody moved, nobody spoke. The man directing operations looked down at the water, as though it were no affair of his.

Then suddenly the man on the stretcher groaned. He stiffened, and tossed his head.

'Right, bring him down,' said Pat. 'We'll fit him in somehow.'

'I'm sorry, Pat, but we can't.' said John.

'Oh, have a heart, mate! We can tie the stretcher on the cabin roof or something. But we can't just leave him to rot!'

'We can't take him. We can't possibly. *Dolphin*'s too far down in the water as it is. We can't risk making her any heavier.'

'One can't make much difference,' said Pat. His mouth was set in a stubborn line. 'If it's a risk, let's take it. We taken plenty already.'

'I'm sorry . . . but no. We have eight men on board, and ourselves. We can't risk ten lives for one. It isn't fair to ask it.'

'It's a risk we got to take. You ain't really saying you can look at that poor devil and say we're going to leave him? Ain't you human?'

'*You're* a flaming idiot!' cried John in exasperation. 'This boat won't take any more, and that's that!'

'We've carried him for three days,' said a voice from the jetty. 'The morphia has worn off. He needs a doctor.'

'I don't see why we can't put him on top of the cabin,' said Pat sullenly.

John struggled to master his rising anger. 'Look, you've only been in a boat for a few hours, Pat, and it's been the calmest day for years. If a bit of wind gets up we'll be shipping water, and in bad trouble.

We are chancing a lot on the hope that there won't be a swell in the Channel as it is . . .'

'It would be all right, then, if I got out?' said one of the soldiers from behind him. John turned to look at him. He was a lanky young man, with a cut on one cheek. He looked tired, and the empty expression on his face was unchanged as he spoke. John nodded.

'Rightie-ho. I'm off then,' said the soldier, scrambling up the side of the nearest lorry. Several hands were extended to help him up, and then to pat him on the back when he got there. Nobody said anything.

The stretcher was lowered down towards them. The man on it screamed when it hit the deck with a jerk. With a little difficulty they made room for the stretcher in the cabin, on one of the bunks. Then at last Pat took *Dolphin* chugging away from the jetty, and roaring across the bay. John was full of admiration for the unknown soldier who had given up his place, full of concern for him. *'I hope another boat comes for him soon'* he thought.

But when they were speeding up the sea-lane to the north, well out to sea, out of range of the guns at La Panne, and the sun shone through the grey afternoon, a great surge of relief and joy lifted John's heart. They had done it; and what was more, it was over. They would be home in a couple of hours; they were out of gunrange already. The thought of home, with real food, and safety, and hearing things on the wireless instead of living through them seemed like heaven on earth.

Felix and the Assassins

Joan Aiken

olerated by his grandfather and despised by his great aunt, Felix has run away from his home in Spain to search out his dead father's family in England. After crossing a treacherous mountain pass on his mule, Felix is looking for shelter . . .

Most of the day had gone before we reached another village, which lay at the foot of a deep glen. The house-roofs, here, were made of huge slates and came down almost to the ground, as a protection from the mountain rains. Up above the houses, on the sides of the mountain, almost like cloths hanging on a line, were the small fields, with cattle grazing; they seemed so steep I wondered that the cattle did not fall down the chimneys. A little church, up above, clung to a crag like a stone-martin perched on a cliffside.

I asked a woman whom I saw carrying a pail of water from the river if the village had an inn (thinking myself now far enough from home to risk notice); she stared at me in surprise, as if quite unused to strangers, and asked if I came from San Antonio? When I, having no idea why she asked the question, answered no, she directed me onward to a small *venta* at the end of the village street.

I rode along, tethered the mule to a tree outside the building, and entered. The place, inside, was one large room like a stable, with heaps of straw on which a number of rough-looking fellows were seated. Some slept, some drank wine from wooden cups, others were sharing a great bowl of stewed hare. A fire burned on a stone hearth in one corner, where travellers might cook their own food (there was no other provision). Another corner was partitioned off for the owner's family.

I was told by a dirty, weary-looking woman that I might stable the mule in a cowshed at the rear, and I obtained some grain (not barley, not maize, which, however, the mule consented to eat). There seemed no prospect of purchasing food for myself, but, retracing my way through the village, I was lucky enough to see a woman milking her cow, and obtained a drink of new milk from her. Thus refreshed I returned to the venta and laid myself down on one of the piles of straw, reflecting that my last night's bed had probably been cleaner, if more exposed to rain, wind, and wolves.

The men eating the hare, travellers like myself, had already gone to sleep, but the wine-drinkers were still drinking and talking; their voices prevented me from falling asleep.

'It is a great insolence,' one of them was saying, 'that he should come to our village! For my part, I think that we should blow his head off – or at least, throw him down from a precipice.'

All in a moment, at these words, I was wide awake, for I thought they were speaking of me, and I trembled in my heap of straw.

'Yes, but, Isidro, he is bringing his daughter,' objected another voice. 'We can hardly throw a girl off the side of the mountain.'

Then I knew they could not be speaking of me.

'It is of no consequence what happens to the girl,'

said Isidro. 'We can leave her on the mountain. Someone from San Antonio will doubtless come looking for her. Or if not, let her perish! She is only a sick girl. But I say that no man from that place should be allowed to set foot here! They are all rogues.'

'That is the truth!' struck in another voice. 'We all know how abominably they behaved over the grazing rights. And about Manuel's ox!'

'And the wild boar that Juan shot!'

'And the sheep that fell into the river!'

'Well, then is it agreed among us?' demanded Isidro.

'Yes, agreed!' came all their voices.

'Where shall we wait for him?'

There was some argument; then the one called Isidro said, 'Let us wait at the top of the path where it comes round the crag above the church. We know he must come that way. And there we may toss him into the next world without the need for fire-arms, and so save ourselves money now and trouble later. If carabineers or *alguacils* should come investigating, what can they find? A broken neck is a broken neck.'

To this they all agreed, and trooped from the building. One of them, passing by me in my corner, said, 'Who is that?' and I made believe to be fast asleep.

'That? Nobody,' said another voice. 'A stranger boy. He came from the south. He is not of San Antonio. I know every soul in that accursed village.'

They went out, and left me wondering very much what was afoot.

To be sure, it was none of my business, but I could not help puzzling about it. Why should they be so resolved upon the death of this man from San Antonio – wherever that was? I recalled the woman in the road who had asked me so suspiciously if I

came from there. What fault had the natives of San Antonio committed?

Presently the sad-looking woman who had shown me the cowshed came in, carrying a great bundle of wood. Discovering that all the men had gone, she looked about anxiously, crossed to one of the sleeping voyagers, shook him awake, and asked in a trembling voice.

'Senor, where are all the men who were here just now?'

'May the devil fly with me if I know,' he growled, not at all pleased, 'and may the devil fly away with *you*, for waking me!' and he burrowed his head back into the hay.

'Ay, Maria purissima, where can they be?' she murmured turning irresolutely towards the door again.

She seemed so distraught that, in spite of some intentions I had had not to meddle in what was no affair of mine, I could not help rising up, and softly following her outside.

'Senora! I can tell you where the men went,' said I, in a low voice, when we were a few yards from the door. 'I heard them say they would go up the

mountain to the church, to meet some person who is coming from San Antonio with his daughter.'

There I stopped. Even in the moonshine I could see her pale face had become even paler, and great drops stood on her wrinkled forehead.

She gripped my wrist with both hands.

'Oh, Dios mio. Are you telling me the truth, boy?'

I said certainly I was.

'He is my brother! Bringing his afflicted child! I begged him not to – I sent a note . . . Oh, the monsters, the devils! But what can I, a poor woman, do about it?' She wound her sackcloth apron between her hands. 'To think of seven of them setting upon one – and he bringing a poor child who has neither moved nor spoken for three years! How *could* they be so wicked?'

'Well,' said I, 'why are they doing it?' For I could see she knew full well what they planned. 'What did your brother do to them?'

'*He* has done nothing! It is just that he comes from San Antonio. Anybody from that town is sure to be killed if he comes here.'

'But you come from there?'

'Oh, I am only a woman. And they took me by

force.'

'I do not understand at all.'

'There is a feud! It all began long ago,' she said impatiently, as if that were not important. 'They said we took a holy relic from their church – or *we* said *they* took it from ours – nobody remembers any more. But now there are many more grievances – about grazing rights, and somebody's ox that strayed and trampled somebody's crop . . . When did they say they expected Jose?'

'I do not know, senora. Tonight – that was all they said. They are going to wait above the church. But why does he come, if there is such danger? Why does he bring a sick child? Is there a doctor in this village?'

'No – yes, there is,' the woman said distractedly, still twisting her apron. 'But it is not that.' Her eyes kept flying about, she turned her head as if listening for some terrible sound. 'No, you see it is the saints' walk. My brother must have hoped that as nothing else helped poor little Nieves – *Hark*, what was that?'

'It was only a dog barking. What is the saints' walk?'

'It is a walk taken to heal illness,' she said rapidly. 'There is a relic of San Antonio here, and one of Santa Teresa over yonder –' She crossed herself. 'It is a pen she wrote with, kept in a box. And they say that if you walk from one church to the other, over the mountain, fasting, and without speaking to any-body, in one night – it is like bearing a message from one saint to the other – it makes them glad, and their virtue will pass through you and heal you of your trouble.'

'How far is it between one church and the other?'

But the woman said, 'It is thirty miles, along a very steep mountain path. Few have done it in one night. And some have fallen over the cliff trying to find their way in the dark. Ay, my poor little niece!'

I said, 'We had better go up to the church. Perhaps we shall think of some way to stop them.'

She stared at me. 'What could *you* do? You are only a boy.'

'We can't just stay here,' said I.

'But they will kill you too.'

I had considered that also, but still – seven against one! And a sick child!

'Never mind, senora,' I said. 'You stay here. Just show me the way to the church.'

'The path is very s-steep.' Her teeth were chattering with terror. But she came with me.

It was steep indeed. A narrow alley ran between two houses, and almost straight up the precipitous hill behind, climbing in steps, turning a little one way, a little the other, then up, up. The track, slippery from rain, threaded between trees whose roots were useful for foot- and hand-holds.

Presently the trees grew fewer. Ahead in the moonlight we could see the little church, nestled on a kind of shelf which just held it. In front grew a great chestnut tree and by its trunk I thought I saw a moving clump of darkness, blacker than the shade round about.

'It is they!' breathed the woman. 'There! I saw a spark as one struck his yesca.' She halted and said, 'I cannot go on. My heart is dying within me.'

'What of your brother? Your niece? You will let them be killed?'

'I will go back and pray. That is the only thing I can do. If my husband found me here. – He is with them!'

'You are afraid for yourself,' said I, thinking poorly of her.

'Yes! No! It is what he would do to the children!'

'Oh, very well, go, go!' I heard her give a whimper, and then she slipped away down the hill among the trees.

By now I could distinguish the group of men clearly enough; they were standing, squatting, and lounging in the shelter of the tree, certain that their quarry must come that way. I could see that the path led on round an overhang on the mountain-side, with a steep drop down below. It was only just wide enough to walk along, where it approached the shelf on which the church was built.

I felt sorry for the man from San Antonio, carrying his sick child.

There would be no sense in my going forward and confronting the men. They would kill me or laugh at me; I did not know which would be worse. I wondered if it might be possible to creep along behind the church and so reach a point up above the group. Pursuing this plan, I turned off to my left, quitting the path and scrambling up through the trees – which were pines, here; more light came through the branches, but the ground below them was treacherous as glass because of the needles. I had to crawl on all fours, gripping the ground with my fingers, but this proved lucky, for one of the men, hearing some sound, discharged his gun in my direction, and the shot went over my head.

Then I heard Isidro's voice:

'You fool! Why did you do that?'

'I heard a twig snap – a bear perhaps.'

'Dolt! Suppose Jose heard you?'

'Oh I daresay he is nowhere near us yet.'

Now I had put the church between myself and them and the sound of their voices died away. Thick brushwood had grown up behind the church and I had the devil's own trouble making my way through, and was in fear all the time that one of the men would hear me again. But they were still arguing, I suppose, and at length I made my way through a mass of prickly gorse bushes and found myself on the steep slope above the group, but screened from their view by the bushes.

Here, as chance would have it, I could see a good stretch of the path by which the man from San Antonio must come, and I bethought me that it might be possible to intercept him, and give him warning of what lay in store for him, and persuade him to turn back.

However this plan did not sit at all comfortably in my mind.

To tell truth, I could not abide the idea that these hateful wretches should successfully turn back a poor fellow who had made his way thirty miles over a dangerous mountain track for such a piteous purpose. So I squatted among the gorse-roots, whittling a piece of pine-wood that I had picked up, and cudgelling my wits for some means of preventing their horrid deed and allowing the man to complete his pilgrimage.

Presently I stole upwards again, beyond the gorse cover, to survey a longer stretch of the path. And there I saw what put a notion into my head.

Above the belt of gorse-bushes the mountain-side lay bare and steep as an elbow, save for a number of boulders, amazingly big, scattered over the slope like lumps of salt on pastry. If only, thought I, one of those could be loosened, so as to roll it down . . .

But if I roll it, they will come looking, to see who set it moving. How can I make them believe that the hand of Providence is against them?

Suddenly a thought came into my head which caused me to chuckle out loud. And I blessed the habit which always inclines me to carry a spare length of cord or two in my breeches pocket.

Crawling like a lizard over the mountain-side I found a boulder which was right for my purpose – big as a mounting block, but so insecurely poised on a smooth slab of rock that it was a wonder it had not rolled away before now. One stout heave, thought I, should suffice to dislodge it from its base.

Having chosen my boulder I returned to the shelter of the gorse and whittled away again at my pine-stave, cutting a hole through one end of it and a row of notches along the side, and a groove round the other end. This done, I wound my cord tightly round the groove and tied it, leaving eighteen inches dangling free. I also removed the stiff leather lining of my hat, which I pressed and moulded into the shape of a cone.

Thus prepared, there was nothing for me to do but wait, hugging my ribs with anticipation. Oh, how I wished Father Tomas had been among the group of men down by the church. I could hear them, from time to time, talking in low voices.

'He is long enough coming!' said one impatiently. 'I wish I had thought to bring a handful of roast chestnuts!'

'Be silent, idiot! A good ambush is better than a hot dinner.'

Becoming impatient myself, I crawled back to the edge of the gorse and strained my eyes, looking along the side of the mountain, which in the moon's bright light shone like a silvered nutmeg at Twelfth Night. And far off, on that silvered surface, I thought I perceived a moving dot, coming slowly but steadily along the track, dragging something behind it. After staring steadily for a few more moments I was certain, and my heart began to thump so hard that my hands shook.

'Come, Felix! Don't be a cow-hearted clunch,' said I to myself, and, returning with all speed to my cover, I took up the notched piece of wood and commenced whirling it round and round at the end of its cord. It made a wonderfully loud roaring sound, like a furious bull a-bellowing, or a great roll of thunder sounding among the trees, and I heard the men below me cry out with fright.

'Ay, Dios, what is that sound?'

Then, still whirling the wood with my right hand, I held the leather cone to my mouth with my left hand, and, through it, bawled at the top of my lungs:

'BEWARE SACRILEGIOUS PROFANERS! Let him beware, who setteth an ambush against his brother! Beware, bloody murderers who hinder the will of the holy saints!'

My voice, through the leather cone, buzzed and boomed like the howl of a ghost – I could hear one man fairly whimpering with terror, and others calling on heaven to protect them, and even on the saints.

'CALL NOT ON THE SAINTS, YE PROFANE DOGS!' I bawled. 'The saints will not help those who lie in wait against unarmed men –' and then I was obliged to stop, for I was bursting with laughter at the thought of what Father Tomas would say if he could hear me making such use of the language he had poured out on me, day after day.

Quick as a monkey I ran up the hillside, bent double, and dislodged my boulder from its rest. It went bounding and hopping down the hillside, in a zigzag course, with a great roaring, rumbling, and crashing – and, even better than I had expected, it dislodged several others in its course, which all burst through the gorse cover and out among the assassins in front of the church. I could not see what befell them, but I heard their yells of surprise and terror as the first boulder landed. Then, from their running footsteps and fading voices I concluded that ghostly fright had overcome them and they had bolted for home.

I heard the frantic cry of one left behind:

'Miguel! Jorge! Help, help! The rock has broken my leg! Do not leave me here!'

Grumbling, two of them returned and assisted him down the hill, which was just as well, for I did not at all wish my presence discovered.

No great time after their dispersal I began to hear another sound – a slow, dragging footfall, weary and limping; also the rattle of wheels over stony ground.

Stealing close through my covert I beheld the arrival of the man from San Antonio. If I had not known about him beforehand I might myself have believed him a ghost – so skeleton-thin, dusty, and gaunt did he seem, poor soul, toiling along the last stretch of the path to the church, and pulling behind him a handcart made from plaited osiers, on which lay a small huddled form.

He looked round him in a puzzled and fearful manner as he neared the church – he must have heard some echo of all the creaking, crashing and shouting that had passed so soon before; but he did not speak, and I, mindful that his pilgrimage must be made in silence, did not reveal my presence.

Halting by the church door he lifted the sick child off the cart and, carrying her in his arms, passed within.

He remained in the church a long time and I did not disturb him. While he was in there I had ample leisure to unwind the cord from my bull-roarer (which I buried under a heap of pine-needles) and replace the leather in my hat. Then I knelt on the pine-needles and said a prayer myself, that his weary walk might be rewarded. It could do no harm. And I thanked God for helping me in regard to the boulders, and mentioned that I hoped He had enjoyed the joke as much as I had. He must have, I thought – after all, He put the plan into my head.

When at last the man came out, he was still carrying the limp form of his child, which caused a check in my flow of spirits. He laid her back on the cart with a sigh, and then stood dolefully scratching his head, as if he did not know what in the world to do next. It was plain to me that he had not the strength to begin on the return journey, yet did not dare linger where he was.

I had not intended to discover myself to him (curiosity as usual had kept me there) but, seeing him at closer quarters, I felt sorry for his plight, and

came out from my hiding-place.

'*Buenas noches, senor,*' I said.

He started with terror.

'Who are you?' he gasped. 'Are you from the village below?'

'No, senor, I am a wayfarer. But I have met your sister down below. And I have a message to you from her. You are to descend to the village, go boldly into the venta, and say that the saints have told you it is their will that the feud should be ended.'

He was amazed.

'Did my sister really say that?'

'That is her wish,' I said. 'Shall I help with your cart down this hill? It is very steep.'

He seemed irresolute still, but the child behind him made a soft whimpering, like somebody who awakens from sleep, and that appeared to decide him. He murmured to himself, 'If the saints wish it, I must not stand in their way,' and so we half-dragged, half-lifted the cart with the child on it down the zigzag path: a most difficult task, for she was far heavier than I had expected.

When we reached the gap between the houses I said,

'I will leave you now, senor,' for I feared that if I were seen with him, somebody in the village might begin to suspect the truth. Therefore I slipped round the other side of the house and ran like a hare to the cowshed at the back of the venta, from which a door led through into the main room. I passed through this, and so into the street. I found that every soul in the village appeared to have gathered on the flat piece of ground in front of the venta, where they were all talking in low amazed voices and crossing themselves repeatedly.

I noticed the innkeeper's wife in the crowd and

made my way to her without attracting attention. When I reached her side I plucked her sleeve and said softly,

'Senora, your brother is coming. He has been protected so far by the saints.'

Her mouth dropped open when she saw me. She began to say,

'Was it *you* –?'

'Hush, senora! Not a word!'

At that moment a kind of gasp went through the crowd, and a lane opened to show the dusty, skinny figure of Jose from San Antonio, dragging his little cart across the ground towards the inn building.

There was total silence as he limped along, and for a moment I felt great fear. Suppose the muttering crowd were to fall on him and stone him to death? Burn his daughter as a witch? Oh, what have I done? I thought. It was impossible to judge their mood.

Then somebody shouted,

'Why does not the child walk? If she has been healed in the church, why is she still in the cart? Let her walk!'

And they all cried out.

'Yes, let her walk. Let the child walk!'

I trembled.

Her father said to her in a low, pleading tone,

'Can you walk, Nieves?' But not as if he expected that she would. He halted, however. And then, in the middle of the silence, she whispered,

'I will try.'

Slowly she stretched up a hand to him. He took it. And she began, inch by inch, little by little, to drag herself upright, with the slow, unaccustomed movements of somebody who has been lying still for years. I was astounded when I saw how tall she was – no wonder she had seemed so heavy coming down

the hill! Why, she must be almost my own age! I had thought her a child of six or seven.

At last she was standing, balanced perilously on her thin legs, holding her father's hand, while he gazed at her, his mouth open, almost petrified with fear and astonishment, it seemed.

I thought she might fall when she swayed and, as no one else seemed ready to help her, I went forward to take her other hand, saying in as matter-of-fact a voice as I could muster,

'Come along then, Nieves, you must be hungry! I will help you walk to your aunt's house.'

Though heavy in the cart, she seemed now, balanced on her stick-like legs, as light as a flower of angelica. Guided by her father and me she moved along slowly – but she was walking herself, we were only helping her to keep her balance.

A kind of sigh came from the crowd, and grew louder and louder, until by the time we reached the venta they were cheering their heads off, shouting, 'Ole, ole!', throwing their hats in the air, embracing each other, and weeping. Dozens of candles were lit, people ran to their houses and fetched stools and chairs and bottles of wine; there was a feast in the street; you would never have guessed that half an hour before every man in the place had cherished the notion of tossing the father of Nieves over a cliff.

In the venta Nieves was given a bowl of milk. Very soon a dignified white-haired man came bustling in. He wore a suit of black and a three-cornered black hat; he, it seemed, was the doctor, much esteemed in the village. He expressed great interest in the recovery of Nieves but said,

'She should rest; all this excitement will be bad for her. Let her pass the night at my house. My housekeeper will look after her.'

This being agreed to, he asked for three helpers to carry her in a chair to his house, which was at the opposite end of the village. Being close by Nieves at the time, I was chosen for one of the helpers, and we walked with her slowly and carefully. The moon had gone down by now, but people were dancing in the street, which was lit from end to end by candles and rush-lights.

I heard the doctor muttering to himself as we walked along:

'Eh, well, the feud is over and *that* is a good thing – though no doubt they will find some other excuse for killing each other soon enough.'

He sounded like a man who had lived too long to believe that people would easily change their ways.

I thought that the doctor's house was most likely the best in the village, for it was stone-floored, furnished with chairs and tables and book-cases, a great contrast to the earth floor and piles of straw in the venta.

'You may sleep in my shed if you wish, boy,' said the doctor, noticing, I suppose, my wistful glance around his room. 'You'd get little enough sleep along *there*; they'll keep on drinking till daybreak, very probably.'

'Thank you, senor. That is kind of you.'

While his housekeeper was heating bricks for the bed and fetching a bowl of whey with warm wine in it for Nieves, the doctor asked a few questions.

'How long is it, my child, since you were able to walk and talk?'

'I don't know, senor,' she said. 'I feel as if I had been asleep a long time.'

'I believe it was three years,' said I, remembering what the girl's aunt had said, for the father, abashed by the grandeur of the doctor's house, had gone back to the venta.

'And what was the last thing you remember?' asked the doctor.

'I saw my mother and my little sister washed away when the river came down in flood. Oh, it was dreadful! – the snow and the black water and the trees tossing like sticks.' Her eyes were huge in her thin white face as she remembered.

'And since then you could neither move nor speak?'

'I – I suppose not, senor.'

'Well – well, it is a very interesting case,' the doctor muttered to himself. 'Hysterical, without a doubt.'

Now the housekeeper took Nieves off to a back room and I slipped away to the shed. The doctor was eyeing me too attentively for comfort. I certainly slept better on his hay than I would have at the inn, where, to judge from the sound, every soul in the village drank and sang till daybreak.

IN THE ABYSS

H. G. Wells

he lieutenant stood in front of the steel sphere and gnawed a piece of pine splinter. 'What do you think of it, Steevens?' he asked.

'It's an idea,' said Steevens, in the tone of one who keeps an open mind.

'I believe it will smash – flat,' said the lieutenant.

'He seems to have calculated it all out pretty well,' said Steevens, still impartial.

'But think of the pressure,' said the lieutenant. 'At the surface of the water it's fourteen pounds to the inch, thirty feet down it's double that; sixty, treble; ninety, four times; nine hundred, forty times; five thousand, three hundred – that's a mile – it's two hundred and forty times fourteen pounds; that – let's see – thirty hundredweight – a ton and a half, Steevens; *a ton and a half* to the square inch. And the ocean where he's going is five miles deep. That's seven and a half' –

'Sounds a lot,' said Steevens, 'but it's jolly thick steel.'

The lieutenant made no answer, but resumed his pine splinter. The object of their conversation was a huge ball of steel, having an exterior diameter of perhaps nine feet. It looked like the shot for some Titanic piece of artillery. It was elaborately nested in a monstrous scaffolding built into the framework of

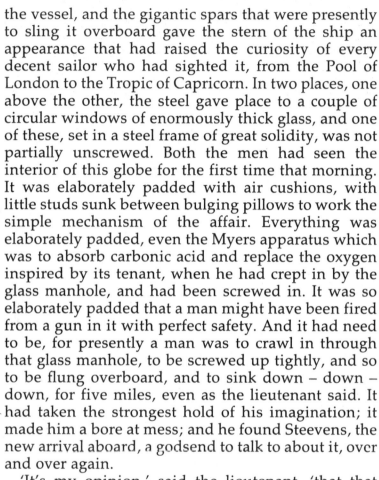

the vessel, and the gigantic spars that were presently to sling it overboard gave the stern of the ship an appearance that had raised the curiosity of every decent sailor who had sighted it, from the Pool of London to the Tropic of Capricorn. In two places, one above the other, the steel gave place to a couple of circular windows of enormously thick glass, and one of these, set in a steel frame of great solidity, was not partially unscrewed. Both the men had seen the interior of this globe for the first time that morning. It was elaborately padded with air cushions, with little studs sunk between bulging pillows to work the simple mechanism of the affair. Everything was elaborately padded, even the Myers apparatus which was to absorb carbonic acid and replace the oxygen inspired by its tenant, when he had crept in by the glass manhole, and had been screwed in. It was so elaborately padded that a man might have been fired from a gun in it with perfect safety. And it had need to be, for presently a man was to crawl in through that glass manhole, to be screwed up tightly, and so to be flung overboard, and to sink down – down – down, for five miles, even as the lieutenant said. It had taken the strongest hold of his imagination; it made him a bore at mess; and he found Steevens, the new arrival aboard, a godsend to talk to about it, over and over again.

'It's my opinion,' said the lieutenant, 'that that glass will simply bend in and bulge and smash, under a pressure of that sort. Daubrée has made rocks run like water under big pressures – and, you mark my words' –

'If the glass did break in,' said Steevens, 'what then?'

'The water would shoot in like a jet of iron. Have you ever felt a straight jet of high pressure water? It

would hit as hard as a bullet. It would simply smash him and flatten him. It would tear down his throat, and into his lungs; it would blow in his ears' –

'What a detailed imagination you have!' protested Steevens, who saw things vividly.

'It's a simple statement of the inevitable,' said the lieutenant.

'And the globe?'

'Would just give out a few little bubbles, and it would settle down comfortably against the day of judgment, among the oozes and the bottom clay – with poor Elstead spread over his own smashed cushions like butter over bread.'

He repeated this sentence as though he liked it very much. 'Like butter over bread,' he said.

'Having a look at the jigger?' said a voice, and Elstead stood behind them, spick and span in white, with a cigarette between his teeth, and his eyes smiling out of the shadow of his ample hat-brim. 'What's that about bread and butter, Weybridge? Grumbling as usual about the insufficient pay of naval officers? It won't be more than a day now before I start. We are to get the slings ready to-day. This clean sky and gentle swell is just the kind of thing for swinging off a dozen tons of lead and iron, isn't it?'

'It won't affect you much,' said Weybridge.

'No. Seventy or eighty feet down, and I shall be there in a dozen seconds, there's not a particle moving, though the wind shriek itself hoarse up above, and the water lifts halfway to the clouds. No. Down there' – He moved to the side of the ship and the other two followed him. All three leant forward on their elbows and stared down into the yellow-green water.

'*Peace*,' said Elstead, finishing his thought aloud.

'Are you dead certain that clockwork will act?' asked Weybridge presently.

'It has worked thirty-five times,' said Elstead. 'It's bound to work.'

'But if it doesn't?'

'Why shouldn't it?'

'I wouldn't go down in that confounded thing,' said Weybridge, 'for twenty thousand pounds.'

'Cheerful chap you are,' said Elstead, and spat sociably at a bubble below.

'I don't understand yet how you mean to work the thing,' said Steevens.

'In the first place, I'm screwed into the sphere,' said Elstead, 'and when I've turned the electric light off and on three times to show I'm cheerful, I'm swung out over the stern by that crane, with all those big lead sinkers slung below me. The top lead weight has a roller carrying a hundred fathoms of strong cord rolled up, and that's all that joins the sinkers to the sphere, except the slings that will be cut when the affair is dropped. We use cord rather than wire rope because it's easier to cut and more buoyant – necessary points, as you will see.

'Through each of these lead weights you notice there is a hole, and an iron rod will be run through that and will project six feet on the lower side. If that rod is rammed up from below, it knocks up a lever and sets the clockwork in motion at the side of the cylinder on which the cord winds.

'Very well. The whole affair is lowered gently into the water, and the slings are cut. The sphere floats, – with the air in it, it's lighter than water, – but the lead weights go down straight and the cord runs out. When the cord is all paid out, the sphere will go down too, pulled down by the cord.'

'But why the cord?' asked Steevens. 'Why not

fasten the weights directly to the sphere?'

'Because of the smash down below. The whole affair will go rushing down, mile after mile, at a headlong pace at last. It would be knocked to pieces on the bottom if it wasn't for that cord. But the weights will hit the bottom, and directly they do the buoyancy of the sphere will come into play. It will go on sinking slower and slower; come to a stop at last, and then begin to float upward again.

'That's where the clockwork comes in. Directly the weights smash against the sea bottom, the rod will be knocked through and will kick up the clockwork, and the cord will be rewound on the reel. I shall be lugged down to the sea bottom. There I shall stay for half an hour, with the electric light on, looking about me. Then the clockwork will release a spring knife, the cord will be cut, and up I shall rush again, like a soda-water bubble. The cord itself will help the flotation.'

'And if you should chance to hit a ship?' said Weybridge.

'I should come up at such a pace, I should go clean through it,' said Elstead, 'like a cannon ball. You needn't worry about that.'

'And suppose some nimble crustacean should wriggle into your clockwork' –

'It would be a pressing sort of invitation for me to stop,' said Elstead, turning his back on the water and staring at the sphere.

They had swung Elstead overboard by eleven o'clock. The day was serenely bright and calm, with the horizon lost in haze. The electric glare in the little upper compartment beamed cheerfully three times. Then they let him down slowly to the surface of the water, and a sailor in the stern chains hung ready to cut the tackle that held the lead weights and the sphere together. The globe, which had looked so large on deck, looked the smallest thing conceivable under the stern of the ship. It rolled a little, and its two dark windows, which floated uppermost, seemed like eyes turned up in round wonderment at the people who crowded the rail. A voice wondered how Elstead liked the rolling. 'Are you ready?' and the commander. 'Ay, ay, sir!' 'Then let her go!'

The rope of the tackle tightened against the blade and was cut, and an eddy rolled over the globe in a grotesquely helpless fashion. Someone waved a handkerchief, someone else tried an ineffectual cheer, a middy was counting slowly, 'Eight, nine, ten!' Another roll, then with a jerk and a splash the thing righted itself.

It seemed to be stationary for a moment, to grow rapidly smaller, and then the water closed over it, and it became visible, enlarged by refraction and dimmer, below the surface. Before one could count three it had disappeared. There was a flicker of white light far down in the water, that diminished to a speck and vanished. Then there was nothing but a depth of water going down into blackness, through which a shark was swimming.

Then suddenly the screw of the cruiser began to rotate, the water was crickled, the shark disappeared in a wrinkled confusion, and a torrent of foam rushed across the crystalline clearness that had swallowed up Elstead. 'What's the idea?' said one A.B. to another.

'We're going to lay off about a couple of miles, 'fear he should hit us when he comes up,' said his mate.

The ship steamed slowly to her new position. Aboard her almost everyone who was unoccupied remained watching the breathing swell into which the sphere had sunk. For the next half-hour it is doubtful if a word was spoken that did not bear directly or indirectly on Elstead. The December sun was now high in the sky, and the heat very considerable.

'He'll be cold enough down there,' said Weybridge. 'They say that below a certain depth sea water's always just about freezing.'

'Where'll he come up?' asked Steevens. 'I've lost my bearings.'

'That's the spot,' said the commander, who prided himself on his omniscience. He extended a precise finger south-eastward. 'And this, I reckon, is pretty nearly the moment,' he said. 'He's been thirty-five minutes.'

'How long does it take to reach the bottom of the ocean?' asked Steevens.

'For a depth of five miles, and reckoning – as we did – an acceleration of two feet per second, both ways, is just about three-quarters of a minute.'

'Then he's overdue,' said Weybridge.

'Pretty nearly,' said the commander. 'I suppose it takes a few minutes for that cord of his to wind in.'

'I forgot that,' said Weybridge, evidently relieved.

And then began the suspense. A minute slowly dragged itself out, and no sphere shot out of the water. Another followed, and nothing broke the low oily swell. The sailors explained to one another that little point about the winding-in of the cord. The rigging was dotted with expectant faces. 'Come up, Elstead!' called one hairy-chested salt impatiently, and the others caught it up, and shouted as though they were waiting for the curtain of a theatre to rise.

The commander glanced irritably at them.

'Of course, if the acceleration's less than two,' he said, 'he'll be all the longer. We aren't absolutely certain that was the proper figure. I'm no slavish

believer in calculations.'

Steevens agreed concisely. No one on the quarter-deck spoke for a couple of minutes. Then Steevens' watchcase clicked.

When, twenty-one minutes after the sun reached the zenith, they were still waiting for the globe to reappear, and not a man aboard had dared to whisper that hope was dead. It was Weybridge who first gave expression to that realisation. He spoke while the sound of eight bells still hung in the air. 'I always distrusted that window,' he said quite suddenly to Steevens.

'Good God!' said Steevens; 'you don't think –?'

'Well!' said Weybridge, and left the rest to his imagination.

'I'm no great believer in calculations myself,' said the commander dubiously, 'so that I'm not altogether hopeless yet.' And at midnight the gunboat was steaming slowly in a spiral round the spot where the globe had sunk, and the white beam of the electric light fled and halted and swept discontentedly onward again over the waste of phosphorescent waters under the little stars.

'If his window hasn't burst and smashed him,' said Weybridge, 'then it's a cursed sight worse, for his clockwork has gone wrong, and he's alive now, five miles under our feet, down there in the cold and dark, anchored in that little bubble of his, where never a ray of light has shone or a human being lived, since the waters were gathered together. He's there without food, feeling hungry and thirsty and scared, wondering whether he'll starve or stifle. Which will it be? The Myers apparatus is running out, I suppose. How long do they last?

'Good heavens!' he exclaimed; 'what little things we are! What daring little devils! Down there, miles and miles of water – all water, and all this empty water about us and this sky. Gulfs!' He threw his hands out, and as he did so, a little white streak swept noiselessly up the sky, travelled more slowly, stopped, became a motionless dot, as though a new star had fallen up into the sky. Then it went sliding back again and lost itself amidst the reflections of the stars and the white haze of the sea's phosphorescence.

At the sight he stopped, arm extended and mouth open. He shut his mouth, opened it again, and waved his arms with an impatient gesture. Then he turned, shouted 'El-stead ahoy!' to the first watch, and went at a run to Lindley and the search-light. 'I saw him,' he said. 'Starboard there! His light's on, and he's just shot out of the water. Bring the light round. We ought to see him drifting, when he lifts on the swell.'

But they never picked up the explorer until dawn. Then they almost ran him down. The crane was swung out and a boat's crew hooked the chain to the sphere. When they had shipped the sphere, they unscrewed the manhole and peered into the darkness of the interior (for the electric light chamber was intended to illuminate the water about the sphere, and was shut off entirely from its general cavity).

The air was very hot within the cavity, and the india-rubber at the lip of the manhole was soft. There was no answer to their eager questions and no sound of movement within. Elstead seemed to be lying motionless, crumpled up in the bottom of the globe. The ship's doctor crawled in and lifted him out to the men outside. For a moment or so they did not know whether Elstead was alive or dead. His face, in the yellow light of the ship's lamps, glistened with perspiration. They carried him down to his own cabin.

He was not dead, they found, but in a state of absolute nervous collapse, and besides cruelly bruised. For some days he had to lie perfectly still. It was a week before he could tell his experiences.

Almost his first words were that he was going down again. The sphere would have to be altered, he said, in order to allow him to throw off the cord if need be, and that was all. He had the most marvellous experience. 'You thought I should find nothing but ooze,' he said. 'You laughed at my explorations, and I've discovered a new world!' He told his story in disconnected fragments, and chiefly from the wrong end, so that it is impossible to re-tell it in his words. But what follows is the narrative of his experience.

It began atrociously, he said. Before the cord ran out, the thing kept rolling over. He felt like a frog in a football. He could see nothing but the crane and the sky overhead, with an occasional glimpse of the people on the ship's rail. He couldn't tell a bit which way the thing would roll next. Suddenly he would find his feet going up, and try to step, and over he went rolling, head over heels, and just anyhow, on the padding. Any other shape would have been more

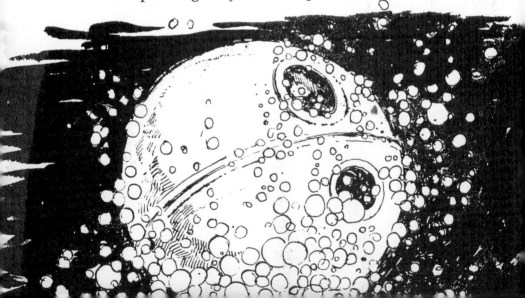

comfortable, but no other shape was to be relied upon under the huge pressure of the nethermost abyss.

Suddenly the swaying ceased; the globe righted, and when he had picked himself up, he saw the water all about him greeny-blue, with an attenuated light filtering down from above, and a shoal of little floating things went rushing up past him, as it seemed to him, towards the light. And even as he looked, it grew darker and darker, until the water above was as dark as the midnight sky, albeit of a greener shade, and the water below black. And little transparent things in the water developed a faint glint of luminosity, and shot past him in faint greenish streaks.

And the feeling of falling! It was just like the start of a lift, he said, only it kept on. One has to imagine what that means, that keeping on. It was then of all times that Elstead repented of his adventure. He saw the chances against him in an altogether new light. He thought of the big cuttle-fish people knew to exist in the middle waters, the kind of things they find half digested in whales at times, or floating dead and rotten and half eaten by fish. Suppose one caught

hold and wouldn't let go. And had the clockwork really been sufficiently tested? But whether he wanted to go on or go back mattered not the slightest now.

In fifty seconds everything was as black as night outside, except where the beam from his light struck through the waters, and picked out every now and then some fish or scrap of sinking matter. They flashed by too fast for him to see what they were. Once he thinks he passed a shark. And then the sphere began to get hot by friction against the water. They had under-estimated this, it seems.

The first thing he noticed was that he was perspiring, and then he heard a hissing growing louder under his feet, and saw a lot of little bubbles – very little bubbles they were – rushing upward like a fan through the water outside. Steam! He felt the window, and it was hot. He turned on the minute glow-lamp that lit his own cavity, looked at the padded watch by the studs, and saw he had been travelling now for two minutes. It came into his head that the window would crack through the conflict of temperatures, for he knew the bottom water is very near freezing.

Then suddenly the floor of the sphere seemed to press against his feet, the rush of bubbles outside grew slower and slower, and the hissing diminished. The sphere rolled a little. The window had not cracked, nothing had given, and he knew that the dangers of sinking, at any rate, were over.

In another minute or so he would be on the floor of the abyss. He thought, he said, of Steevens and Weybridge and the rest of them five miles overhead, higher to him than the very highest clouds that ever floated over land are to us, steaming slowly and staring down and wondering what had happened to him.

He peered out of the window. There were no more bubbles now, and the hissing had stopped. Outside there was a heavy blackness – as black as black velvet – except where the electric light pierced the empty water and showed the colour of it – a yellow-green. Then three things like shapes of fire swam into sight, following each other through the water. Whether they were little and near or big and far off he could not tell.

Each was outlined in a bluish light almost as bright as the lights of a fishing smack, a light which seemed to be smoking greatly, and all along the sides of them were specks of this, like the lighter portholes of a ship. Their phosphorescence seemed to go out as they came into the radiance of his lamp, and he saw then that they were little fish of some strange sort, with huge heads, vast eyes, and dwindling bodies and tails. Their eyes were turned towards him, and he judged they were following him down. He supposed they were attracted by his glare.

Presently others of the same sort joined them. As he went on down, he noticed that the water became of a pallid colour, and that little specks twinkled in his ray like motes in a sunbeam. This was probably due to the clouds of ooze and mud that the impact of his leaden sinkers had disturbed.

By the time he was drawn down to the lead weights he was in a dense fog of white that his electric light failed altogether to pierce for more than a few yards, and many minutes elapsed before the hanging sheets of sediment subsided to any extent. Then, lit by his light and by the transient phosphorescence of a distant shoal of fishes, he was able to see under the huge blackness of the superincumbent water an undulating expanse of greyish-white ooze, broken here and there by tangled thickets of a growth of sea lilies, waving hungry tentacles in the air.

Farther away were the graceful, translucent outlines of a group of gigantic sponges. About this floor there were scattered a number of bristling flattish tufts of rich purple and black, which he decided must be some sort of sea-urchin, and small, large-eyed or blind things having a curious resemblance, some to woodlice, and others to lobsters, crawled sluggishly across the track of the light and vanished into the obscurity again, leaving furrowed trails behind them.

Then suddenly the hovering swarm of little fishes veered about and came towards him as a flight of starlings might do. They passed over him like a phosphorescent snow, and then he saw behind them some larger creature advancing towards the sphere.

At first he could see it only dimly, a faintly moving figure remotely suggestive of a walking man, and then it came into the spray of light that the lamp shot out. As the glare struck it, it shut its eyes, dazzled. He stared in rigid astonishment.

It was a strange vertebrated animal. Its dark purple head was dimly suggestive of a chameleon, but it had such a high forehead and such a braincase as no reptile ever displayed before; the vertical pitch of its face gave it a most extraordinary resemblance to a human being.

Two large and protruding eyes projected from sockets in chameleon fashion, and it had a broad reptilian mouth with horny lips beneath its little nostrils. In the position of the ears were two huge gill-covers, and out of these floated a branching tree of coralline filaments, almost like the tree-like gills that very young rays and sharks possess.

But the humanity of the face was not the most extraordinary thing about the creature. It was a biped; its almost globular body was poised on a tripod of two frog-like legs and a long thick tail, and its fore limbs, which grotesquely caricatured the human hand, much as a frog's do, carried a long shaft of bone, tipped with copper. The colour of the creature was variegated; its head, hands, and legs were purple; but its skin, which hung loosely upon it, even as clothes might do, was a phosphorescent grey. And it stood there blinded by the light.

At last this unknown creature of the abyss blinked its eyes open, and, shading them with its disengaged hand, opened its mouth and gave vent to a shouting noise, articulate almost as speech might be, that penetrated even the steel case and padded jacket of the sphere. How a shouting may be accomplished without lungs Elstead does not profess to explain. It then moved sideways out of the glare into the mystery of shadow that bordered it on either side, and Elstead felt rather than saw that it was coming towards him. Fancying the light had attracted it, he turned the switch that cut off the current. In another moment something soft dabbed upon the steel, and the globe swayed.

Then the shouting was repeated, and it seemed to him that a distant echo answered it. The dabbing recurred, and the whole globe swayed and ground against the spindle over which the wire was rolled. He stood in the blackness and peered out into the everlasting night of the abyss. And presently he saw, very faint and remote, other phosphorescent quasi-human forms hurrying towards him.

Hardly knowing what he did, he felt about in his swaying prison for the stud of the exterior electric light, and came by accident against his own small

glow-lamp in its padded recess. The sphere twisted, and then threw him down; he heard shouts like shouts of surprise, and when he rose to his feet, he saw two pairs of stalked eyes peering into the lower window and reflecting his light.

In another moment hands were dabbing vigorously at his steel casing, and there was a sound, horrible enough in his position, of the metal protection of the clockwork being vigorously hammered. That, indeed, sent his heart into his mouth, for if these strange creatures succeeded in stopping that, his release would never occur. Scarcely had he thought as much when he felt the sphere sway violently, and the floor of it press hard against his feet. He turned off the small glow-lamp that lit the interior, and sent the ray of the large light in the separate compartment out into the water. The sea-floor and the man-like creatures had disappeared, and a couple of fish chasing each other dropped suddenly by the window.

He thought at once that these strange denizens of the deep sea had broken the rope, and that he had escaped. He drove up faster and faster, and then stopped with a jerk that sent him flying against the padded roof of his prison. For half a minute, perhaps, he was too astonished to think.

Then he felt that the sphere was spinning slowly, and rocking, and it seemed to him that it was also being drawn through the water. By crouching close to the window, he managed to make his weight effective and roll that part of the sphere downward, but he could see nothing save the pale ray of his light striking down ineffectively into the darkness. It occurred to him that he would see more if he turned the lamp off, and allowed his eyes to grow accustomed to the profound obscurity.

In this he was wise. After some minutes the velvety blackness became a translucent blackness, and then, far away, and as faint as the zodiacal light of an English summer evening, he saw shapes moving below. He judged these creatures had detached his cable, and were towing him along the sea bottom.

And then he saw something faint and remote across the undulations of the submarine plain, a broad horizon of pale luminosity that extended this way and that way as far as the range of his little window permitted him to see. To this he was being towed, as a balloon might be towed by men out of the open country into a town. He approached it very slowly, and very slowly the dim irradiation was gathered together into more definite shapes.

It was nearly five o'clock before he came over this luminous area, and by that time he could make out an arrangement suggestive of streets and houses grouped about a vast roofless erection that was grotesquely suggestive of a ruined abbey. It was spread out like a map below him. The houses were all roofless enclosures of walls, and their substance being, as he afterwards saw, of phosphorescent bones, gave the place an appearance as if it were built of drowned moonshine.

Among the inner caves of the place waving trees of crinoid stretched their tentacles, and tall, slender, glassy sponges shot like shining minarets and lilies of filmy light out of the general glow of the city. In the open spaces of the place he could see a stirring movement as of crowds of people, but he was too many fathoms above them to distinguish the individuals in those crowds.

Then slowly they pulled him down, and as they did so, the details of the place crept slowly upon his apprehension. He saw that the courses of the cloudy buildings were marked out with beaded lines of round objects, and then he perceived that at several points below him, in broad open spaces, were forms like the encrusted shapes of ships.

Slowly and surely he was drawn down, and the forms below him became brighter, clearer, more distinct. He was being pulled down, he perceived, towards the large building in the centre of the town, and he could catch a glimpse ever and again of the multitudinous forms that were lugging at his cord. He was astonished to see that the rigging of one of the ships, which formed such a prominent feature of the place, was crowded with a host of gesticulating figures regarding him, and then the walls of the great building rose about him silently, and hid the city from his eyes.

And such walls they were, of water-logged wood,

and twisted wire-rope, and iron spars, and copper, and the bones and skulls of dead men. The skulls ran in zigzag lines and spirals and fantastic curves over the buildings; and in and out of their eye-sockets, and over the whole surface of the place, lurked and played a multitude of silvery little fishes.

Suddenly his ears were filled with a low shouting and a noise like the violent blowing of horns, and this gave place to a fantastic chant. Down the sphere sank, past the huge pointed windows, through which he saw vaguely a great number of these strange, ghostlike people regarding him, and at last he came to rest, as it seemed, on a kind of altar that stood in the centre of the place.

And now he was at such a level that he could see these strange people of the abyss plainly once more. To his astonishment, he perceived that they were prostrating themselves before him, all save one, dressed as it seemed in a robe of placoid scales, and crowned with a luminous diadem, who stood with his reptilian mouth opening and shutting, as though he led the chanting of the worshippers.

A curious impulse made Elstead turn on his small glowlamp again, so that he became visible to these creatures of the abyss, albeit the glare made them disappear forthwith into night. At this sudden sight of him, the chanting gave place to a tumult of exultant shouts; and Elstead, being anxious to watch them, turned his light off again, and vanished from before their eyes. But for a time he was too blind to make out what they were doing, and when at last he could distinguish them, they were kneeling again. And thus they continued worshipping him, without rest or intermission, for a space of three hours.

Most circumstantial was Elstead's account of this astounding city and its people, these people of perpetual night, who have never seen sun or moon or stars, green vegetation, nor any living, air-breathing creatures, who know nothing of fire, nor any light but the phosphorescent light of living things.

Startling as is his story, it is yet more startling to find that scientific men, of such eminence as Adams and Jenkins, find nothing incredible in it. They tell me they see no reason why intelligent, water-breathing, vertebrated creatures, inured to a low temperature and enormous pressure, and of such a heavy structure, that neither alive nor dead would they float, might not live upon the bottom of the deep sea, and quite unsuspected by us, descendants like ourselves of the great Theriomorpha of the New Red Sandstone age.

We should be known to them, however, as strange, meteoric creatures, wont to fall catastrophically dead out of the mysterious blackness of their watery sky. And not only we ourselves, but our ships, our metals, our appliances, would come raining down out of the night. Sometimes sinking things would smite down and crush them, as if it were the judgment of some unseen power above, and sometimes would come things of the utmost rarity or utility, or shapes of inspiring suggestion. One can understand, perhaps, something of their behaviour at the descent of a living man, if one thinks what a barbaric people might do, to whom an enhaloed, shining creature came suddenly out of the sky.

At one time or another Elstead probably told the officers of the *Ptarmigan* every detail of his strange twelve hours in the abyss. That he also intended to write them down is certain, but he never did, and so unhappily we have to piece together the discrepant fragments of his story from the reminiscences of Commander Simmons, Weybridge, Steevens,

Lindley, and the others.

We see the thing darkly in fragmentary glimpses – the huge ghostly building, the bowing, chanting people, with their dark chameleon-like heads and faintly luminous clothing, and Elstead, with his light turned on again, vainly trying to convey to their minds that the cord by which the sphere was held was to be severed. Minute after minute slipped away, and Elstead, looking at his watch, was horrified to find that he had oxygen only for four hours more. But the chant in his honour kept on as remorselessly as if it was the marching song of his approaching death.

The manner of his release he does not understand, but to judge by the end of cord that hung from the sphere, it had been cut through by rubbing against the edge of the altar. Abruptly the sphere rolled over, and he swept up, out of their world, as an ethereal creature clothed in a vacuum would sweep through our own atmosphere back to its native ether again. He must have torn out of their sight as a hydrogen bubble hastens upward from our air. A strange ascension it must have seemed to them.

The sphere rushed up with even greater velocity than, when weighted with the lead sinkers, it had rushed down. It became exceedingly hot. It drove up with the windows uppermost, and he remembers the torrent of bubbles frothing against the glass. Every moment he expected this to fly. Then suddenly something like a huge wheel seemed to be released in his head, the padded compartment began spinning about him, and he fainted. His next recollection was of his cabin, and of the doctor's voice.

But that is the substance of the extraordinary story that Elstead related in fragments to the officers of the *Ptarmigan*. He promised to write it all down at a later date. His mind was chiefly occupied with the improvement of his apparatus, which was effected at Rio.

It remains only to tell that on February 2, 1896, he made his second descent into the ocean abyss, with the improvements his first experience suggested. What happened we shall probably never know. He never returned. The *Ptarmigan* beat about over the point of his submersion, seeking him in vain for thirteen days. Then she returned to Rio, and the news was telegraphed to his friends. So the matter remains for the present. But it is hardly probable that no further attempt will be made to verify his strange story of these hitherto unsuspected cities of the deep sea.

ALL THE DOGS IN THE WORLD

Paul Berna

hile tracking the thieves who stole their wooden horse, Gaby and his gang of Paris back-street children discover an abandoned factory packed with carnival novelties. Determined to get their own back on the thieves, they decide to use the factory to spring a trap. . .

Saturday isn't much of a day for school-children in Louvigny. Most of them see their father start a lazy morning, look in the local paper to find what's on at the cinema, or set out on his motor-bike, fishing-tackle strapped on the back. Meanwhile they themselves go through a regular third degree in a dingy building in the rue Poit from a gentleman in spectacles, who grills them about the Pass of Thermopylae and the murder of the Duc de Guise.

That morning, and again in the afternoon, Monsieur Juste, the schoolmaster, noticed how preoccupied the older boys – Gaby, Fernand, and Zidore – were, and guessed from experience that they had a lot planned.

Next door Madame Juste was not surprised to find Marion was absent. It was true that this happened quite often; the child was either helping her poor mother or somebody else. In the infants' class, young Mademoiselle Berry suddenly burst out laughing and then made Bonbon stand in the corner for ten minutes, to teach him not to wear a great bulbous red false nose in form. The nose was confiscated until the end of the period, which was fortunately not long in coming.

None of the gang went home after school. Madame Lariqué, Madame Babin, and Madame Gédéon would have been able to keep their offspring indoors by saying what dreadful weather it had been all day, and that wouldn't have suited Gaby in the very least. He wanted to have every single member of the gang to hand. It wasn't snowing much; every now and then one gust of wind would bring a handful of flakes to dance at the end of the street, until a moment later another gust would come and scatter them. But already it was getting very dark and their knees were blue with the bitter cold.

Marion was waiting for the gang at the corner of the rue des Petits-Pauvres. She made them all come home with her to leave their satchels there and have a good cup of steaming hot chocolate. Little Bonbon had put on his false his nose again, and was brandishing his enormous revolver most threateningly.

'You might just as well have left that old thing at home, for all the good it did you last time,' said Zidore, laughing.

'I know it can't kill anyone,' agreed Bonbon regretfully, 'but I don't feel so frightened when I'm holding it.'

The first thing Gaby did was to check on what they had for lighting. In all, there were five candle-ends and two boxes of matches, and he divided them among the elder children.

While the younger ones were being wrapped up in their scarves, Madame Fabert came in. She took these brigands' visit very well, considering that she found they had eaten up her supply of bread for the week-end during the five minutes they had been there. Marion was always truthful, and smiling at her mother she said:

'We're just going to have a run round the Clos to get warmed up.'

Madame Fabert shrugged her shoulders resignedly. 'Well, off you go, then,' she said, 'but take care you don't fall down and hurt yourselves in those bomb-craters. I think I'd rather have you going at sixty miles an hour on that wretched horse of yours.'

The ten crossed the road together and slipped under the barbed wire without any attempt at concealment. The Clos Pecqueux stretched in front of them until it was lost in the evening mist, as quiet and deserted as on the previous evenings.

Gaby, Fernand, and Zidore boldly led the way, each swinging a good thick cudgel picked from Madame Fabert's wood-pile. Juan hugged the long knife they used for the potatoes to his chest, while Tatave brandished an elegant poker with a copper handle. Bonbon came next, shooting with his heavy revolver at the crows in the distance.

'Take aim! Fire! Bang! He's dead!' cried Bonbon, closing his left eye.

But the crow would flap off cawing his denial.

Marion brought up the rear, alone, her hands thrust deep into the pockets of her jacket. A smile played round her lips and it was not one of complete kindness.

They reached the middle of the Clos. Gaby went straight on without stepping a yard out of his course. Instinctively they stopped talking, and the younger ones kept close to their elders. A little fresh snow had caught in the cracks and crannies of the Black Cow and lay along the top of her rusty boiler. As they went past they hurled the usual rain of stones against her and set her booming like the great bell of a cathedral. Then the ten trotted away to the fence round César Aravant's goods-yard. They reached the alley, and Marion let the others file past, while, pressing close to the wall, she watched the empty spaces of the Clos Pecqueux.

A moment later two indistinct figures came out of the Black Cow. One of them hurried back towards the houses of Louvigny, while the other followed the tracks of the gang, taking care not to be seen and stopping now and then to get the lie of the deserted buildings.

Quickly Marion left her observation post and caught up with her friends in the Ponceau road. She said nothing, for one still couldn't tell what was going to happen. She contented herself with tipping the wink to Gaby to set him on his guard. Whereupon he opened the gate, let them all in and then carefully shut and double-locked it. It was so dark that they had to light their candles immediately to see their way into the workshop.

Gaby stayed outside a moment to have a brief word with Marion and Fernand. 'The main gate won't hold ten seconds with men who've got the tools they have,' he said anxiously. 'The wood's all rotten round the lock.'

'That doesn't matter a bit,' said Marion. 'You just barricade yourselves in the store-room and lock the three communicating doors behind you. They'll lose a good ten minutes breaking through, and there's a lot you can do in ten minutes. The main thing is to get them inside and keep them there. I'll do the rest.'

Fernand nodded.

'I'll go straight up and keep a look out of the little round window above the gate.'

He tiptoed up to the door and climbed the narrow staircase leading to the two empty rooms on the floor above. Half-way up was a skylight. Slowly he poked his head out and looked up and down the Ponceau road.

Complete darkness had fallen on the Clos Pecqueux. Yellow lights glowed in the nearest houses in Louvigny. The road was quite dark, in spite of the glaring lights above the railway lines. Fernand listened in vain. Every sound in the neighbourhood was drowned by the hissing of the shunting engines and the roar of the trains passing through. Sticking his head out still farther, he looked towards Louvigny. The harsh glare of a pair of headlights lit up the sunken road, and as they came sweeping nearer and nearer they flashed for a second on the faces of the neighbouring buildings. Instead of turning and going through the tunnel, the car kept straight on, and pulled up in front of the fence across the end of the road. The headlights were switched off and Fernand heard the doors bang.

'Can you see anything?' a voice behind him asked. 'Let me have a look.'

Marion had crept up. Gently she pushed him aside and poked her head through the opening. At that moment another car came from Louvigny; its headlights swept across the skyline, catching the girl's face in their glare.

'Look out,' whispered Fernand. 'They'll see you!'

As before, the car came through the tunnel, pulled up in the darkness by the goods-yard, and switched off its lights.

'It's them all right!' whispered Marion.

Then without a word she pointed to something outside opposite the skylight.

A passenger train was slowing down to take the

Louvigny curve, and its lights flickered confusedly across the ground below them. Fernand looked: on the other side of the road a man was waiting, leaning up against the retaining wall of the embankment. He was so close that it took Fernand's breath away. The man switched on a torch and flashed it off and on to call up the others. Then he ran the beam over the factory walls.

The two children listened. There was a crunch of gravel below the window. Fernand leant still further out and suddenly spotted five dark figures moving along beside the wall in single file.

'They're inside,' muttered a voice. 'You can see a light moving in the other end of the building.'

Noiselessly Fernand and Marion climbed down and took up their position in the entrance hall. There was a dull rumbling in the distance, gradually growing louder and louder until it set every window in the building rattling. The Melun express hurtled past along the embankment beside the Ponceau road. The very ground trembled, then the thunder of its wheels grew less and less and slowly faded away.

'Warn the others,' said Marion, 'and don't bother about me. Barricade yourselves in the end room as strongly as you can; you must hold out as long as possible.'

'What are you going to do?'

'I'll get out through the little yard at the back and cut across the fields. I shan't have long – but don't worry, I'll be back.'

She disappeared among the shadows in the passage. The door gave another crack: a ray of light filtered through the broken panels, which were being violently shaken from outside.

'Come on, give her a shove!' someone shouted.

Fernand turned and ran into the first workshop.

Gaby joined him, his face showing his alarm, his hand clutching a candle-end.

'Well?'

'They're here!' panted Fernand. 'We've just got time to bar the doors.

There was no key in the first one in the hall, so they dragged the work-benches across the opening and pushed them flush against the iron of the door.

There was a dull crash from the direction of the road. Both leaves of the door had given way under the pressure of the besiegers. Gaby and Fernand dashed into the next workshop. A communicating door, its upper panel of glass, separated this room from the other. It locked, however.

'It won't take them long to smash their way through this,' shrugged Gaby.

'They'll waste two or three minutes,' answered Fernand, 'and Marion says we must gain time.'

The younger ones were calmly trying on wigs and false beards in the store-room at the end, standing round Zidore, who was dressed up as a demon; Tatave had already broken a dozen gazookas; Berthe and Mélie were hurling paper streamers furiously at each other; and Criquet decked out in a three-cornered hat, was having a row of medals pinned on his chest by General Bonbon Louvrier de Louvigny.

'Stop this fooling!' growled Gaby in an awful voice. 'The crooks who pinched our horse will be on top of us any minute now. Man the barricades, all of you! Come on, shift that pile of cardboard boxes over there in front of the door!'

The grill that separated the stock-room from the rest of the building was made of solid slats of wood that ran from floor to ceiling. The double door, strengthened with wooden cross beams, was fastened top and bottom by two thick bolts which could not be reached from outside. But it still wasn't enough to stop the intruders.

Without wasting a second they all fell to work, piling boxes of carnival novelties up against the partition, the heaviest at the bottom as a firm foundation for their barricade and the lighter ones tossed in showers on the top. As they fell some of them broke open and the place was soon festooned with a tangle of paper chains of all colours, plumes of horse-hair, chinese umbrellas, cardboard crowns, jack-in-the-boxes, streamers of artificial flowers, a snow of spangles, armfuls of gazookas and rattles, castanets, false beards, false noses, false teeth, and all the thousand and one treasures of this Ali Baba's cave of a store-room.

An appalling crash and the tinkle of broken glass came from the neighbouring room. A flash-light beam played furtively upon the bluish glass of the roof; heavy boots clumped across the concrete floor, and slowly drew near the store-room.

'One more door,' said Fernand, 'and then we'll see what these toy thieves really look like.'

'Out with the candles,' hissed Gaby, trembling with excitement. 'Get back to the far end of the store, behind the last pile of boxes. If anyone laughs I'll do them.'

Bottling their laughter the children tiptoed off, tripping over the oddments that littered the passage down the middle. From one end of the room to the other the cases of goods were carefully stacked head high, leaving a gap about a yard wide between each pile. These cardboard fortifications not only gave an illusion of safety, but as Gaby said, could easily be pushed over if it came to a tussle, and so create the most glorious chaos.

The last door made the toughs sweat a bit. It was metal-sheathed and Gaby had securely double-locked it. They had to join forces to smash it in. They used a work-bench which they swung like a battering-ram, backwards and forwards, their curses setting the rhythm. All at once one of the panels gave way completely and most of the doorframe with it. The crash stifled the giggles of Berthe and Mélie, set off by the cascade of paper streamers that had fallen out of the half-open cupboard and buried them up to their necks.

Gaby and Fernand were side by side, entrenched behind the first wall of boxes. By pushing two of them out of the pile they had made themselves a narrow peep-hole. On the other side of the slatted partition they saw the toughs come into the room, one behind the other. The dancing light of a torch flashed on the burly forms and now caught one scowling face and now another. The one in the lead put his foot in the pig's head mask, which happened to be lying in his path. He tripped and measured his length on the floor, bringing down with him a pile of paint-cans in a glorious clatter. He spat and swore, and, cursing his comrades and puffing and blowing, he heaved himself to his feet. Quite by accident he got a long black beard stuck to the end of his nose. This mishap cheered Gaby's gang; the tension had been growing unbearable.

'You won't get anywhere until you get some decent light,' came a deep voice in the background. 'The fuse-box is out here in the entrance hall. Knock the front off and put in some fresh wires. No one will see us. The nearest house is a good half-mile away.'

Two minutes later a harsh light was playing from the bulbs that ran the length of the roof upon the grand chaos the children's visits had made, and on the fading treasures of the factory. Satisfied, the crooks dashed forward to the partition. There were five of them. Fernand and Gaby had no difficulty in picking out Pépé and Ugly in their leather jackets, and a little behind them, as though rather unsure of himself, the tall shape of Roublot. The other two wore heavy overcoats, the collars turned up so that their faces could not be seen properly.

Roughly, Ugly rattled the slats, muttering under his breath.

'Those little blighters have locked themselves behind here. Well, we'll soon shift 'em!'

He went for the door with a crow-bar. But the crossbeams were thick and the bolts were solid steel, and the door held firm. Red with anger, Ugly hurled his tool away, and poking his face through the slats he yelled: 'You in there! Get this door open, and make it snappy, or I'll wring your blasted necks!'

'Open up, you little ruffians!' added Pépé.

Nothing stirred in the store-room.

'That's not the way to talk to children,' said one of the men in overcoats, quietly. (He seemed to be the leader.) 'Here, let me.'

Then, pushing the two others aside, he looked inquisitively between the slats. A solitary bulb hung over the door and dimly lit the long store-room with its grey steel cupboards and regular walls of boxes across the room.

'Come, come, come, come, come!' he sang out, as though calling in the hens for feeding. 'Don't be naughty. Open the door like good children and no one will be cross. Here's a hundred francs for the first one to come out.'

There was not a sound from the store. No one wanted the hundred francs, and Tatave for one would have willingly given a hundred thousand to be somewhere else. Zidore and Juan had just found a box of bangers in their 'wall'. These bangers were little round paper balls filled with sand and holding a detonator cap. A hard throw would send them off with a fine explosion. Taking a handful each, they jumped up and threw them over the top of the boxes. They made a terrific bang-bang as they went off against the partition. It was like a burst of tommy-gun fire. Taken by surprise, the men instinctively drew back, shielding their heads with their arms. At the same time Gaby and Fernand leapt back to rejoin their friends.

'Help yourselves!' Zidore whispered. 'But let's shift a bit, or they'll spot us!'

The five crooks, boiling with rage, once more returned to the partition, this time with pistols drawn.

'Well, if you like that sort of game,' the leader shouted at the children, 'we'll join in too!'

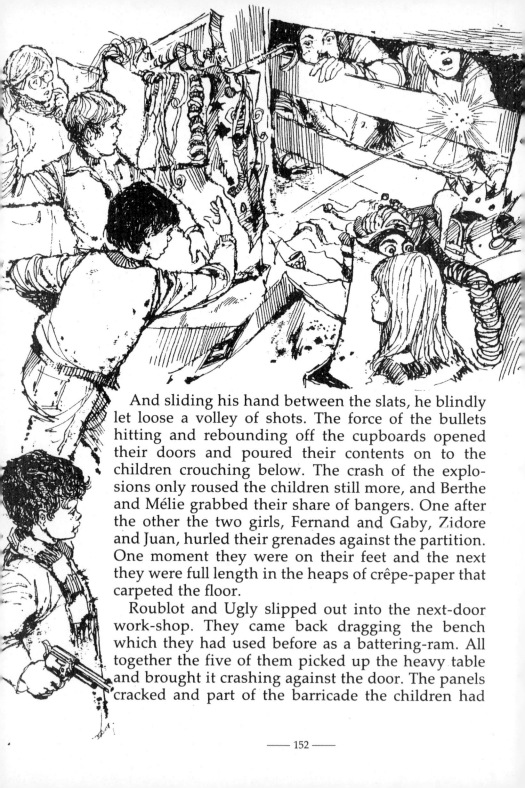

And sliding his hand between the slats, he blindly
let loose a volley of shots. The force of the bullets
hitting and rebounding off the cupboards opened
their doors and poured their contents on to the
children crouching below. The crash of the explosions only roused the children still more, and Berthe
and Mélie grabbed their share of bangers. One after
the other the two girls, Fernand and Gaby, Zidore
and Juan, hurled their grenades against the partition.
One moment they were on their feet and the next
they were full length in the heaps of crêpe-paper that
carpeted the floor.

Roublot and Ugly slipped out into the next-door
work-shop. They came back dragging the bench
which they had used before as a battering-ram. All
together the five of them picked up the heavy table
and brought it crashing against the door. The panels
cracked and part of the barricade the children had

made collapsed under the shock.

A real storm of bangers burst with a blinding flash against the partition. The second blow from the battering-ram tore the bolt out of the bottom of the door, smashed in the lower panel, and brought down a whole mound of boxes. All the children were now on their feet and, throwing caution to the winds, they hurled their bombs by the handful, harassing the five men as they drew back for their last assault.

'What can Marion be doing?' muttered Fernand as he scraped the last handful of bangers from the bottom of the box.

Marion jumped over the low wall at the end of the yard and landed as lightly as a cat on the other side. It was very dark by now, but a fresh fall of snow covered the ground and by its pale glitter you could make out the mounds and hollows in the ground, above all the dangerous bomb-craters that riddled the bottom of the field beside the railway tracks. Marion took to her heels and dashed into the darkness, heading for the ghostly mass of the rusty old Black Cow faintly outlined by the lights of the town behind it.

The snow went on falling gently, but the wind had fallen away. The noise of the traffic died down towards Triage and gradually this little corner of the suburbs became as quiet as the country.

When she reached the old engine, Marion stopped to rest for a second. Then she put two fingers between her teeth, took a deep breath, and began to whistle. Her shrill, wavering call travelled across the Clos Pecqueux, making itself heard above the roar of the traffic on the main roads and penetrated the streets, the alleys, the backyards, the gardens, the sheds, and the barns.

Turning towards the lights of Louvigny that shone in her face, Marion whistled with all her might, not weakening but rather gaining power from the echo from the embankment, which prolonged the sinister note. Through the bitter night, she whistled up help for the children from the rue des Petits-Pauvres.

Butor and Fanfan, Marion's two farm dogs, were the first to hear her urgent summons. They were hunting a cat at the head of the rue de la Vache Noire. The hair on their backs rose and, leaving the big tom, they cleared the barbed wire at one bound and hurled themselves into the darkness of the Clos Pecqueux. At the foot of the rue des Petits-Pauvres, Marion's twelve patients snored on, and the alert Fifi was the only one to jump the fence and run like a hare towards the Black Cow.

Close on her heels came the three aristocrats of the rue Cécile – Hugo, Fritz, and César. Shoulder to shoulder they took the corner of the cross-roads and vanished as fast as they had come. Dingo, Cobbler Gally's old spaniel, got under way more slowly, crossed the road behind them, and slipped under the barbed wire with an angry growl. One after the other, Pipotte, old Monsieur Gédéon's bitch, and

Moko, the fox-terrier belonging to the Babin family, came down the rue des Petits-Pauvres, and after them five ugly mongrels from Cité Ferrand: Mataf, Doré, Jeremie, Ursule, and Drinette. The whole mob of them turned the corner at full speed, heads down, never a bark, and nearly knocked down the solitary pedestrian who was coming up the Ponceau road. Mustafa, the one-eyed Alsatian from the Bar de l'Auvergnat, and Zanzi, Madame Louvrier's poodle, came galloping along with Emile and Fido, the two retrievers owned by Monsieur Manteau, the Mayor of Louvigny. And those four nobly swelled the muster.

All the while Marion whistled.

Gamin, Monsieur Joye's black-and-white terrier, soon turned the corner of the rue Aubertin and raced up the rue de la Vache Noire slightly ahead of the reinforcements from Louvigny-Cambrouse. The latter came helter-skelter across the main road, not bothering about the glaring headlights or the screeching brakes.

Mignon, the bulldog belonging to Maubert the small-holder, brought with him the rough-and-tough mongrels from the neighbourhood of les

Maches: Filon, Canard, Betasse, Flip, and Briquet. And behind them came the farm dogs from the Bas-Louvigny, dark, shaggy, snarling, snapping brutes: Raleur, and Nougat, limping Croquant (though he didn't limp now) and yellow-eyed Charlot – scarred, and with most of his ears chewed off – Taquin, a mangy beast, and Canon the chicken-thief. This robber band came pattering along the tarmac of the main road. It was a wonderful sight to see the entire dog population of Louvigny in migration from one side of the town to the other.

And it was even better to see the toffs of the Quartier-Neuf joining in the game and sending such clipped and combed champions as Otto de la Ville-Neuberg du Pacq des Primevères, the boxer whose pedigree covered four whole pages, and whose daily dish was a pound of the best-quality minced beef; Bébé, the black Schnauzer with eyes like a goat; Hubert, the boar-hound, four times a medal winner, who could jump any wall; Popoff, the greyhound, once famous in the stadium; Zoum, the griffon, with an insatiable appetite for slippers and soft furnishings; and then five little dogs of all shapes and sizes, all a little over-plump, and all highly scented. Every one of them had passed through Marion's hand for some cure or other. Yes, the toffs of the Quartier-Neuf were hastening eagerly to the rallying place.

And still Marion went on whistling in the darkness of the Clos Pecqueux. A faint echo even reached the little houses of Petit Louvigny and the Faubourg-Bacchus, and all at once every dog in the place seemed to go mad: rag-pickers' mongrels for the most part, good for nothing and living like outlaws on the fringes of the shopping streets. Leaving whatever they were doing, the rag-tag and bob-tail came out of the wooden huts and the waste land, entered the town-centre, crossed the Grand'rue and the rue Piot, turned up the rue des Alliés, and dashed full-cry down the rue des Petits-Pauvres, quite blocking the pavement. Pipi, Juan's lemon-and-white fox-terrier, was leading the pack with old Chable's dog, Arthur, a short-legged mongrel with a jackal's head, a coat as rough as a bass-broom, and one eye black and one blue. Then came Caillette, Frisé, Loupiotte l'Apache, Chopine, old Zigon's bitch, Golo, the Lariqués' lurcher, the old pug Adolf, Polyte, Bidasse, Gros-Père, and a dozen other flea-ridden curs, who changed name and home regularly once a week.

Planted beneath the threatening bulk of the Black Cow, Marion was still whistling as hard as she could when the first dogs reached her. She had half seen them in the darkness of Clos Pecqueux, wave upon wave of them, racing silently towards her. Not one of them gave tongue – Marion didn't allow that – and their feet pattered on the ground like a rain-storm. In a few seconds she found herself hemmed in by a growling mass that eagerly twisted and turned to touch her friendly hand or sniff her coat. The more dogs there were about her, the gentler and more caressing her whistle grew. Louvigny-Cambrouse and the Quartier-Neuf arrived almost together, and then came the flea-bitten rabble from the Faubourg-Bacchus.

Every so often the beam of a distant headlight caught the group, and hundreds of eyes gleamed red and green around her, like so many fire-flies. The dogs whimpered with delight, and occasionally one or the other of them would give a plaintive little whine.

'Whisht!' said Marion, throwing wide her arms,

'here, here!'

The dogs closed round her, leaping, gazing adoringly up at her. Marion held out her arms, recognizing them by touch, stroking noses, patting backs, and calling them by name as she did so.

Then with a sharp call of 'Come!' she broke through them and set off running towards the bottom of the Clos Pecqueux. Obediently the dogs panted after her. The whole pack threaded their way through the narrow lane that led into the Ponceau road. As the dogs eagerly crowded after Marion, an express thundered along the embankment in a shimmer of golden lights.

Her pace slackened when she approached the factory. The splintered gates yawned black, but there was a glow of light above the workshop roof. From the depths of the building came a series of muffled thuds. She went in – or rather, she was pushed in by the wild rush of the dogs, who hurled themselves panting from room to room.

A cloud of acrid smoke hung about the end workshop. The partition was still holding – but only just. The five crooks were swinging their battering-ram for the final blow. With a crash, one half of the door fell in and brought down with it the barricade of boxes.

'Hey!' called Marion.

The astonished men turned, and their hands hung useless and their jaws dropped to see the girl and her sixty silent, straining hounds standing behind them. The dogs were waiting as though they were held back only by some invisible leash.

'Go on!' cried Marion in a shrill voice. 'Catch 'em! Pull 'em down! Rotten swine who pinch kids' toys in the rue des Petits-Pauvres!'

With a joyful bound the dogs fell to work.

Danger Afloat

Allan Campbell McLean

iall is convinced that one of the fishermen on the Isle of Skye where he lives has tried to murder his brother. He persuades the local land agent, the Factor, to let him sail with the men in their fishing boat, or coble, but a storm is blowing up. Long John, the skipper, and Big Willie prepare to cast off, but the red-headed Murdo tries to warn Niall not to go. . .

To tell the truth I was sorely tempted. I had been born within sight and sound of the sea, and I had spent all my life on the rocky east coast of our island. In our township, the sea is never out of sight, and hardly ever out of mind. I knew enough about it to realize the risks they were taking.

If a heavy breaker caught the coble before she had fully cleared the river mouth, she would be dashed on the rocks and smashed to pieces within minutes. But that was only the first of the dangers they faced. To try to fish a bag net with such a swell running was to risk capsizing the coble, and if that did not happen there was always the danger of the engine stalling. If the engine failed, they could not hope to keep her off the rocks with the oars alone. And if all those perils were overcome, the greatest one of all had still to be surmounted – the river had to be regained without the coble being swept on to the rocks by the force of the breakers.

If it had been any other man than the red fellow. I might have heeded his advice. But I knew well enough that all he wanted was to see me away from the bothy, and I would have cut the nose off my face to spite him in that.

To be honest, though, I listened to him with only one ear. It was the words of Long John that burned in my mind, and rankled within me. *The boy can please himself* he had said, not even looking at me as he spoke, tossing the words out carelessly, as if I had been of no more concern to him than an old boot. It was his words, and his alone, that determined me on my course. *The boy can please himself*. Very well, I would please myself.

'If the rest of you are going out, my place is in the coble,' I said.

I think the red fellow could see by my face that it was useless arguing. So it was. At any rate, all he said was: 'You are a fool, boy. But before the coble is out of the river, you will be wishing you were on your way home.'

His forecast was more than half true. It makes me wild to have to admit, but a part of me had no stomach for the sea, and I could not get out of my mind the thought of our cosy kitchen at home, Lassie stretched out on the rug, and the peat fire glowing in the open range. No wonder. As I sat in the stern of the coble, watching the breakers come surging in, I did not see how she could come through them, and live.

As we neared the mouth of the river, Long John shouted: 'Oars, boys.' They were already fitting the long oars into the rowlocks before he opened his mouth, and they put their backs into it with a will.

There is no need for orders when your life is depending on the speed with which you jump to it.

The coble rose high on the first roller, tossed up as lightly as a cork. She came down into the trough, the screw racing as it came clear of the water. A torrent of spray streamed over her curving bow, dashing against the bent backs of the oarsmen. It even reached Long John and me in the stern.

Up we went. Down again, timbers groaning. A flood of spray half swamped the rowers. They strained grimly on the oars, pulling with every ounce of their strength, arms shooting forward again like out-thrust pistons. Up again, and over the crest of the roller, the stern riding clear of the water. Then down, down, down, until I thought she would never lift her bows again.

I gripped the gunwhale with frozen fingers, seeing a huge green wall of water bearing down on us. Slowly – so slowly that at first I thought she was not moving at all – every timber in her groaning like a live thing, her high prow lifted through it. A flood of water and spray poured over the port bow. The coble staggered, dipped into a trough again, and wallowed out of it.

We were hardly making way at all, the thrust of the engine lost every time the screw lifted out of the water. I glanced astern, seeing the tide ebbing back from the rocks at the river mouth, and surging forward again to swamp them in a creamy wash of foam and spray. The half-covered rocks were no more than a cable's length away.

The rowers had seen them, too. Indeed, they never took their eyes off them. They redoubled their efforts, lips drawn back as they gulped air, straining on the oars like men possessed.

We took seven bad ones, one after the other, not a

break between them. I counted them, and I am not likely to forget the number. The seventh roller was the worst of the lot, a monster just. I shut my eyes as the towering wall of water swept down on us.

I heard the coble groan from stem to stern, as she struggled to climb through it. I pitched forward, almost losing my grip, as the stern kicked up, suddenly riding free. Then it was down, down, down, and a crack like the shot of a cannon, as another wave broke against our bows. I opened my eyes, and ducked quickly, taking a shower of spray across my back.

Big Willie's sou'wester had slipped over his eyes. His mouth gaped open like the mouth of a stranded fish, and he grunted every time he pulled back on his oar. Short, savage grunts, as if he were fighting a battle with the heavy oar, and knew that it was going to be a losing one. Farther for'ard, on the starboard oar, the red fellow was in no better shape. His face had a mottled look, and his long frame seemed to sag every time he took his blade back for another pull.

But we had struggled clear of the river mouth, clear of the menacing rocks, and the steep, inshore rollers. The screw was biting deep, no longer riding clear of the water, and we gradually drew away from the shore.

Long John swung her slowly round to the north and the men shipped their oars. The coble ploughed through the swell, pitching steeply, but riding it well. Great showers of spray broke over her bows, and the bilge swirled about my ankles whenever she lifted on the swell.

Big Willie went for'ard, and joined the red fellow on his seat. They huddled together, backs bent against the lash of the spray, their heads close together. The noise of the labouring engine and the wind and sea smothered their voices, but I could guess what they were talking about by the angry looks they shot in the direction of Long John.

Their glares did not seem to disturb him. I doubt if he even noticed them. He was bareheaded, his black hair plastered wetly about his head, rain and spray trickling down his neck inside the collar of his yellow oilskin smock.

It did not seem to worry him. Indeed, he looked as if he was enjoying himself. He was like a beached boat on dry land, smart though he was with the crutch, not really coming to life until he was back in his element, and at grips with the sea.

He leaned over, his lips close to my ear. 'We will fish the Rock net first,' he shouted.

I nodded, my eyes on the red fellow and Big Willie. The Harris man had certainly found his tongue now. He was talking away good style, bringing his fist down on the big fellow's knee to ram some point home. Big Willie nodded, and from the looks he was giving Long John it was clear who was figuring in the talk.

The coble plunged steeply, shipping a bad one over the bow. 'Getting sick?' Long John yelled.

I shook my head. 'Wait you,' he roared. 'When she is not making way, that is the time you will feel it, boy.'

I ducked as a cloud of spray crashed high over the bows, and showered us in the stern. Long John took it full in the face and never even blinked. In fact, he grinned. I believe he would not have exchanged his wet seat in the stern for the ease of a cushioned throne.

We were the best part of two hours battling against the wind and sea to the Rock net. As we drew near, I could see the tremendous wash of tide and swell

around the dark reef. The sea surged forward,
flooding over the jutting point of the reef, breaking
around the rocks in a fury of crashing waves and
drenching them in torrents of spray. The undertow
swirled back, the water boiling, baring the black
spine of the reef until another breaker swept down
on it.

The black rocks were bare. The seabirds had fled
inland. Not even a gull could have survived on the
rocks with the angry wash of the sea breaking all
around. I did not fancy the look of them at all. The
sooner the net was fished and we were away, the
better, I thought.

It seemed that Long John had taken the bag net too
wide, and we were going to miss it by yards. But as
he cut the engine, the swell plucked the coble round
and flung her against the net. Big Willie's clutching
hands seized the rope on the head pole, and the red
fellow hung on grimly to a side rope. Long John was
out of the stern seat and in between the two of them
like a flash, pulling in the head pole and freeing the
padlock.

He was as much a part of the pitching, rolling coble
as the timber that went into the making of her. With

his good knee wedged against the gunwale, hands working at the head pole ropes, he kept his balance as easily as I could have done with two good legs planted firmly on dry ground.

With the three of them hanging over the port gunwale, clinging to the ropes of the bag net, the coble was at the mercy of the swell. She was flung up and down like a tossing cork. One moment I was gazing up at a wall of water, certain that it could not fail to swamp the heeling boat, and the next moment I was looking down into a deep trough. Then down again, shipping water freely. Long John's salmon club floating in the bilge around my feet.

Now that the coble had stopped making way, and was rolling wildly, like a drifting log, my stomach started to turn queasy. Gripping a seat, I slid across to the gunwale, alongside the red fellow. I wedged my knees against the gunwale, and helped to haul in the net, hoping that the work would take my mind off my stomach. Anything was better than sitting idly in the stern, getting sick.

We rose up on the swell, and the coble took a steep plunge. The red fellow was thrown off balance, and he crashed against me. I pitched forward, arms and

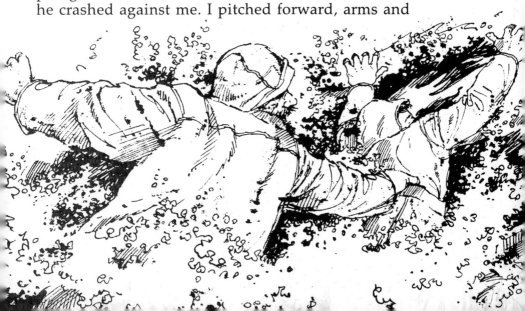

shoulders under water. If I had been wearing a smock like the rest of them, I would have been over the side there and then, but Long John managed to get a hand to the belt of my oilskin coat. He dragged me back aboard.

'Get in the stern,' he shouted. 'You are more use there. Cover the engine.'

I fought my way back against the steep list of the boat, and covered the engine as best I could with the skirt of my oilskin. Long John had the fish door open. As the coble went down in a trough, they heaved up the net. Three salmon plunged into the coble, all of them young grilse, seven pounders, at the very outside. I groped for the club and handed it to Long John. Three quick thumps, and the threshing fish were still.

Long John fastened the fish door and they released the net. But it was no easy task sinking the head pole with the coble rolling and plunging so wildly. It took the combined weight of the three of them to force it down, and it was a wonder to me that the coble did not capsize in the doing of it. Long John secured the padlock and ropes. He let go, and the head pole bobbed upright.

I had the starter cord wound ready, and I gave it a sharp tug. The noise of the engine firing was sweeter in my ears than the music of a massed pipe band. I opened the throttle as long John dropped into the stern seat beside me. He took over the helm without a word.

As his hand closed over the rubber grip, we caught a bad one, almost full abeam. The sea smashed over the stern, half drowning me, and the coble shuddered from stem to stern. The engine faltered and coughed, and slowly picked up again. Another sea broke over the stern. The engine spluttered, and died.

The silence struck me worse than a thunderclap, but it galvanized the others into action. Long John fumbled at the starter cord. The other two scrambled for the oars. A wave caught the coble, whipped her round broadside on to the swell; and swept her back towards the reef. It seemed to my fear-stricken eyes that she had never moved so fast before. We were being carried closer to the jagged black spine of the reef with every second that passed.

Long John yanked the starter cord. The engine coughed and died. Big Willie was pulling on his oar like a madman, and the curving beak of the prow faced the swell again. The red fellow cried: 'Hold her at that,' and the two of them bent their backs to the oars and pulled as they had never pulled before.

Long John tried to start the engine a second time, and failed. He glanced at the looming reef as he wound the cord for a third attempt. For all the efforts of the oarsmen, we were barely holding our own. Once they started to tire, we were finished. The jagged rocks of the reef would tear the bottom out of the coble, and the sea would pound her to matchwood.

I held my breath as he pulled the starter cord for the third time. The engine gave a faint cough, drowned in a loud curse from Long John. He fished under his smock, and thrust a dry rag into my hands. Working feverishly, he removed the magneto cap and took out the sparking plug. He snatched the rag out of my hands and unrolled it. There was a fresh plug inside. He fitted the plug and connected the lead, drying it carefully with the rag. He wiped his hands on the rag and replaced the cap. I wanted to close my eyes and shut my ears as he wound the starter cord.

The engine fired at the first pull, and the coble,

with the thrust of the screw added to the pull of the oars, drew away from the reef. Soon we were running easily before the wind and sea, and the long oars had been shipped once more. I had learned one lesson, at any rate. Never again would I despise an oar; no, not for all the outboards in creation.

Big Willie and the red fellow were huddled together again. They were facing the prow now, and all I could see of them was their bent backs. They were so close together you could have got the one sou'wester over the two heads, supposing you could have found one big enough.

Big Willie got up and made his way aft. He steadied himself with a hand on my shoulder and bent over Long John. 'You can make straight for the river,' he declared, 'whether you like it or not. Murdo and me are done with fishing for the day, even supposing the rest o' the nets are thick wi' salmon. We have had enough, MacGregor. Aye, more than enough.'

Long John nodded. 'As you wish,' he said mildly, and I wondered if he was already regretting the rash words he had spoken before we set out.

Willie made his way for'ard to his seat, and he and the red fellow soon had their heads together again. Long John did not seem to be in a mood for talking, and neither was I, for that matter. I was thinking how the red fellow had been thrown against me when we were fishing the net, and how only the quick action of Long John had saved me from going over the side. Had he genuinely lost his balance, or did he deliberately blunder into me? He was the only man who could answer that question, so I would never know. Accident or no, it was as well to remember what had happened to Ruairidh, and I resolved to keep well clear of him in future.

We made good time back to the river mouth, but the tide was on the ebb now. It had uncovered the rocks at the narrow entrance to the river, and the channel lay dangerously close to them. To make matters worse, the wind had freshened. It was licking white tops on the crests of the rollers.

As he took the coble in, Long John shouted to Big Willie to have an oar ready. I believe Willie thought he would give him a fright, and not pull until the last moment. At any rate, he was slow in dipping his oar, when two good pulls would have been enough to straighten the coble. As it was, she was caught by a steep roller and swept off course before Willie's oar was in the water. He saw the danger too late, and jabbed his oar out like a spear, trying to fend the boat off the rocks. The blade snapped like a matchstick, and he fell against the gunwale, crushing his fingers between the stump of the oar and the rowlock.

The coble plunged down on the rocks, changed course slightly, whether by the pull of the tide or Long John's work at the helm I shall never know, and scraped past them into the calm water of the river. A deep groove, the length of my arm, had been gouged in her timbers, and Big Willie's crushed fingers were spouting blood, but that was all the damage we suffered.

Nobody spoke as we moved upstream and nosed into the berth below the bothy. Big Willie muttered something to the red fellow, as they leapt ashore and made for the rollers, but not a word was spoken as we hauled the coble up the slip on the hand winch.

We all stripped off our soaking oilskins in the store shed, and trooped silently to the bothy. Long John sat down on the big cork float at the end of the table. Big Willie and the red fellow stood in the doorway. I was behind them. The silence was the sort that you feel deep in the stomach – the brooding silence of a gathering storm. I waited tensely for it to break.

Long John was playing with his ebony-hafted knife, digging the point into the table.

'Well?' he said.

I saw the red fellow's elbow busily working at Big Willie's ribs. He would always be the one, I thought, to stand in the shadows, and urge another to fire the shot. Willie took a step forward, wrapping a dirty handkerchief around his bleeding fingers.

'You were keen on making out, MacGregor,' he said. 'And what have we to show for it? Three grilse – poor ones at that – and a broken oar – and this!' He held up his clenched fist, the dirty handkerchief already a bright crimson with seeping blood. 'A fine fishing, eh?' he sneered.

'Aye, and very near drowned the lot of us,' the red fellow chipped in over his shoulder. 'If she had gone on the reef we were finished.'

Long John dug the knife savagely into the table. It stuck there, quivering. 'Well?' he said again.

'You told me I could march to the Factor and tell him I was finished, if I did not make out with you,' Big Willie went on. 'Well, I made out with you, so you can make no lies about me being afraid. But I am marching off now, MacGregor, and Murdo along wi' me, and we are not marching back in a hurry. I wish you luck at the fishing. You will be needing it.'

He swung round, nearly knocking me off my feet, in his blind rage to be gone from the bothy. The red fellow turned after him. He whipped back like a scavenging dog loth to leave his pickings, and snarled: 'Seeing you are so keen on drowning, MacGregor, you can drown alone.'

There was a long silence.

'Well, boy?' Long John said.

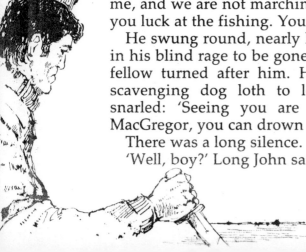

The red fellow was back at my side. 'What are you waiting for, boy?' he said. 'Big Willie is across the bridge.'

I took a step forward. 'Come on,' he said, catching me by the shoulder.

I tried to shake myself free, but he tightened his grip. I stumbled back against the door. It slammed shut behind us.

'Take your hands off the boy, Murdo,' Long John said quietly.

He got a better grip on me and gave me a shake. 'Wake up, boy,' he said, 'and let us away. That old cratur is finished. Let him be.'

I saw Long John's fingers close over the ebony haft of the knife, and jerk it out of the table. His arm drew back, and the next thing I knew the knife had thudded into the door. I swear it was not an inch from the red fellow's ear.

'I told you to take your hands off the boy, Murdo,' Long John said.

I looked at the red fellow. His bulging eyes were fixed on the quivering knife. There were beads of sweat as big as winkles coming off him. He swallowed, and made to say something, but the words were not there. He seemed to have a job to find the handle, but he got the door open and stumbled out.

THE ESCAPE

Ian Serraillier

his is the story of a Polish family, and of what happened to them during the Second World War and immediately afterwards. Their home was in a suburb of Warsaw, where the father, Joseph Balicki, was headmaster of a primary school. He and his Swiss wife Margrit had three children. In early 1940, the year when the Nazis took Joseph away to prison, Ruth the eldest was nearly thirteen, Edek was eleven, and the fair-haired Bronia three.

Warsaw under the Nazis was a place of terror, and without their father to protect them the Balickis had a grim time of it. But worse was in store for them. They were to endure hardships and conditions which made them think and plan and act more like adults than children. Great responsibilities were to fall upon Ruth. Many other girls had to face difficulties as great as hers. But if there were any who faced them with as much courage, unselfishness, and common sense as she did, I have not heard of them.

First I must tell of Joseph Balicki and what happened to him in the prison camp of Zakyna.

The prison camp which the Nazis sent him to was in the mountains of South Poland. A few wooden huts clung to the edge of the bleak hillside. Day and night the wind beat down upon them, for the pine trees were thin and gave little shelter. For five

months of the year snow lay thick upon the ground.
It smothered the huts. It gave a coating of white fur to
the twelve-foot double fence of wire that surrounded
the clearing. In stormy weather it blew into the bare
huts through cracks in the walls. There was no
comfort in Zakyna.

The camp was crowded with prisoners. Most of
them were Poles, but there were some Czechs,
Hungarians, and a few Russians too. Each hut held
about 120 – yet it was hardly big enough for more
than forty. They passed the time loafing about,
playing chess, sewing, reading, fighting for old
newspapers or cigarette stumps, quarrelling, shouting. At mealtimes they huddled round trestle tables
to eat their cabbage and potato soup. It was the same
for every meal. You could blow yourself out with it
and never be satisfied. For drinking they had warm
water with bread crumbs in it – the Nazi guards
called it coffee. Twice a week they had a dab of
butter, and there was a teaspoonful of jam on
Saturdays. What use was this for keeping out the
cold?

Few had the strength or the spirit to escape.
Several prisoners had got away – a few even reached
the plains. Those that were not caught and sent back
died of exposure in the mountains.

But Joseph was determined to escape. During the
first winter he was too ill and dispirited to try. He
would sit around the hut, thinking of his family and
staring at the few tattered photos of them that he had
been allowed to keep. He would think of his school
in Warsaw and wonder what was happening there
now. When the Nazis came, they had not closed it.
But they had taken away the Polish textbooks and
made him teach in German. They had hung pictures
of Hitler in all the classrooms. Once, during a

scripture lesson, Joseph had turned the picture of Hitler's face to the wall. Someone had reported this to the Nazis. Then the Nazi Storm Troops had come for Joseph in the middle of the night and bundled him off to Zakyna. They had left Margrit and the three children behind. How he longed to see them again!

During the summer his health mended, but the number of guards was doubled. A group of six – he was one of them – tried to break away together, but the attempt failed. For this he had a month of solitary confinement.

The following winter he was ill again, but no less determined to escape. He decided to wait till early spring, when the snow was beginning to melt and the nights were not so bitter.

Very carefully he laid his plans.

It was no use thinking of cutting the wire fence. There was a trip-line inside the double fence, and anyone who crossed it would be shot. If he got as far as touching the fence, the alarm bell in the guard-house would ring. There was only one way out – the way the guards went, through the gate and past the guard-house. His idea was to disguise himself as one of them and follow them as they went off duty. But how was he to get hold of the uniform?

At the back of each block was a leaky and unheated hut known as 'the cooler'. It had three or four cells to which unruly prisoners were sent to 'cool off'. To be sent there you only had to be late for roll-call or cheek a guard. It was quite a popular place in summer, as it was so quiet. But in winter you could freeze to death there. In spring, with a bit of luck, you might survive a night or two of frost.

One March day, during the morning hut inspection, he flicked a paper pellet at the guard. It stung him behind the ear and made him turn round. The next one made his nose smart. That was all there was time for. Within five minutes Joseph was in a cell in 'the cooler'.

For two days he stamped up and down, to keep himself warm. He clapped his arms against his sides. He dared not lie down for more than a few moments at a time in case he dropped off to sleep and never woke again. Twice a day a guard brought him food. For the rest of the time he was alone.

On the evening of the third day the guard came as usual. When Joseph heard the soft thud of his footsteps in the snow, he crouched down on the floor at the back of his tiny cell. He had a smooth round stone and a catapult in his hands. He had made the catapult from pine twigs and the elastic sides of his boots. His eyes were fixed on the flap in the door. In a moment the guard would unlock it, peer inside and hand in the food.

Tensely Joseph waited. He heard the key grate in the rusty lock of the outside door of 'the cooler'. The hinges creaked open. There was the sound of a match spluttering – the guard was lighting the lamp. Heavy boots clumped across the floor towards his cell.

Joseph drew back the elastic. He heard the padlock on the flap being unlocked. The flap slid aside.

The guard had not seen Joseph when the stone struck him in the middle of the forehead and knocked him down. The floor shook as he tumbled. He groaned and rolled over.

Joseph must act quickly, before the guard came to his senses. He knew the guard kept his bunch of keys in his greatcoat pocket. He must get hold of them without delay. He must lift the guard till they were within reach.

He took a hook and line from under his bed. He

had made the line by cutting thin strips from his blanket and plaiting them together. The hook was a bent four-inch nail that he had smuggled in from his hut.

After several attempts, the hook caught in the top fastened button of the guard's greatcoat. He tugged at the line and drew the guard, still groaning, up towards him . . . higher and higher.

Suddenly the line snapped. The guard fell back, striking his head sharply on the floor. The hook was lost.

Joseph had one spare hook, that was all.

He tried again. This time the cotton broke and the button went spinning across the floor.

He had begun to despair when he saw the keys. They were lying on the floor. They had been shaken out of the greatcoat pocket when the guard fell.

Quickly Joseph fished for the ring of keys and hauled it up. A few moments later he was kneeling beside the senseless body, hastily stripping off the uniform. There was no time to lose. Already the locking up of the prisoners had started and he could hear the guards shouting at them outside.

Joseph felt warm in the guard's uniform. The greatcoat reached to his ankles. The fur cap had flaps for covering his ears. He smiled to himself as he locked the guard in the freezing cell. Then, turning up his collar so that the tips touched his cheekbones, he went out into the bitter night.

He walked through the snow towards Block E, where the Hungarian and Rumanian prisoners were kept. In the dark shadows behind the huts he hid until the trumpet sounded the change of guard.

Hundreds of times he had watched the soldiers of the guard fall in and march out of camp. He had memorized every order, every movement. It seemed to him quite natural now to be lining up with the others.

'Anything to report?' the officer asked each of them in turn.

'All correct, sir,' they answered.

'All correct, sir,' said Joseph in his best German.

'Guard, dismiss!' said the officer.

Joseph dropped to the rear and followed the other soldiers out – out of the great spiked gate and into freedom. It seemed to good to be true.

Some of the soldiers stopped outside the guard-house to gossip. A few went in. Joseph walked straight ahead, turning his head away from the window light as he passed.

'Where are you going?' one of them called.

'Shangri La,' he muttered. It was the soldiers' name for the night club in the village where they sometimes spent their off-duty times.

Without looking behind him, he walked on.

The village of Zakyna was a mile below the camp. It was a mass of tiny huts clinging to the steep cliffside. There was no moon that night, but Joseph could see lights in the windows.

He walked straight through the village.

Suddenly he was challenged in German. 'Karl, give me the cigarettes,' said a rough voice.

He took no notice and walked on.

'Karl, the cigarettes!' the voice shouted, threateningly.

He hurried on.

There were footsteps behind him.

He turned round to look. A drunken soldier was tottering after him.

Joseph began to run. The soldier ran too, swearing whenever he stumbled.

Just below the last huts in the village, the road curled away from the cliff edge. A mail car had pulled up. Her lights were on and the engine running. There was a pile of luggage in the road, and an angry group of people had gathered round.

'You're two hours late!' someone cried.

'I told you – there was an avalanche. The road was blocked,' returned the driver.

Joseph dived behind the white wall of snow that the snow plough had thrown up at the side of the road. He was right on the edge of the cliff, which dropped steeply into the darkness. He heard the sound of crates being dumped in the road. And he heard the drunken soldier roll up and cry, 'Driver you've pinched my cigarettes!'

'Chuck him over the cliff,' said someone.

A scuffle. Laughter. Steps coming towards him.

Joseph slid quietly away – to where a square shape jutted out from the road. In the dark it looked like a cart without wheels. Quickly he hid underneath.

At once he wished he hadn't moved. A heavy crate banged down on to the boards above his head. The boards quivered and shook. Boots scraped the wood, shuffled on the snow.

There was a babble of voices – jokes and leg-pulling mixed with directions for the loading of the crates.

Joseph waited tensely while the crates were lifted in and the tarpaulin draped over them. When the soldiers were back in the road, he heaved himself over the wooden edge and under the tarpaulin.

A loud voice shouted, 'Are you ready, there?'

From the other side of the dark valley came an answering call.

Suddenly Joseph realized that the wooden boards he lay on were moving. They were sliding out into the darkness, away from the road. Where was he?

As soon as he dared, he lifted the edge of the tarpaulin and looked out. He was in a kind of roofless cage. It was hung by pulleys and wire to an overhead cable and was swinging giddily from side to side. An aerial luggage lift. These were quite common in the mountains. They were driven by electricity and used for carrying goods from one side of a steep valley to the other.

Joseph sighed with relief. The giddy movement of the cage made him feel sick, but he knew that every second it was taking him farther from his enemies.

Then suddenly the cage squeaked to a standstill. It began to slide back, back to the road. The voices on the road grew louder. A jerk, a rattle of pulleys, the scrape of wood on snow, and he was back where he had started. Someone leapt into the cage and lifted the tarpaulin on the other side of the crates from Joseph.

'There's room for it alongside – hurry up!' cried the same voice.

Joseph's hand was in his revolver holster. He meant to fight his way out if he had to. But all he could feel in the holster was a stick of chocolate.

Another crate was chucked in and kicked alongside the other pair. It banged against his foot and nearly made him scream with pain. He fell back and bit his lip, groaning.

But no one heard his groans, for the cage was already rattling out into the darkness again. While he rubbed his bruised toes, it pitched and swung from side to side. After a few minutes of climbing, a shape loomed down towards him and rattled past. It was the balance lift – the descending cage which balanced the weight of the climbing one – and it meant he had passed the half-way mark. Ahead of him was the black shape of the mountain. With every swing of the cage and every creak of the cable, it came nearer. Were there soldiers on that side, too? If so, what was he to do? He could not escape discovery and he was quite unarmed.

In a flash he made up his mind.

He lifted the tarpaulin from his shoulders and sat with his back to the crates, facing the dark mountain.

The cage banged to a standstill. The light of a torch was flashed full into Joseph's face.

'I have you covered with my pistol,' said Joseph steadily. 'If you make a sound, I'll shoot.'

A Polish voice swore.

'Be quiet. Do you want me to shoot?' said Joseph. 'Hand me your torch.'

He seized it from the trembling hands and flashed the beam on to a grey-bearded peasant face. Joseph's spirits rose. The man was Polish, a countryman of his.

Joseph spoke more gently. 'Do as I tell you and you'll come to no harm. Unload the cage.'

Joseph questioned him while he was unloading. 'Is the cage worked from this end? The control is in your hands? Good. We shan't be disturbed, then. Take me to where you live.'

The crates were safely stacked and the shed by the cage locked. The peasant had kept one crate for himself. It contained provisions and clothing from town. He lifted it on to his shoulder and then led the way along a track of beaten snow that wound upwards through pine trees. Soon they came to his home. It was a large chalet, with wide overhanging eaves. Wood was stacked at the sides.

He laid down the crate and led Joseph inside.

A wood fire was burning brightly in a wide open hearth. A large pot hung above it from a hook in the chimney. An old lady was sitting by the fire. She looked startled.

Joseph threw his cap and greatcoat over a chair.

'Here's the pistol I almost shot you with,' he said. 'It's a slab of chocolate.'

He broke it into three pieces, giving one to each of them. They were suspicious and waited till Joseph had swallowed his piece before they ate theirs.

'I don't understand,' said the peasant slowly. 'You speak like a Pole. You look like a Pole. But your uniform –'

At that moment a bell clanged out from the other side of the valley. It echoed among the mountains.

'That's the prison bell,' said Joseph. 'It's a long time since it rang like that – when the last prisoner escaped.'

'You've come to search for him?' asked the old lady.

'I am the prisoner,' said Joseph. 'I knocked out a guard and stole his uniform. Look – if you don't believe me, here's my camp number burnt into my arm – ZAK 2473. I want you to hide me.'

The number convinced them that he was telling the truth. They knew that if they were found hiding him they would die. But they were brave people and did not hesitate.

Joseph slept in a warm bed that night for the first time for two years.

In the morning the old man went to work the luggage lift as usual. Before going, he arranged a danger signal. If there were any soldiers coming across in the cage, he would whistle three times. And he showed Joseph a hiding-place in the woodshed.

While he was away, Joseph showed the old woman the tattered photos of his family. He had taken them out of his wallet so many times to look at them that they were creased and crumpled and finger-marked all over. He spoke about his wife and children, his school, his capture by the Nazis; about the shortage of food, the destruction everywhere, and the continual fear of arrest. Every day had brought news of more families being split up.

The old woman was moved by his story. While he was speaking, she began to think of ways in which she could help him. He looked starved and needed good food. She had a little cheese and oatcakes, a side of bacon hanging in the cellar, and the remains of a tin of real coffee saved from before the war.

Suddenly there was a loud bank on the door. Was it a search party? If so, why had the old man given no warning?

A voice called out in German.

There was no time to escape to the woodshed.

'Quick – up there!' The old woman pointed up the chimney. 'There's an opening on the right, half-way up.'

Joseph dived into the hearth and hauled himself up over the iron spit. The fire was only smouldering and there was not much smoke. He had not found the opening when the door burst open and two soldiers came in. While they searched the room, he stood very still, his legs astride the chimney. He wanted to cough. He thought his lungs would burst.

Suddenly a head peered up the chimney. It was the old woman. 'They've gone upstairs,' she said. 'But don't come down yet.'

She showed him where the opening was. He crept inside, coughing. He could see the sky through the wide chimney top above him.

He was congratulating himself on his good luck
when he heard the soldiers return to the room below.
With difficulty he controlled his cough.

'What about the chimney?' said a German voice.
'Plenty of room to hide up there.'

'Plenty of soot too,' said the other soldier. 'Your
uniform's older than mine. What about you going
up?'

'Not likely.'

'Then we'll send a couple of bullets up for luck.'

Two ear-splitting explosions. It seemed as if the
whole chalet was falling down. Joseph clung to his
perch. There was a great tumbling about his ears. He
clung and clung and clung – till his fingers were torn
from their grip, and he fell.

When he came to his senses, he was lying on the
floor. The old woman was bending over him,
washing his face with cold water.

'It's all right – they've gone,' she said. 'The fall of soot saved you. The soldiers ran for it when the soot came down. They were afraid for their uniforms.'

'I'm sorry I didn't have time to warn you,' said the old man. 'The soldiers had hidden themselves in the cage. I didn't see them till it was too late.'

Joseph spent two whole weeks in the chalet. The old couple treated him like a son, sharing all they had with him. They fed him so well that his thin cheeks filled out and he gained several pounds in weight. They were simple, homely folk, and in their company his mind grew more peaceful than it had been for years. In the brutality of his prison life he had almost forgotten what kindness was.

He passed his time indoors, mostly eating and resting. More than once he was tempted to go outside. The spring sun beamed down all day long from clear skies. It melted the icicles that hung from the roof; it roused the first crocuses from the bare brown patches in the snow. But there was no sense in exposing himself, and he wisely stayed indoors. The nights were freezing, and he was glad of his warm blankets.

On the fifteenth night he left the chalet on the first stage of the long journey home. The moon was in her first quarter, and it was freezing hard. He was wearing the warm woollen clothes of a Polish highlander. The old man went with him as guide for three days till they were clear of the high mountains.

On the afternoon of the second day they reached the edge of the snow line. Little rivers coursed down from under the snow. Wherever they trod, the ground was soggy and their boots squelched. But it was a joy to leave the snow behind and to see the snowdrops and crocuses everywhere. Lower down in the valleys the grass was already green, gay with primroses, violets, and wild daffodils.

In the gorge where the River Sanajec tumbles down between steep wooded rocks to meet the great rivers of the plains, they said good-bye to each other. The old man took Joseph's head between his hands, blessed him and wished him good fortune.

Joseph Balicki walked all the way back to Warsaw, where he found his home destroyed and his wife and children gone. The family had been split up the night Joseph was taken away, but they all made their way to Switzerland, where, after many adventures, they were eventually reunited.

THE BATTLE OF TRESCO

Ann Schlee

ivil War is raging in England, and the Roundhead fleet is set to attack the Scilly island of Tresco. Two Royalists, Lum Melchett and his mother Lady Melchett, have been hiding on the island with the fisherman Nants and his daughter Kate. With the Royalist ships becalmed off the island of St Mary's, Nants and Lum must somehow foil the Roundhead invasion . . .

Nants rowed slowly and steadily towards the fleet, taking his bearings from the shore and never once turning around to look at it. Lum crouched down in the boat, tying the fish to a boathook. He watched his own fingers with great detachment. They seemed a separate tool, made solely to do this one thing. It was so very quiet. No breath of wind to bring the Royalist ships from St Mary's. But he wasn't frightened. Everything was calm and simplified, narrowed down to doing what Nants told him. There was no more need to think or act for himself. He felt happier than he had for days.

'That's Northwithel, lad.'

The channel opened between the black rock and the headland. Lum remembered Kate's scorn when he asked if he could walk from Tresco to Northwithel. 'You'd drown,' she'd said. Now he saw why. They would never believe Nants. It was too wide.

The fisherman pulled evenly on the oars and the dancing water sucked and swirled from the blades. A few strokes more and the channel had sealed up again, rock on rock. It was as if it had never been. Rock and headland were again one. It would work. He was sure of it. But not really concerned. This was happening to someone else. He was on the shore, watching between the grasses. He was in the stable lofts at Melchett, imagining his first battle, his sword, his horse. He was in a fishing boat, tying fish to a pole, why, he hardly knew.

The fleet grew nearer. He saw the gulls that had fled at the din of the cannonade return above the ships in clouds. Then suddenly they burst up into the air again like handfuls of chaff as the men on the decks began to raise cheer after cheer.

'What might that be for?' said Nants. Lum strained forward. He could see the ships clearly now, ten or so, between the rocks, and as he watched the sides of them began to crawl with men.

'They're going over the sides. Down into barges.'

There were so many of them. Lum felt the first watery stirrings of fear. The cheering went on like one huge mad voice. Then it grew ragged and died away.

'That'll be why they stopped firing,' said Nants. 'We'd best waste no time.'

'What do I do?'

'When we're right in among them, heave the fish aloft. But don't you say a word if you can help it. Look as silly as you can and leave me to talk. But keep an eye out for the *Phoenix*, Blake's ship. It's her we want.'

They were at the entrance to the Pool.

The black walls of the Parliament ships swayed

high over their heads, still swarming with men. The water between was paved with heaving bargeloads of more men. Musketeers struggled to buckle on their heavy equipment before the barges became too crowded to move in. Pikemen stood crowded together with the rising sun dazzling on their pointed helmets and their great pikes towering stiffly above them.

Above the creaking of the ships, the shouts, the clatter of weapons, gulls screamed and clamoured, dropping suddenly between the ships on some rotting morsel and fighting over it with their wings beating up into the air again.

The stench was sudden and appalling. The open gunports breathed out the foul air of the lower decks where the soldiers and crew had lived packed together during the past three days in sickness and filth. Mingled with the smell of spent gunpowder it settled over the Pool like a cloud with no wind to disperse it.

A dead rat floated past them, its pale gleaming belly just breaking the surface. From one of the ships came the terrified whinnying of a horse. Lum felt sick and dazed. It was difficult and painful to breathe. He heard Nants say anxiously, 'Come on, lad. Heave up the pole.'

He wedged it between his knees and gripped it with his hands.

They began to move in amongst the shifting walls of waiting staring men. Still no one challenged them. No one seemed to question their being there. But how the men stared, hungry for anything to distract them. Their eyes seemed to fasten on the little boat and draw it in among them.

Lum stared back. Was this an army? Were they enemies? They stretched when they could and

gnawed at scraps of food in their hands and spat over the sides of the barges. They lifted their helmets and scratched their heads or stood with hands clasped, rapt in prayer. Their faces were drawn and ill-shaven and many of them had the awful pallor of seasickness. A few laughed and joked. One entire bargeload stood bareheaded, fervently chanting a psalm. Their voices were English, familiar, not like the strange shouts on the quay at St Mary's. Yet these were enemies.

'Fish. Fresh-caught and salted,' called Nants.

Men waved and called out to him but he did not stop. Lum clutched the pole and tried to copy poor Will Corner's vacant anxious expression. He let his mouth fall slack and his head loll to one side and he searched for some sign of the *Phoenix*. There she was, with a red and gold flag drooping from her stern. He signalled to Nants with his eyes.

The fisherman edged the boat close to the flagship, in beside a bargeload of musketeers. 'Fish. Fresh fish!'

A grizzled soldier leant on his musket close to the gun wales of the barge. He squinted at the fish. 'What's your price, grandfather?'

'Tuppence,' shouted Nants.

The soldier fumbled in his pouch and tossed two coins into the boat.

'You're a fool to pay,' said a scrawny pock-marked fellow beside him. 'We'll be able to help ourselves by noon.'

The old soldier shrugged. 'I'm hungry now. By noon, who knows?'

Lum lowered the boat hook towards him and he slashed off a fish with his dagger. Lum felt the tug of his blade at the end of the pole but he watched the leering pock-marked face of the other man and saw the hand leap out to snatch a fish. Instinctively he swung the pole back over his head. The boat rocked wildly. He struggled to balance it. He saw the thief reach out after it too far, totter a moment on the edge of the barge while the wooden powder cases on his bandolier rattled like frightened teeth, and crash overboard between the two boats.

There was a great guffaw of laughter from the barge.

'You so anxious to get ashore then?'

'Not like him to be first!'

They could see his arms clawing below the surface of the dirty water. His wide hat with a hank of match still tucked into its greasy orange ribbon floated away unheeded. Everyone began to shout. Nants reached out an oar, but a moment later the man's head thrust out of the water and his friends, leaning over the side of the barge, caught him under the armpits and tried to drag him aboard. He flung his long hair out of his eyes and still in the water began to swear viciously at Lum.

'He did it a purpose,' he shouted as they hauled him up. 'The boy did it a purpose. I saw him. What's he doing here? He's a spy. A delinquent.'

Spy . . . Delinquent . . . The words were muttered back through the barge. The peering faces melted and blurred. The words were chanted on and on. The heavy pole jerked. He had nearly dropped it.

'Nay,' said the old musketeer angrily. 'You tried to steal his fish.'

'He's a spy. He did it a purpose.'

'And you're a thief, Tom Watt. What would you know of honest men?'

'A spy. A spy!'

High over their heads a loud voice hailed down to them, 'What's this of a spy?' Everyone went silent and looked up. A tall florid man stood flourishing a spyglass at them from the poop deck of the *Phoenix*. The broad orange sash of a Parliamentary officer curved across his stomach.

'I'm no spy, sir,' Nants called up to him. 'An honest fisherman trying to sell my catch, sir.'

'He's lying,' shouted the pock-marked musketeer, but the officer paid no attention to him.

'You, fisherman, are you of this island?'

'Born and bred,' called Nants squinneying up at him. 'Do you know these waters, then? Are you a pilot?'

'Aye, aye.'

'Come aboard to me, then.'

'That I can't. The boy's good for naught but to hold the fish. Can't trust him with the boat.'

The officer swore. 'Wait there, then,' he shouted. He disappeared. Then they saw him striding towards the rail on the main deck. Another officer, short and swarthy, caught him by the arm and held him back, arguing earnestly with him. 'Now,' thought Lum, 'now they've guessed. They know.' But the tall officer broke away, straddled the rail and clambered down the rope net into the barge. The soldiers packed together to make way for him. Lum dared not lower his eyes from the swarthy man on the deck. He was leaning on the rail now, watching with a look of cool suspicion that sent Lum's heart sick. He knew. At any moment the terrible cry would go up again: *Spy! Delinquent!*

Nants waited impassively, dipping his oars from time to time, until the officer came close enough to speak.

'Can you take us ashore?'

'Depends where you're wanting to go.'

'The beach below the blockhouse.'

'Taking all these with you, then?'

'Yes, with all haste.'

Nants puckered out his lips and shook his head. 'Not with the tide this low. Can't take you in that way. You'd never get there.'

'Where, then? There must be some way.'

Nants screwed up his eyes craftily and leant forward on his oars. 'If I were you, now, I'd aim at the point. Good deep water about there. You could beach them easy behind those rocks.' He stretched out an arm to where the black outline of Northwithel pressed against the greens and browns of Tresco. The officer levelled his spy glass. Then without lowering it he asked casually, 'Is that bit of the shore defended, do you know?'

'Not so as you'd notice. They say there's a man or two left at the blockhouse, but most's gone round to the other side or fled to St Mary's.'

The officer lowered the spyglass suddenly and swung round to stare Nants straight in the eye. Patiently, stupidly, the fisherman held his gaze. At last he said, 'Can you lead us there? We'll pay you generously when the last man's ashore.'

Nants ducked over his oars. 'Yes, sir. That I will, sir.'

'Take up your position then at the mouth of the Pool and wait till my boat comes alongside.'

He turned abruptly, shouldering his way back among the musketeers to the side of the *Phoenix*, and Nants began to pull away from the barge. Lum felt a sudden sharp pain in his chest and his hands. He had been holding his breath locked inside him and his hands so tightly gripped around the pole that they were quite white and rigid with cramp. He lowered the pole and began to clench them open and shut. The staring eyes were a torment to him now. He felt them on his very skin. How could they stare and stare and not seem to see what was before them? It could not last. Perhaps they knew already. They would let them row to the very mouth of the Pool, thinking they were safe, before they gave the order. Spit gathered in his mouth thick and sour. The

swarthy officer still leant over the rail of the *Phoenix*, moodily watching them go.

He looked across to Nants, but the fisherman's face was quite expressionless as he manoeuvred the boat about and worked his way back among the barges. He whistled into his sooty beard the same snatch of song again and again as he had rowing to St Mary's. But once, as he raised his oars and leant slowly forward for the next stroke, he said softly to Lum, 'We've netted them, lad. Now to haul them in.'

A narrow barge manned by eight oarsmen came alongside the fishing boat at the mouth of the Pool. The tall officer, with his spyglass in his hand, stood at the raised stern, with him the helmsman and two young officers. Musketeers crowded around the cannon in the bows.

'Not a seaman amongst them,' muttered Nants. 'They've even set soldiers to the oars. We might have saved ourselves the trouble. I doubt they'll get to Northwithel, let alone Tresco.'

'They're falling in behind, Colonel Bowden, sir,' said one of the young officers.

'Tell them to make haste. The water's low enough

as it is, with the boats so burdened.'

The young man shouted the order back to the first
of the clustering barges. The other lieutenant turned
to his superior. He made no effort to lower his voice,
as if he scarcely expected fishermen to understand
civilized speech. Lum, in the stern of the fishing boat
bobbing a few feet from him, heard every word.

'You trust these fellows, sir?'

'Why not? The island looks deserted. The turncoat
said it was undefended.'

'Then why is there no sign of him?'

'He's not had his chance yet.'

'Blake mistrusted these two,' said the young man,
jerking his head towards Nants and Lum.

Bowden laughed shortly and scornfully. 'He's been
tricked before, you know. He trusted a Portuguese
fruitseller who rowed out to him in the Tagus and
turned out to be a Royalist vending a fire-bomb.
Now he suspects everyone. Oh, but it's a cautious
merchant's nature! Pay him no heed. His job was to
get us here and ours to get ashore and do the
fighting. Besides, it's a stone's throw away. It cannot
be so great a matter.'

'Twenty boats assembled, sir,' called the officer in
the stern. 'Colonel Clarke follows with twenty more.'

'Lead on, then,' Bowden said sharply to Nants. The
order to row was passed back along the flotilla. As
they moved forward another cheer rang out behind
them and the barges slowly followed in compact
ranks of five.

Nants had stopped whistling. His face was set. He
kept close to the bows of the shallop, just wide of her
oars. The brown hill, the pale grasses, the white
beach with the black mass of Northwithel stuck in
front of it, heaved and fell closer with every stroke. A
few thin trails of smoke rose from the invisible

cottages. The Royal standard hung limply from its mast on the block-house.

Once, as Lum watched, there was a flicker of white down the beach. He thought it was Kate running towards them. He could hear her name in her shrill frightened voice. The shape lifted and changed. It was nothing but a pair of seabirds startled out of the grasses. His ears were filled with the thrashing of water and the creaking of oarlocks, the grunts and shouts of the rowers and, from behind him, a growing confusion of voices.

'Look behind you now, boy.'

He looked back over his shoulder. In those few minutes the orderly pack of barges had been caught by the current and scattered like driftwood after a wreck, grounded on sandbanks and broken on the rocks. A troop of pikemen struggled to pole themselves free with their weapons. The men floundering around their sunken barge were being hauled aboard others already so overladen that they scarcely cleared the water. The barges that still rode clear drifted helplessly. The rowers slumped over their oars, all strength exhausted in minutes by the strength of the current and the great weight of their cargo. As the flat keels rolled in the slight swell, men retched over the sides, overcome with seasickness.

Bowden shouted to Nants to halt. His own men raised their oars clear of the water and leant across them. Lum could hear them panting like hounds. Bowden motioned his lieutenants aside and began to shout his own orders over the stern. The barge closest behind was to halt where it was in the lee of a rock, and the others to rendezvous there with it. Then he turned and studied the deserted rock ahead of him minutely through his spyglass.

'Are you sure this is Tresco?' he shouted suddenly

to Nants.

'Of course it be Tresco.'

'Then why has no one fired on us?' He stood fingering the spyglass uncertainly. The first few barges were dragging painfully to the meeting place. Then he shouted down to the oarsmen, 'Forward again. Take me in to land.'

Immediately the young officers began to protest. 'What if it's an ambush, sir? Wait till we can take more men in with us.'

'No, we'll land without delay. I don't think this is an ambush. I think it's something else altogether. You, fisherman, do you swear this rock is part of Tresco?'

'Upon my life, sir.'

The barge lurched past them, but Nants made no attempt to follow. He kept his boat bobbing in its wake while the barge beached on a spit of sand running out from Northwithel. Bowden leapt over the side and waded ashore alone. Nants sat resting on his oars, tense and watchful. The current was drawing them away from the rock, back towards the barges clustering at the rendezvous. As they watched Bowden climb to the crest of Northwithel the water between them widened steadily. Lum saw the man stand still against the sky. Then he came bounding down. He was knee-deep in water beside his barge, shouting furiously.

'Damnation, where's that old villain? It's no more Tresco! There's half a musket-shot of water between it and the island. I'll have you strung up for this! What do you mean by it?'

'It's part of Tresco as I say, sir,' Nants called back to him. 'The men can wade across at the low tide. It's going out fast, sir.'

'We'll see about that!' They were helping him

aboard the barge again. 'Row me around the other side of this rock. Signal the others to wait.'

Five or six soldiers splashed over the sides and began straining to push her off.

'She's stuck fast, sir. We can't move her. She's grounded too deep.'

'Damnation, you fools! Out, all of you, and get her afloat!'

In the confusion no one seemed to have noticed that the fishing boat was drifting further and further away. Nants began to row again, very gently, pulling clear of the barges to the west and heading slowly towards the southern tip of Northwithel.

'What's happening now, boy?'

'They're in the water to free her. She's afloat. They're getting aboard.'

'Where's he headed? Can you see?'

'Around Northwithel, on the far side.'

'He'll sound the channel. We've not much time. We'll keep to this side of Northwithel out of his way while we can. Have a look behind.

The second troop of barges was slowly overtaking the first, coming up in good order in the deeper water west of the rock.

'We haven't stopped them,' said Lum bleakly. 'They're coming straight on.'

'Nay lad, we've cut them in half, and they can't be so slow as not to know it. Bowden will have us in his sights in a minute. He's forgotten us for the moment but he'll soon think of us when he's taken the soundings.'

Nants had been rowing steadily now past North-withel. The rock stayed for a moment longer between them and Bowden's barge. Then they came out into the channel. The shore of Tresco seemed very close. Lum caught sight of the barge. Then Nant's voice shouted, 'Down, boy. Down flat.'

He flung himself into the bottom of the boat, curled between the thwarts with cold water seeping into his clothes. He heard the oarlocks creak violently. The little boat began to hurtle through the water with amazing speed. Nants's body jerked back and forth over his head. His jaw was tight and twisted and the veins in his forehead and neck like thick, dark cords. Sweat poured off his face, streaking it with soot. Lum could not watch him. He buried his head in his arms. When he heard the first crack of musket fire, he did not understand what it was but thought that something in the straining body above him had broken.

One of the oars rattled over his head. He looked up. Nants still hung grimly to one oar but the other swung loose on the thole pin. His left arm was limp and bleeding at his side. The boat began to swirl around. Lum caught the loose oar with both hands. He swung himself under it and wedged himself in beside the fisherman. The boat rocked wildly out of control, but his hands clung to the oar and all his being went into dragging it through the water.

He could see Bowden's barge wavering against the side of Northwithel and the men raising their muskets trying to aim in the unsteady motion of the boat. Spouts of water burst up in the sea around them. Again and again came the small deadly crack and sing of the muskets.

One . . . two . . . three strokes. Something solid swelled and burnt in his chest.

Four . . . five . . . The boat shuddered against the Tresco shore.

'Out!' Nants shouted 'Over the side. Get to the rocks.'

The water was about his legs. He was scrambling

and crawling between the boulders. The firing had
stopped. He was climbing up among the rocks,
seeing nothing but his hands clinging on the rough
lichens in front of his face, scraping his ankles as he
dragged himself up.

Then his finger scrabbled among grass and rabbit
pellets. There was a voice. Hands were pulling him
upwards.

For a long time he lay with his eyes shut, listening
to someone suck in long rasping breaths. Someone
lay in pain near him. He remembered Nants and
reached out his hand, groping on the grass. The
breathing was nearer and louder. It came and went,
taking on the rhythm of the pain that throbbed in his
chest. It was his own breathing that made the sound
and the pain. Nants was not there.

A strange face was between him and the sky. An
arm slid behind his neck, lifting his head. He smelt
sweat. There were more voices.

'Poor lad, he's all in.'

'Here, give him something to drink.'

'Easy. He can't swallow till his breath comes back.'

Something pressed against his mouth. He twisted
his head to get away from it, but it followed him,
pinching his lips against his teeth until at last he took
a painful gulp of warm beer.

'Where is he?' he said.

'Easy, lad, easy.'

'Where is he?'

'Whom does he mean?'

'The fellow that was in the boat with him. The one
that was hit.'

'He was just behind me. He must be here. He was
in the rocks. You must find him.' Lum spoke very
slowly and carefully so that they would understand.

'We can't go down there now, boy. They're almost

upon us. We've orders not to show ourselves.'

'He was just behind me. He's hurt.'

He tried to get to his feet but they held him down: three seamen in a grassy hollow behind some rocks. Neat pyramids of cannonballs were stacked on the ground beside him. The hard thing behind his shoulders was the carriage of a cannon. He knew that he was on Tresco, that this was a guncrew from one of the Royalist frigates, that there was a battle that was over or perhaps yet to come. The seamen held like iron, but tried, kindly, to soothe him. 'Don't you fret. He'll be all right. Never saw a man row so. Like the damned. He'll be safe. You'll see.'

Two other cannon were hidden in the rocks of the headland and men with muskets were lying and crouching behind them. An officer paced back and forth below them with his naked sword in his hand, talking quietly. 'Steady, my boys; steady, my brave boys. Wait, wait. It's not time yet. Wait till they come in closer. Move that boy,' he called up to them. 'Take up your positions. Steady now.'

Lum was dragged aside and propped against a boulder while the seamen crouched down beside their guns. As soon as they left him he rolled over and began to crawl back to the rocky edge. He dragged himself between two stones and lay in their shelter looking down into the bay. Colonel Clarke's troupe of barges were past Northwithel, crowding in towards the rocky beach below. He saw Nants's boat, swamped with water, lying between two rocks, but there was no sign of Nants.

A shout sounded behind him. He turned to see the officer's sword flash in the air. There was a sudden commotion and then the gun fired.

Instantly Lum's ears were blocked with pain, but still he heard each thud of the cannon shudder on his spine. Tears burst from his eyes. Beside him the guncrew worked in a grim intense rhythm, loading, firing, swabbing, loading, as if they and the cannon were joined together. The great gun hurtled back and forth on the grass. He felt its hot breath and the fierce pleasure of the seamen. A thick taste of metal coated the roof of his mouth and the back of his throat. He lay, staring confusedly down into the bay, looking for Nants among the rocks by the broken boat, hardly aware of what had become of the attack.

The barges in the rear were already turning back to the bleak shelter of Northwithel. More and more churned around in the crowded water and fled. Only a few had anchored in the bay with the men spilling over their sides and running for shelter among the rocks. Those that were still aboard struggled for room to raise their muskets, while bullets hailed about them.

The Roundhead officer in the foremost boat stood urging them on with his arms. Musket-fire raked down the side of his barge. One after the other the oars snapped and drifted away. Lum saw the officer's arms fall to his sides in despair. A moment later the retreat sounded from beyond Northwithel. The few men that had reached shore scrambled back through the water, dragging a wounded man with them and leaving their dead on the rocks. The attack had failed.

Lum got to his feet with silence ringing in his ears. A bitter cloud of gunsmoke hung over the headland. He could scarcely see. He was looking for Nants. He wanted to get down to the shore again but he could not find the way. The men around him were cheering and embracing each other. He hardly knew why. He broke into a stumbling run, shouldering his way between them. He would get down by the boat and search among the rocks for Nants, who had gone.

Then he saw him standing no more than a few feet away. The fisherman had his good arm slung across the shoulders of a seaman; his face was black with grime; a dirty neckerchief was tied about his wound. Lum stared at him. Nants had a bottle clutched in his hand. He wrapped his arm clear round the seaman's neck and took a long swig of it. Then he rubbed the back of his hand over his lips and grinned foolishly at Lum. He didn't seem at all surprised to see him.

'I couldn't find you,' said Lum. His voice sounded cold and accusing. 'I thought you were dead.' He was suddenly afraid he might cry.

'Whatever made you think that? You all right, boy? I saw you safe among the rocks.' He transferred his arm heavily onto Lum's shoulders and laughed. 'We'll make an oarsman of you yet.'

'Come away,' muttered Lum. His mind had cleared. He knew they must get back to the cottage. He began to lead Nants along the path to the village. 'Come away before they come back.'

'Oh, they'll not be back. Not today at any rate. They'll need to lick their wounds awhile. Eh, but we led them a pretty dance.' He spat with relish onto the path.

'What good was it? We haven't stopped them.'

'Lad, there's nigh on two thousand in the fleet, they say. There's no stopping them. But we've done what we wanted to. We've held them up for today. By the time they come you'll be half way to France.'

It did not feel like what he wanted. He turned angrily to look at Nants. 'You can't hide from them that your arm's hurt. If it's badly hurt you won't be able to get a livelihood.' He dropped his head, staring at the trampled dust on the path. 'Come with us. To France. You could all come.'

But the fisherman pulled him forward. 'Nay, lad,

what would I do in any place but this? But you'll see.
It will never come to that. You'll tell about this to
your sons, boy, as if it were the day of your life.'

But Lum did not believe him.

MY SHORE ADVENTURE

Robert Louis Stevenson

ollowing a chart found in an old sea chest, cabin-boy Jim Hawkins and the crew of the *Hispaniola* have at last dropped anchor off Treasure Island. Jim has overheard the rascally Long John Silver plotting with some of the crew, and he senses trouble brewing . . .

The appearance of the island when I came on deck next morning was altogether changed. Although the breeze had now utterly failed, we had made a great deal of way during the night, and were now lying becalmed about half a mile to the south-east of the low eastern coast. Grey-coloured woods covered a large part of the surface. This even tint was indeed broken up by streaks of yellow sandbreak in the lower lands, and by many tall trees of the pine family, out-topping the others – some singly, some in clumps; but the general colouring was uniform and sad. The hills ran up clear above the vegetation in spires of naked rock. All were strangely shaped, and the Spy-glass, which was by three or four hundred feet the tallest on the island, was likewise the strangest in configuration, running up sheer from almost every side, and then suddenly cut off at the top like a pedestal to put a statue on.

The *Hispaniola* was rolling scuppers under in the ocean swell. The booms were tearing at the blocks, the rudder was banging to and fro, and the whole

ship creaking, groaning, and jumping like a manu-
factory. I had to cling tight to the back stay, and the
world turned giddily before my eyes; for though I
was a good enough sailor when there was a way on,
this standing still and being rolled about like a bottle
was a thing I never learned to stand without a qualm
or so, above all in the morning, on an empty
stomach.

Perhaps it was this – perhaps it was the look of the
island, with its grey, melancholy woods, and wild
stone spires, and the surf that we could both see and
hear foaming and thundering on the steep beach – at
least, although the sun shone bright and hot, and the
shore birds were fishing and crying all around us,
and you would have thought anyone would have
been glad to get to land after being so long at sea, my
heart sank, as the saying is, into my boots; and from
that first look onward, I hated the very thought of
Treasure Island.

We had a dreary morning's work before us, for
there was no sign of any wind, and the boats had to
be got out and manned, and the ship warped three or
four miles round the corner of the island, and up the
narrow passage to the haven behind Skeleton Island.
I volunteered for one of the boats, where I had, of
course, no business. The heat was sweltering, and
the men grumbled fiercely over their work. Ander-
son was in command of my boat, and instead of
keeping the crew in order, he grumbled as loud as
the worst.

'Well,' he said, with an oath, 'it's not for ever.'

I thought this was a very bad sign; for, up to that
day, the men had gone briskly and willingly about
their business; but the very sight of the island had
relaxed the cords of discipline.

All the way in, Long John stood by the steersman

and conned the ship. He knew the passage like the palm of his hand; and though the man in the chains got everywhere more water than was down in the chart, John never hesitated once.

'There's a strong scour with the ebb,' he said, 'and this here passage has been dug out, in a manner of speaking, with a spade.'

We brought up just where the anchor was in the chart, about a third of a mile from either shore, the mainland on one side, and Skeleton Island on the other. The bottom was clean sand. The plunge of our anchor sent up clouds of birds wheeling and crying over the woods; but in less than a minute they were down again, and all was once more silent.

The place was entirely land-locked, buried in woods, the trees coming right down to high-water mark, the shores mostly flat, and the hill-tops standing round at a distance in a sort of amphitheatre, one here, one there. Two little rivers, or, rather, two swamps, emptied out into this pond, as you might call it; and the foliage round that part of the shore had a kind of poisonous brightness. From the ship, we could see nothing of the house or stockade, for they were quite buried amongst trees; and if it had not been for the chart on the companion, we might have been the first that had ever anchored there since the island arose out of the seas.

There was not a breath of air moving, nor a sound but that of the surf booming half a mile away along the beaches and against the rocks outside. A peculiar stagnant smell hung over the anchorage – a smell of sodden leaves and rotted tree trunks. I observed the doctor sniffing and sniffing, like someone tasting a bad egg.

'I don't know about treasure,' he said, 'but I'll stake my wig there's fever here.'

If the conduct of the men had been alarming in the boat, it became truly threatening when they had come aboard. They lay about the deck growling together in talk. The slightest order was received with a black look, and grudgingly and carelessly obeyed. Even the honest hands must have caught the infection, for there was not one man aboard to mend another. Mutiny, it was plain, hung over us like a thunder-cloud.

And it was not only we of the cabin party who perceived the danger. Long John was hard at work, going from group to group, spending himself in good advice, and as for example no man could have shown a better. He fairly outstripped himself in willingness and civility; he was all smiles to everyone. If an order were given, John would be on his crutch in an instant, with the cheeriest 'Ay, ay, sir!' in the world; and when there was nothing else to do, he kept up one song after another, as if to conceal the discontent of the rest.

Of all the gloomy features of that gloomy afternoon, this obvious anxiety on the part of Long John appeared the worst.

We held a council in the cabin.

'Sir,' said the captain, 'if I risk another order, the whole ship'll come about our ears by the run. You see, sir, here it is. I get a rough answer, do I not? Well, if I speak back, pikes will be going in two shakes; if I don't, Silver will see there's something under that, and the game's up. Now we've only one man to rely on.'

'And who is that?' asked the squire.

'Silver, sir,' returned the captain; 'he's as anxious as you and I to smother things up. This is a tiff; he'd soon talk 'em out of it if he had the chance, and what I propose to do is to give him the chance. Let's allow

the men an afternoon ashore. If they all go, why, we'll
fight the ship. If they none of them go, well, then we
hold the cabin, and God defend the right. If some go,
you mark my words, sir, Silver'll bring 'em aboard
again as mild as lambs.'

It was so decided; loaded pistols were served out
to all the sure men; Hunter, Joyce, and Redruth were
taken into our confidence, and received the news
with less surprise and a better spirit than we had
hoped for, and then the captain went on deck and
addressed the crew.

'My lads,' said he, 'we've had a hot day, and are all
tired and out of sorts. A turn ashore'll hurt nobody –
the boats are still in the water; you can take the gigs,
and as many as please can go ashore for the
afternoon. I'll fire a gun half an hour before sun-
down.'

I believe the silly fellows must have thought they
would break their shins over treasure as soon as they
were landed; for they all came out of their sulks in a
moment, and gave a cheer that started the echo in a
far-away hill, and sent the birds once more flying
and squalling around the anchorage.

The captain was too bright to be in the way. He

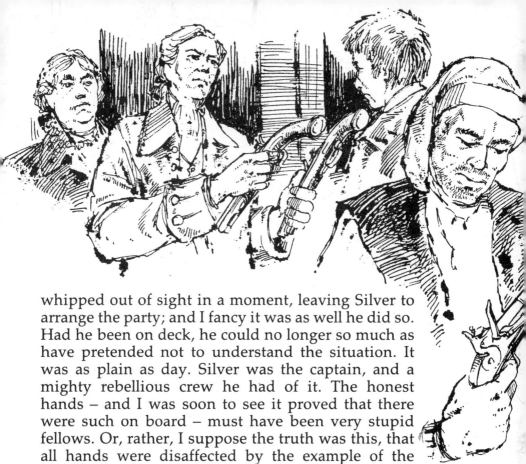

whipped out of sight in a moment, leaving Silver to arrange the party; and I fancy it was as well he did so. Had he been on deck, he could no longer so much as have pretended not to understand the situation. It was as plain as day. Silver was the captain, and a mighty rebellious crew he had of it. The honest hands – and I was soon to see it proved that there were such on board – must have been very stupid fellows. Or, rather, I suppose the truth was this, that all hands were disaffected by the example of the ringleaders – only some more, some less: and a few, being good fellows in the main, could neither be led nor driven any further. It is one thing to be idle and skulk, and quite another to take a ship and murder a number of innocent men.

At last, however, the party was made up. Six fellows were to stay on board, and the remaining thirteen, including Silver, began to embark.

Then it was that there came into my head the first of the mad notions that contributed so much to save our lives. If six men were left by Silver, it was plain our party could not take and fight the ship; and since only six were left, it was equally plain that the cabin party had no present need of my assistance. It

occurred to me at once to go ashore. In a jiffy I had
slipped over the side, and curled up in the fore-
sheets of the nearest boat, and almost at the same
moment she shoved off.

No one took notice of me, only the low oar saying,
'Is that you, Jim? Keep your head down.' But Silver,
from the other boat, looked sharply over and called
out to know if that were me; and from that moment I
began to regret what I had done.

The crews raced for the beach; but the boat I was
in, having some start, and being at once the lighter
and the better manned, shot far ahead of her consort,
and the bow had struck among the shoreside trees,
and I had caught a branch and swung myself out, and
plunged into the nearest thicket, while Silver and the
rest were still a hundred yards behind.

'Jim, Jim!' I heard him shouting.

But you may suppose I paid no heed; jumping,
ducking, and breaking through, I ran straight before
my nose, till I could run no longer.

I was so pleased at having given the slip to Long
John, that I began to enjoy myself and look around
me with some interest on the strange land that I was
in.

I had crossed a marshy tract full of willows,
bulrushes, and odd, outlandish, swampy trees; and I
had now come out upon the skirts of an open piece of
undulating, sandy country, about a mile long, dotted
with a few pines, and a great number of contorted
trees, not unlike the oak in growth, but pale in the
foliage, like willows. On the far side of the open
stood one of the hills, with two quaint, craggy peaks,
shining vividly in the sun.

I now felt for the first time the joy of exploration.
The isle was uninhabited; my shipmates I had left

behind, and nothing lived in front of me but dumb brutes and fowls. I turned hither and thither among the trees. Here and there were flowering plants, unknown to me; here and there I saw snakes, and one raised his head from a ledge of rock and hissed at me with a noise not unlike the spinning of a top. Little did I suppose that he was a deadly enemy, and that the noise was the famous rattle.

Then I came to a long thicket of these oak-like trees – live, or evergreen, oaks, I heard afterwards they should be called – which grew low along the sand like brambles, the boughs curiously twisted, the foliage compact, like thatch. The thicket stretched down from the top of one of the sandy knolls, spreading and growing taller as it went, until it reached the margin of the broad, reedy fen, through which the nearest of the little rivers soaked its way into the anchorage. The marsh was streaming in the strong sun, and the outline of the Spy-glass trembled through the haze.

All at once there began to go a sort of bustle among the bulrushes; a wild duck flew up with a quack, another followed, and soon over the whole surface of the marsh a great cloud of birds hung screaming and circling in the air. I judged at once that some of my shipmates must be drawing near along the borders of the fen. Nor was I deceived; for soon I heard the very distant and low tones of a human voice, which, as I continued to give ear, grew steadily louder and nearer.

This put me in a great fear, and I crawled under cover of the nearest live-oak, and squatted there, hearkening, as silent as a mouse.

Another voice answered; and then the first voice, which I now recognised to be Silver's, once more took up the story, and ran on for a long while in a stream, only now and again interrupted by the other. By the sound they must have been talking earnestly, and almost fiercely; but no distinct word came to my hearing.

At last the speakers seemed to have paused, and perhaps to have sat down; for not only did they cease to draw any nearer, but the birds themselves began to grow more quiet, and to settle again to their places in the swamp.

And now I began to feel that I was neglecting my business; that since I had been so foolhardy as to come ashore with these desperadoes, the least I could do was to overhear them at their councils; and that my plain and obvious duty was to draw as close as I could manage, under the favourable ambush of the crouching trees.

I could tell the direction of the speakers pretty exactly, not only by the sound of their voices, but by

the behaviour of the few birds that still hung in alarm above the heads of the intruders.

Crawling on all-fours, I made steadily but slowly towards them; till at last, raising my head to an aperture among the leaves, I could see clear down into a little green dell beside the marsh, and closely set about with trees, where Long John Silver and another of the crew stood face to face in conversation.

The sun beat full upon them. Silver had thrown his hat beside him on the ground, and his great, smooth, blond face, all shining with heat, was lifted to the other man's in a kind of appeal.

'Mate,' he was saying, 'it's because I thinks gold dust of you – gold dust, and you may lay to that! If I hadn't took to you like pitch, do you think I'd have been here a-warning of you? All's up – you can't make nor mend; it's to save your neck that I'm a-speaking, and if one of the wild'uns knew it, where 'ud I be, Tom – now, tell me, where 'ud I be?'

'Silver,' said the other man – and I observed he was not only red in the face, but spoke as hoarse as a crow, and his voice shook, too, like a taut rope – 'Silver,' says he, 'you're old, and you're honest, or has the name for it; and you've money, too, which lots of poor sailors hasn't, and you're brave, or I'm mistook. And will you tell me you'll let yourself be led away with that kind of a mess of swabs?' Not you! As sure as God sees me, I'd sooner lose my hand. If I turn agin my dooty –'

And then all of a sudden he was interrupted by a noise. I had found one of the honest hands – well, here, at that same moment, came news of another. Far away out in the marsh there arose, all of a sudden, a sound like the cry of anger, then another on the back of it; and then one horrid, long-drawn scream. The rocks of the Spy-glass re-echoed it a

score of times; the whole troop of marshbirds rose again, darkening heaven, with a simultaneous whirr; and long after that death yell was still ringing in my brain, silence had re-established its empire, and only the rustle of the redescending birds and the boom of the distant surges disturbed the languor of the afternoon.

Tom had leaped at the sound, like a horse at the spur; but Silver had not winked an eye, He stood where he was, resting lightly on his crutch, watching his companion like a snake about to spring.

'John!' said the sailor, stretching out his hands.

'Hands off!' cried Silver, leaping back a yard, as it seemed to me, with the speed and security of a trained gymnast.

'Hands off, if you like, John Silver,' said the other. 'It's a black conscience that can make you feared of me. But, in heaven's name, tell me what was that?'

'That?' returned Silver, smiling away, but warier than ever, his eye a mere pin-point in his big face, but gleaming like a crumb of glass. 'That? Oh, I reckon that'll be Alan.'

At this poor Tom flashed out like a hero.

'Alan!' he cried. 'Then rest his soul for a true seaman! And as for you, John Silver, long you've been a mate of mine, but you're mate of mine no more. If I die like a dog, I'll die in my dooty. You've killed Alan, have you? Kill me, too, if you can. But I defies you.'

And with that, this brave fellow turned his back directly on the cook, and set off walking for the beach. But he was not destined to go far. With a cry, John seized the branch of a tree, whipped the crutch out of his armpit, and sent that uncouth missile hurtling through the air. It struck poor Tom, point foremost, and with stunning violence, right between the shoulders in the middle of his back. His hands flew up, he gave a sort of gasp, and fell.

Whether he were injured much or little, none could ever tell. Like enough, to judge from the sound, his back was broken on the spot. But he had no time given him to recover. Silver, agile as a monkey, even without leg or crutch, was on the top of him next moment, and had twice buried his knife up to the hilt in that defenceless body. From my place of ambush, I could hear him pant aloud as he struck the blows.

I do not know what it rightly is to faint, but I do know that for the next little while the whole world swam away from before me in a whirling mist; Silver and the birds, and the tall Spy-glass hill-top, going round and round and topsy-turvy before my eyes, and all manner of bells ringing and distant voices shouting in my ear.

When I came again to myself, the monster had pulled himself together, his crutch under his arm, his hat upon his head. Just before him Tom lay motionless upon the sward; but the murderer minded him not a whit, cleansing his bloodstained knife the while upon a wisp of grass. Everything else was unchanged, the sun still shining mercilessly on the streaming marsh and the tall pinnacle of the mountain, and I could scarce persuade myself that murder had been actually done, and a human life cruelly cut short a moment since, before my eyes.

But now John put his hand into his pocket, brought out a whistle, and blew upon it several modulated blasts, that rang far across the heated air. I could not tell, of course, the meaning of the signal; but it instantly awoke my fears. More men would be coming. I might be discovered. They had already slain two of the honest people; after Tom and Alan,

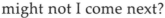

might not I come next?

Instantly I began to extricate myself and crawl back again, with what speed and silence I could manage, to the more open portion of the wood. As I did so, I could hear hails coming and going between the old buccaneer and his comrades, and this sound of danger lent me wings. As soon as I was clear of the thicket, I ran as I never ran before, scarce minding the direction of my flight, so long as it led me from the murderers; and, as I ran, fear grew and grew upon me, until it turned into a kind of frenzy.

Indeed, could anyone be more entirely lost than I? When the gun fired, how should I dare to go down to the boats amongst those fiends, still smoking from their crime? Would not the first of them who saw me wring my neck like a snipe's? Would not my absence itself be evidence to them of my alarm, and therefore of my fatal kowledge? It was all over, I thought. Good-bye to the *Hispaniola*; good-bye to the squire, the doctor, the captain! There was nothing left for me but death by starvation, or death by the hands of the mutineers.

All this while, as I say, I was still running, and, without taking any notice, I had drawn near to the foot of the little hill with the two peaks, and had got into a part of the island where the live-oaks grew more widely apart, and seemed more like forest trees in their bearing and dimensions. Mingled with these were a few scattered pines, some fifty, some nearer seventy, feet high. The air, too, smelt more freshly than down beside the marsh.

And here a fresh alarm brought me to a standstill with a thumping heart.

From the side of the hill, which was here steep and stony, a spout of gravel was dislodged, and fell rattling and bounding through the trees. My eyes turned instinctively in that direction, and I saw a figure leap with great rapidity behind the trunk of a pine. What it was, whether bear or man or monkey, I could in no wise tell. It seemed dark and shaggy; more I knew not. But the terror of this new apparition brought me to a stand.

I was now, it seemed, cut off upon both sides; behind me the murderers, before me this lurking nondescript. And immediately I began to prefer the dangers that I knew to those I knew not. Silver himself appeared less terrible in contrast with this creature of the woods, and I turned on my heel, and, looking sharply behind me over my shoulder, began to retrace my steps in the direction of the boats.

Instantly the figure reappeared, and, making a wide circuit, began to head me off. I was tired, at any rate; but had I been as fresh as when I rose, I could see it was in vain for me to contend in speed with such an adversary. From trunk to trunk the creature flitted like a deer, running manlike on two legs, but unlike any man that I had ever seen, stooping almost double as it ran. Yet a man it was, I could no longer be in doubt about that.

I began to recall what I had heard of cannibals. I was within an ace of calling for help. But the mere fact that he was a man, however wild, had somewhat reassured me, and my fear of Silver began to revive in proportion. I stood still, therefore, and cast about for some method of escape; and as I was so thinking, the recollection of my pistol flashed into my mind. As soon as I remembered I was not defenceless, courage glowed again in my heart; and I set my face resolutely for this man of the island, and walked briskly towards him.

He was concealed by this time, behind another

tree trunk; but he must have been watching me closely, for as soon as I began to move in his direction he reappeared and took a step to meet me. Then he hesitated, drew back, came forward again, and at last, to my wonder and confusion, threw himself on his knees and held out his clasped hands in supplication.

At that I once more stopped.

'Who are you?' I asked.

'Ben Gunn,' he answered, and his voice sounded hoarse and awkward, like a rusty lock. 'I'm poor Ben Gunn, I am; and I haven't spoke with a Christian these three years.'

I could now see that he was a white man like myself, and that his features were even pleasing. His skin, wherever it was exposed, was burnt by the sun; even his lips were black; and his fair eyes looked quite startling in so dark a face. Of all the beggar-men that I had seen or fancied, he was the chief for raggedness. He was clothed with tatters of old ship's canvas and old sea cloth; and this extraordinary patchwork was all held together by a system of the most various and incongruous fastenings, brass buttons, bits of sticks, and loops of tarry gaskin. About his waist he wore an old brass-buckled leather belt, which was the one thing solid in his whole accoutrement.

'Three years!' I cried. 'Were you shipwrecked?'

'Nay, mate,' said he – 'marooned.'

I had heard the word, and I knew it stood for a horrible kind of punishment common enough among the buccaneers, in which the offender is put ashore with a little powder and shot, and left behind on some desolate and distant island.

'Marooned three years agone,' he continued, 'and lived on goats since then, and berries, and oysters.

Wherever a man is, says I, a man can do for himself. But, mate, my heart is sore for Christian diet. You mightn't happen to have a piece of cheese about you, now? No? Well, many's the long night I've dreamed of cheese – toasted, mostly – and woke up again, and here I were.'

'If ever I can get on board again,' said I, 'you shall have cheese by the stone.'

All this time he had been feeling the stuff of my jacket, smoothing my hands, looking at my boots, and generally, in the intervals of his speech, showing a childish pleasure in the presence of a fellow-creature. But at my last words he perked up into a kind of startled slyness.

'If ever you can get aboard again, says you?' he repeated. 'Why, now, who's to hinder you?'

'Not you, I know,' was my reply.

'And right you was,' he cried. 'Now you – what do you call yourself, mate?'

'Jim,' I told him.

'Jim, Jim,' says he, quite pleased apparently. 'Well, now, Jim, I've lived that rough as you'd been ashamed to hear of. Now, for instance, you wouldn't think I had had a pious mother – to look at me?' he asked.

'Why, no, not in particular,' I answered.

'Ah, well,' said he, 'but I had – *re*markable pious. And I was a civil, pious boy, and could rattle off my catechism that fast, as you couldn't tell one word from another. And here's what it come to, Jim, and it begun with chuck-farthen on the blessed grave-stones! That's what it begun with, but it went further'n that; and so my mother told me, and predicked the whole, she did, the pious woman! But it were Providence that put me here. I've thought it all out in this here lonely island, and I'm back on piety. You don't catch me tasting rum so much; but just a thimbleful for luck, of course, the first chance I have. I'm bound I'll be good, and I see the way to. And, Jim,' – looking all round him, and lowering his voice to a whisper – 'I'm rich.'

I now felt sure that the poor fellow had gone crazy in his solitude, and I suppose I must have shown the feeling in my face, for he repeated the statement hotly:

'Rich! rich! I says. And I'll tell you what: I'll make a man of you, Jim. Ah, Jim, you'll bless your stars, you will, you was the first that found me!'

And at this there came suddenly a lowering shadow over his face, and he tightened his grasp upon my hand, and raised his forefinger threateningly before my eyes.

'Now, Jim, you tell me true: that ain't Flint's ship?' he asked.

At this I had a happy inspiration. I began to believe that I had found an ally, and I answered him at once.

'It's not Flint's ship, and Flint is dead; but I'll tell you true, as you ask me – there are some of Flint's hands aboard; worse luck for the rest of us.'

'Not a man – with one – leg?' he gasped.

'Silver?' I asked.

'Ah, Silver!' says he; 'that were his name.'

'He's the cook; and the ringleader, too.'

He was still holding me by the wrist, and at that he gave it quite a wring.

'If you was sent by Long John,' he said, 'I'm as good as pork, and I know it. But where was you, do you suppose?'

I had made my mind up in a moment, and by way of answer told him the whole story of our voyage, and the predicament in which we found ourselves.

He heard me with the keenest interest, and when I had done he patted me on the head.

'You're a good lad, Jim,' he said, 'and you're all in a clove hitch, ain't you? Well, you just put your trust in Ben Gunn – Ben Gunn's the man to do it. Would you think it likely, now, that your squire would prove a liberal-minded one in case of help – him being in a clove hitch, as you remark?'

I told him the squire was the most liberal of men.

'Ay, but you see,' returned Ben Gunn, 'I didn't mean giving me a gate to keep, and a shuit of livery clothes, and such; that's not my mark, Jim. What I mean is, would he be likely to come down to the toon of, say one thousand pounds of money that's as good as a man's own already?'

'I am sure he would,' said I. 'As it was, all hands were to share.'

'*And* a passage home?' he added, with a look of

great shrewdness.

'Why,' I cried, 'the squire's a gentleman. And, besides, if we got rid of the others, we should want you to help work the vessel home.'

'Ah,' said he, 'so you would.' And he seemed very much relieved.

'Now, I'll tell you what,' he went on. 'So much I'll tell you, and no more. I were in Flint's ship when he buried the treasure; he and six along – six strong seamen. They were ashore nigh on a week, and us standing off and on in the old *Walrus*. One fine day up went the signal, and here come Flint by himself in a little boat, and his head done up in a blue scarf. The sun was getting up, and mortal white he looked about the cut-water. But, there he was, you mind, and the six all dead – dead and buried. How he done it, not a man aboard us could make out. It was battle, murder, and sudden death, leastways – him against six. Billy Bones was the mate; Long John, he was quarter-master; and they asked him where the treasure was. 'Ah,' says he, 'you can go ashore, if you like, and stay,' he says; 'but as for the ship, she'll beat up for more, by thunder!' That's what he said.

'Well, I was in another ship three years back, and we sighted this island. 'Boys,' said I, 'here's Flint's treasure: let's land and find it.' The cap'n was displeased at that; but my messmates were all of a mind, and landed. Twelve days they looked for it, and every day they had the worse word for me, until one fine morning all hands went aboard. 'As for you, Benjamin Gunn,' they says, 'here's a musket,' they says, 'and a spade, and a pickaxe. You can stay here, and find Flint's money for yourself,' they says.

'Well, Jim, three years have I been here, and not a bite of Christian diet from that day to this. But now, you look here; look at me. Do I look like a man before the mast? No, says you. Nor I weren't, neither, I says.'

With that he winked and pinched me hard.

'Just you mention them words to your squire, Jim' – he went on: 'Nor he weren't neither – that's the words. Three years he were the man of this island, light and dark, fair and rain; and sometimes he would, maybe think upon a prayer (says you), and sometimes he would, maybe, think of his old mother, so be as she's alive (you'll say); but the most part of Gunn's time (this is what you'll say) – the most part of his time was took up with another matter. And then you'll give him a nip, like I do.'

And he pinched me again in the most confidential manner.

'Then,' he continued – 'then you'll up, and you'll say this: Gunn is a good man (you'll say), and he puts a precious sight more confidence – a precious sight, mind that – in a gen'leman born than in these gen'lemen of fortune, having been one hisself.'

'Well,' I said, 'I don't understand one word that you've been saying. But that's neither here nor there; for how am I to get on board?'

'Ah,' said he, 'that's the hitch, for sure. Well, there's my boat, that I made with my two hands. I keep her under the white rock. If the worst comes to the worst, we might try that after dark. Hi!' he broke out, 'what's that?'

For just then, although the sun had still an hour or two to run, all the echoes of the island awoke, and bellowed to the thunder of a cannon.

'They have begun to fight!' I cried. 'Follow me.'

And I began to run towards the anchorage, my terrors all forgotten; while, close at my side, the marooned man in his goatskins trotted easily and lightly.

'Left, left,' says he; 'keep to your left hand, mate Jim! Under the trees with you! Theer's where I killed my first goat. They don't come down here now; they're all mastheaded on them mountains for the fear of Benjamin Gunn. Ah! and there's the cetemery' – cemetery, he must have meant. 'You see the mounds? I come here and prayed nows and thens, when I thought maybe a Sunday would be about doo. It weren't quite a chapel, but it seemed more solemn like; and then, says you, Ben Gunn was short-handed – no chapling, nor so much as a Bible and a flag, you says.'

So he kept talking as I ran, neither expecting nor receiving any answer.

The cannon-shot was followed, after a considerable interval, by a volley of small arms.

Another pause, and then, not a quarter of a mile in front of me, I beheld the Union Jack flutter in the air above a wood.

Tunnel To Freedom

Eric Williams

his true story of escape from a prisoner of war camp describes how four prisoners dig a tunnel under the wire, hiding the tunnel entrance with a wooden vaulting horse. Constant danger of discovery has delayed the escape, but now they are determined to break through . . .

When they reopened the tunnel at the end of seven days they found that the sand on the roof and walls had dried and considerable falls had occurred. It took them another week to clear the fallen sand and to shore the tunnel in the dangerous places.

It was now early October and the long Silesian summer was ending. All through the summer their working had been controlled by the weather. Once the trap was lifted and the workers were in the tunnel it took them all of fifteen minutes to get back to the shaft, close the trap and get ready to be carried in. They could not afford to be caught out by a shower of rain. It if started to rain the vaulters could not continue without arousing the suspicion of the guards. Nor could they run for the shelter of the canteen leaving the vaulting horse to stand out in the rain. The obvious thing was to carry the horse in with them, and they could not do this with the trap open and two men in the tunnel. So they studied the weather carefully and if it looked at all like rain they had to vault without digging. Nearly every time they took the horse out it was only after long discussions on the weather. The nearer they got to the wire the more reluctant they were to risk being caught by the rain. They were also determined to be out by the end of October and as the time passed they began to get dogmatic and short-tempered in their discussions.

Philip was more upset than the other two by a sudden change of plan. They would part in the evening having arranged a vault immediately after breakfast the following morning. Philip would arrive in their room, dressed for digging, only to find that owing to a change in the weather they had decided not to dig. Ten minutes afterwards, if the weather showed signs of clearing, they would decide to start work, and all the vaulters would be assembled at a moment's notice.

It was trying for all of them. They were physically tired after three and a half months of digging and now their nerves were becoming frayed by continual anxiety and changes of plan. Peter told again and again the story of the old and the young bull, and fumed inwardly at the delays caused by the more and more frequent showers of rain.

With the new system of digging the tunnel made slow progress. They had enlarged the end of the tunnel to form a 'bulge' large enough to allow the man working at the face to rest on his elbows and draw his knees up under his chest. Instead of using the usual wooden toboggan for carrying the sand down the tunnel they used a metal basin eighteen inches in diameter and eight inches deep. The basin was just small enough to fit into the tunnel. Two holes had been drilled in opposite sides of the rim of the basin to take the rope which they had plaited from string off the Red Cross parcels.

When the bulge was finished – it took them four days to remove the extra sand – the tunnel was driven on. One man worked in the tunnel extension, dragging the sand backwards into the bulge. Once in the bulge he pulled the basin up the tunnel, past his feet and over his legs on to his stomach, where he filled it with the sand he had brought back. Two pulls on the rope was the signal for the man in the shaft to pull back the basin full of sand. He then tipped the basin over and filled his bags while the worker in the bulge crawled up the tunnel extension for more sand.

At first they merely threaded the rope through the holes in the rim of the basin. But the holes were raggedly punched through with a nail and soon cut the string, leaving the basin stranded – usually half-way up the tunnel. Then there followed a whispered argument as to who was nearer the basin and whose turn it was to crawl up the tunnel and repair the string. Later they made strong wire hooks with which to attach the basin to the rope.

Up to the time of making the bulge they had been troubled by lack of air in the tunnel. Under the new system they found that sufficient air was pushed up the tunnel by the passage of the basin to supply the man in the bulge. They were now working gradually up towards the surface and it was impossible to remain in the extension for more than a few minutes. If for any reason the basin was not kept moving the shortage of air became dangerous.

After a time they drove the new tunnel so far beyond the bulge that it became impossible to work in the extension and they made a new bulge at the end of the tunnel, filled in the old bulge, lengthened the rope and carried on as before. They made three such bulges before the tunnel was complete.

Try as they might they could not persuade Philip
to enter the tunnel in the nude. He insisted on
wearing a shirt, shorts and tennis shoes; and for this
reason they did all they could to arrange that he
remained in the shaft.

It was a feat of some endurance to drag the
thirty-odd full basins of sand from the face to the
shaft. In addition to this the bags had to be filled and
lifted one by one and stacked inside the vaulting-
horse. So Peter and John pleaded fatigue and
persuaded Philip to allow one of them to work at the
face whenever it was his turn to dig.

When they had been digging for some months John
became convinced that the tunnel was veering to the
left. Peter, who was in charge of the construction, was
convinced that the tunnel was straight. They had taken
their direction by a home-made compass. After considerable argument they decided to put it to the test.

Peter crawled to the end of the tunnel with the
rope of the basin tied to his ankle. He took with him
a thin metal poker about four feet long. John sat in
the shaft holding the other end of the rope while
Nigel sat on the horse apparently resting after an
energetic bout of vaulting.

Philip stood gazing out through the wire, hands in
pockets, in the hopeless, forlorn and typically Kriegie
attitude. Prisoners strolled slowly round the wire.
The guards brooded in their boxes. The whole camp
wore its usual afternoon air of lassitude.

Peter, lying full length at the end of the tunnel,
scooped a deep pit in the floor in front of his face. He
placed the end of the poker in the pit and forced it
slowly upwards through the roof of the tunnel, using
a corkscrew motion to avoid bringing down the roof.
It was hard work. Steady trickles of sand fell from the

ceiling, covering his head and shoulders. Inch by inch he forced the poker upwards until the end was flush with the ceiling of the tunnel. He scraped the sand away from around the poker and pushed it up still higher. By the sudden lack of resistance he knew that it was through and protruding above the surface of the ground. He gave two tugs on the rope to tell John that he was through. John knocked on the inside of the horse and Nigel, hearing this, sent a messenger across to Philip.

Philip, without appearing to do so, frantically scanned the ground in front of him for the end of the poker. He could not see it.

Peter became impatient and began to move the poker slowly up and down. Then Philip saw it. He scratched his head. Nigel kicked the side of the horse. John pulled the rope and Peter pulled down the poker.

The end of the tunnel was under the wire, but fifteen feet to the left of where Peter had expected it to be.

The following morning Peter, John and Philip walked together round the wire completing their plans for the break.

'We shall have to "mole" the last ten feet,' Peter said. 'We're under the wire now and we've twelve days to go to the end of the month. If we're lucky we shall do another six feet by then. That puts us about three feet outside the wire. There's a shallow ditch about twelve feet beyond the wire and if we can manage to strike that it will give us some cover for the break.'

'It's still in the light of the arc lamps,' John objected.

'The light from the lamps extends for about thirty feet outside the wire and we can't possibly push the tunnel on as far as that. Besides, the only railway timetable Stafford's got expires at the end of the month and we *must* time the break so that we just have time to leap down to the station and catch a train. If we get out and then have to hang about waiting for a train we stand a good chance of getting picked up right away.'

'I agree with Pete,' Philip said. 'We'll just have to organise a diversion in the huts nearest the wire at the time we mean to break.'

'That won't be too easy,' John said. 'Who's going to estimate how long it's going to take us to mole ten feet?'

'We'll have to over-estimate it,' Peter said. 'Then add half as much time again and if we reach the ditch before the time we've said – we'll just have to lie doggo until we hear the diversion start.' He turned to Philip. 'Will you organise the diversion?'

'O.K. I'll get that laid on. What about the outside sentries?'

'They don't come on until an hour after dusk. John and I have been sitting up all night watching them. There are two on the side where we are. They each patrol half the wire, meet in the middle, turn back to back and walk to the end. If it's raining they stand under a tree. They walk pretty slowly and when the diversion starts they and the goons in the boxes will be looking inwards towards the noise. We should get past them all right.' He spoke confidently, but thought of tommy-gun bullets and the sharp cry in the night when Alan had been shot on the wire. 'We shall have to wear dark clothes,' he said.

'I'd thought of that,' Philip said. 'We've just had some long woolen combinations sent in by the Red Cross. If we dye them black with tea-leaves or coffee we could put them on over our clothes. It will keep us clean while we're down there and be good camouflage when we get out.'

'John and I thought of going down naked,' Peter said.

'*I'm* not going to get caught and dragged off to the cooler without a stitch of clothing. It's all right for you nudists. Besides, my skin's not like yours – it's too white and would show up like hell. There's another thing too – I want to go right along the hole tomorrow and have a look at the end. I don't trust you two. I want to make certain it's big enough to take me and all my kit.'

'What's all this talk of "all my kit"?' John asked.

'Well, I'm going as a commercial traveller, aren't I? I shall need a bag of samples and I've got a black Homburg hat I bribed off one of the goons. That will have to go in a box to save it from getting crushed. Then I'm wearing an R.A.F. greatcoat . . .'

'He'd better go down tomorrow and see how big
the hole is,' John said.

'Right,' Peter said, 'but look here, Phil, none of
your little games. No widening it while you're down
there and saying it fell in. It's quite big enough as it
is.'

'Let's get this thing straight,' Philip said. 'You
can't go down there naked – you'll have to wear
shoes at least in case you have to run. And I wouldn't
fancy running through those woods with dogs after
me without any clothes on.'

'We must remember to get some pepper for the
dogs,' Peter said.

'Yes, but what about the kit?'

'I like the idea of the combinations,' John said. 'We
could wear socks over our shoes and black hoods
over our heads.'

'We shan't be able to wear all our clothes,' Peter
said. 'The hole's not big enough.'

'We'll wear our shirts and trousers then,' Philip
said, 'and pack the rest of our kit in kitbags dyed
black. We can drag them down the tunnel tied to our
ankles.'

'We haven't solved the most important problem

yet,' Peter said.

'What's that?'

'How to get four people out in the horse.'

'Four people?' Philip sounded excited. 'I thought only we three were going!'

'Yes, but somebody's got to close the trap down after us.'

'Do you mean to say that you haven't arranged all that?' Philip was even more excited.

'As a matter of fact I never thought we'd get as far as we have.' Peter winked at John. 'When we decided to ask you to come in we never considered how we were going to get out once the tunnel was finished. We could have got three into the horse at a pinch, but I'm damned if I can see how we could get four.'

'We'll have to draw lots,' John said.

Philip nearly choked. 'D'you mean to say that you've got as far as this and never considered how we were to get out?'

'Did *you* consider it?' Peter asked.

'I thought you'd got it all fixed.'

'We'll have to put the kit down the day before,' John said.

'We can't do that,' Peter said. 'If we put three

kitbags in the tunnel we shan't be able to get down ourselves.'

'Then we'll have to make a chamber near the end of the tunnel large enough to take them.'

'That's a week's work in itself,' Peter said. 'I can't see us finishing up much outside the wire. We've got to get past the path where the outside sentries walk and we've got to do it before the end of the month. Our timetable expires at the end of the month and after that God knows how the trains will run.'

'Pray God it doesn't rain much during the next few days,' Philip said.

'We'll just have to vault in the rain, that's all. The goons think we're mad already. We'll just have to risk it and hope they don't get suspicious.'

'What train do you and John want to catch?'

'There's a fast train to Frankfurt at six-thirty p.m. German time,' Peter said. 'It's dark by five-thirty and the outside guards usually come on soon after that. If we break at six o'clock it will be dark enough and we stand a chance of getting out before the guards arrive. We don't want to go too early because if they find the hole and get to the station before the train goes we'll get picked up.'

'That train will do me too,' Philip said.

'You're definitely not coming with us then?' Peter asked. It's just as well, he thought. We'd only row if we all went together. Old Phil's much better on his own. He'll make his plans and he'll stick to them, which is something we'd never do. Ours is the better way though. Keep it fluid. You need less luck our way. And we can do it . . .

'I'll go on my own,' Philip said. 'I'll make for Danzig and try to get a boat there.'

'We shall get off at Frankfurt,' John said. 'Take the fast train as far as Frankfurt, spend the night there, and see how things go. We shall most likely make Stettin in two or three short hops. Most likely we shall get off before we get to Stettin station and walk into town.'

'I shall go straight on up to Danzig,' Philip said. 'I hope to be in Sweden three days after leaving the camp.'

'I think you're doing the right thing,' Peter said. 'The right thing for you. Speaking German and travelling as a neutral, a long-distance fast train is the obvious thing. You should get away with it. Once we get to Frankfurt we shall go by slow local trains.'

'I think I've got it!' John said.

'Got what?' Peter asked.

'If I go down in the afternoon before roll-call – say about two o'clock in the afternoon – and take the baggage with me, you can seal me down and I'll dig the whole of the afternoon. You can cook my absence at roll-call and then you two come down as soon as you can. Roll-call's at three forty-five, so you'll be down about four o'clock, or soon after. You take someone out with you – the smallest man we can find – to seal the trap down after you, and then we'll have two hours in which to get ready to break.'

'It'll be pretty grim,' Peter said, 'stuck down there alone for a couple of hours.'

'Oh, I shall be all right. I'll put an air-hole up inside the wire where it won't be seen, and mole on quite happily. I should do five or six feet before you come down.'

'Don't go and bloody well overdo it.' Peter knew John's unsparing energy once he'd set his heart to a thing. He was all energy once he started. Nervous energy and guts. He took more out of himself than he knew. 'Remember we may have to run for it,' he said. 'Don't fag yourself out digging – leave most of it for when we get down there.'

'Oh, I'll take it easy,' John lied. Peter knew he lied and could do nothing about it.

'That's everything then, is it?' Philip asked. 'I'll go along and see the Committee and fix up the diversion for six o'clock. I want to see about my samples too.'

'What are they?' Peter asked.

'Samples of margarine packed in wooden boxes,' Philip replied. 'I'll eat them if I get hungry.'

For the next twelve days they vaulted every day and removed as much sand as they could. They increased the number of bags to fourteen and finally fifteen, although the bearers staggered as they carried the horse into the canteen.

On October the twenty-eighth they made the final bulge at the end of the tunnel. This was as far as they could go. They reckoned that between them they could dig a further ten feet after they had been sealed down. The bulge they made to hold their kitbags while they were digging the last ten feet and finally breaking through to the surface.

They spent the next morning bringing in the last twelve bags and recovering their civilian clothing from their various scattered hiding places round the camp. At twelve-thirty John had his last meal, a substantial meal of bully beef, potatoes and Canadian biscuits and cheese. At one o'clock he went over to the canteen with the camp glee-singing club. He wore his civilian clothes under a long khaki Polish greatcoat. Earlier in the day their baggage had been taken to the canteen, hidden in bundles of dirty laundry.

While John was eating the last of his lunch Peter went along to see the duty pilot. There were two ferrets in the compound. Hell, he thought, they would have to be here now. 'Where are they?' he asked.

'One's in the kitchen, the other's hanging around outside the canteen.'

Peter thought for a moment. 'O.K.,' he said. 'If any more come into the compound send a stooge off to Philip. He'll be in the canteen.'

He ran across to the S.B.O.; knocked on the door. 'Come in.'

He stood in the doorway, panting slightly. 'Sir – we're just putting Clinton down and there's a goon hanging round the canteen. I wonder if you could get him out of the way for a few minutes?'

The S.B.O. smiled and put down his book. 'Let me see,' he said, 'the cooking stove in Hut 64 isn't drawing very well. I'll just stroll over and ask him to have a look at it. He might like to smoke an English cigarette in my room.'

'Thank you, sir.'

Back at the canteen he found the glee-club singing an old English folk song. John, Philip, Nigel and the vaulters were standing near the door.'

'We can't get started,' John said. 'There's a ferret outside and he keeps walking past and looking in at the window. I don't think he likes the singing.'

'It'd be worse without it,' Peter said. 'There's another next door in the kitchen. The S.B.O. is going to take the one outside away and then we'll get cracking.' He looked out of the window. The S.B.O. was walking across the Sportsplatz, a golf club in his hand. Suddenly he appeared to see the ferret and altered course. 'Here comes "Groupy," 'Peter said. 'Good man!'

The group captain exchanged a few words with the ferret and they both walked away across the Sportsplatz.

'O.K.,' said Peter. 'Let's go!'

John hurriedly doffed his coat and pulled the long black combinations on over his clothes. He pulled black socks over his shoes and adjusted the hood which was made from an old undervest dyed black. 'It's bloody hot in here,' he said.

'You look like the Ku Klux Klan,' Peter told him. 'O.K.?'

They both crawled under the vaulting-horse, Peter holding a blanket, a cardboard box and twelve empty bags; John sinister in his black clothes. The three kitbags hung between them suspended from the top of the horse. They both crouched with their backs to the ends of the horse, their feet one each side on the bottom framework. Then the bearing poles were inserted and the horse was raised. Tightly holding the kitbags to prevent them from swaying, they lurched down the steps and went creaking across the compound towards the vaulting-pits.

With a sigh of relief the bearers placed the horse in position and withdrew the poles ready for vaulting.

John crouched in one end of the horse while Peter piled the kitbags on top of him. Peter then spread the blanket on the ground at the other end of the horse and began to uncover the trap. He first collected the grey top layer in the cardboard box and threw the damp subsoil on to the blanket. Feeling round with his fingers he uncovered the bags of sand on top of the trap. He scraped the sand away from the damp wood. As he removed the trap he smelled the familiar damp musty smell of the tunnel. He lifted the kitbags off John's crouching figure and balanced them on top of the trap on the pile of sand. 'Down you go,' he said, and crouched astride the hole while John dropped feet first into the shaft. 'My God, those clothes stink!'

'It'll be worse by the time you come down,' John said. 'It's the dye. Must have gone bad or something.'

While John crawled up the tunnel Peter detached the metal basin from the end of the rope and tied one of the kitbags in its place. One by one John pulled the kitbags up the tunnel and put them in the bulge at the end. Peter then replaced the basin and between them they filled the twelve empty bags they had taken out with them.

While Peter was stacking the bags in the body of the horse, John crawled back for his last breath of fresh air. It was the first time he had been in the tunnel wearing clothes and Peter could hear him cursing softly as he struggled to get back. Finally his feet came into view and then his body, clothed and clumsy under the black combinations. Peter crouched inside the horse looking down on him as he emerged. Outside he could hear the shouting of the vaulters and the reverberating concussion as they landed on top of the horse. John straightened up, head and shoulders out of the trap. He had left the hood at the end of the tunnel and his face was red.

'It's bloody hot down there with clothes on.'

'Take it easy,' Peter said. 'For Christ's sake don't overdo it. I don't want to have to carry you once we get outside.'

'I'll be all right. You seal me down now and I'll see you later.'

'O.K., but for Christ's sake don't make the air-hole bigger than you have to,' Peter said.

He watched John's legs disappear down the narrow tunnel and then he replaced the trap. He replaced the heavy bags of sand and stamped the loose sand firmly on top of them. It's burying a man alive, he thought. Then he heard an anxious voice from outside.

'How's it going, Peter?'

'Five minutes, Phil,' he said, and started to hang the twelve bags of sand from the top of the horse. He gathered the blanket in his arms and spread the rest of the sand evenly over the ground unde the horse. He sprinkled the dry grey sand from the cardboard box over this and gave Philip a low hail that he was ready. The bearing poles were inserted and he was carried back into the canteen.

As they neared the canteen he could hear the voices of the male voice choir. 'He shall set His angels guard over thee . . . Lest thou catch thy foot against a stone . . .' He grinned widely in the dark belly of the horse.

With a final creaking lurch they were up the steps and inside the canteen. The old horse is falling to pieces, Peter thought. Hope it lasts out this evening.

One end of the horse was lifted and he passed the

bags of sand out to Philip. Between them they carried the bags into the band practice room where the choir was going at full blast. 'He shall set His angels, there's a ferret outside the window,' sang David.

'O.K.,' said Peter. 'Keep an eye on him. Is Nig in the roof?'

David nodded his head and continued singing.

'Right. We'll just get these bags to safety in the roof and then we're O.K.'

Nigel's anxious face was peering down from the trap door in the ceiling. Peter held out his fist, thumb extended upwards, and grinned. Nigel grinned too, and lowered his arm for the first of the bags.

Roll-call was at three forty-five and Peter and Philip spent the time until then lying on their bunks. For Peter this was the worst moment of all. This waiting after the work had been done. This lying on his bunk while John was down below digging, and at any moment the scheme might blow and their four and a half months' effort be wasted. Once they were outside he felt it wouldn't matter so much. He hardly expected to get back to England. That was looking too far ahead. That was too much in the lap of the gods. Anything might happen once they were outside. Outside the wire they would rely almost entirely on their luck. It was no use making detailed plans of what they would do when they were outside. They could make a rough outline plan of what they wanted to do, but that was all. From the moment they left the end of the tunnel they would have to adapt their policy to the conditions they met. He could not plan ahead a single day.

And so he lay on his back on the bunk and let his mind run over the list of things he was taking with him.

There was the 'dog food', a hard cake made from dried milk, sugar, Bemax and cocoa. It had been packed in small square tins from the Red Cross parcels and he intended to wear a girdle of them between two shirts.

Next there were several linen bags containing a dry mixture of oatmeal, raisins, sugar and milk powder. When they ate this it would swell in the stomach and prevent that hollow aching sickness that comes from eating ill-balanced concentrated food. He had sewn on one of these bags into each armpit of his jacket as an emergency ration if he became separated from the attaché case which held the bulk of their food.

The attaché case was already down in the tunnel, at the bottom of the kitbag. He mentally checked its contents: the food, clean socks, shaving gear, a roll-neck sweater, soap, a small packet of paper and pen and ink for minor alterations to their papers, and spare cigarettes and matches.

He got to his feet and checked over his jacket pockets. The wallet which held his papers and German money, a small pocket compass, a penknife, handkerchiefs, his pipe (a German one bought in the town by one of the guards), a length of string, a pencil, a German tobacco pouch, his beret and a comb.

He went out on the circuit. It was no use, he couldn't be still. He walked round, over the tunnel, and thought of John moling away down there, sweating away, not knowing the time, not knowing whether the tunnel had been discovered, out of touch with everyone. John digging away, trying to get as much done as he could before the others joined him.

He went unnecessarily to the abort, checked with

Philip on the timing of the diversion for their break, and then walked with Nigel several times round the circuit while they waited for the appel.

'I shall miss you after you've gone,' Nigel said. 'It's been quite good fun, this vaulting.'

'I expect they'll take the horse away when they discover the tunnel,' Peter said. He wanted to thank Nigel for all the help he had given, but he knew that he could not do it. To thank him would put the thing on a formal basis and it was beyond that. So they walked, trying to talk naturally, and waited for the roll-call.

At roll-call the Senior British Officer, suitably disguised, took John's place in the ranks and his absence was not noticed.

As soon as roll-call was finished the vaulters assembled at the canteen. Peter's knees felt loose and he did not want to go in the horse. They had taken it out twice already that day and he felt that the third time would be unlucky. It was the first time they had vaulted after evening roll-call and he was certain that the guards would be suspicious. As he pulled on the evil-smelling black combinations he could hear Nigel instructing the four men who were to carry the horse. He looked at Philip, unrecognisable in his black hood; and then at the third man, a New Zealander called McKay, whom they had chosen as the lightest man in the camp. He was stripped for lightness and holding the cardboard box for the dry sand to be sprinkled over the trap after he had sealed them down.

Nigel came in and handed him a bottle of cold tea for John. 'Give him my love,' he said, 'and tell him to write.'

Peter and Philip crawled under the horse, stood one at each end and held McKay suspended between them. The poles were placed in position and the horse protestingly started on its last journey. One of the bearers slipped as they came down the steps and Peter thought that he would drop them. The man recovered his balance and they went swaying and jerking across the football pitch.

Once the horse was in position Philip sat on McKay's back at one end while Peter again removed the trap. As he took out the wooden boards he listened for sounds of movement in the tunnel. It was silent. He looked at Philip.

'I'll go up the tunnel and see how John is,' he added. 'You fill twelve bags from the bottom of the shaft for Mac to take back, and then stay down this end. I'll send the sand back to you in the basin and you spread it along the floor of the tunnel as you come up.'

'Right.'

'You'll never get down there!' McKay looked with wonder at the narrowness of the shaft.

Peter dropped feet first into the vertical shaft. He slid to his knees, edging with his legs backwards into the back burrow. Stooping awkwardly in his tight clothing, he managed to get his head under the lintel

of the opening and slipped head first into the tunnel. He waved his legs in farewell, and squirmed inch by inch along the hundred feet that had taken them so long to build. Now that it was finished he was almost sorry. The tunnel had been first in his thoughts for months, cherished, nursed; and now it was finished and he was crawling down it for the last time.

He had brought the torch with him as he inched along he could see heaps of loose sand dislodged by John's clothing. He noticed all the patches of shoring, strangely unfamiliar in the light but which had been built with difficulty in darkness.

As he neared the end of the tunnel he flashed the torch ahead and called softly to John. He was afraid to call loudly for he was now under the wire and close to the sentry's beat. He passed the bend where they had altered course and came to the end of the tunnel.

Where he had expected to find John there was nothing but a solid wall of sand.

John must have been digging steadily on and in banking up the sand behind him had completely blocked the tunnel.

Peter bored a small hole through the wall of sand

which was about three feet thick. As he broke through a gust of hot fetid air gushed out and there was John, wringing wet with perspiration and black from head to foot with the dye that had run out of his combinations. Sand clung to his face where he had sweated and his hair, caked with sand, fell forward over his eyes. He looked pale and tired under the yellow light of Peter's torch.

'Where the bloody hell have you been?' he asked.

'It's only just about four-thirty,' Peter said.

'I thought it must have gone six. I seem to have been down here for hours. I thought the roll-call had gone wrong and I'd have to go out alone.'

'It's all O.K.,' Peter said. 'I've got a bottle of tea here.' He pushed it through the hole to John. 'I'll just send this back to Phil and then I'll join you.' He pulled the empty basin up the tunnel and sent the first load back to Philip, who filled the empty bags he had brought down and stacked them in the shaft.

As they worked on they found that now the end of the tunnel where Peter and John were working had a certain amount of fresh air from the air-hole under the wire. Philip, with the trap sealed down, had none.

They worked feverishly trying to get as much as possible done before the breaking time. John, in front, stabbing at the face with a trowel and pushing the damp sand under his belly back towards Peter, who lay with his head on John's heels collecting the sand and squirming backwards with it to Philip, who banked it up as a solid wall behind them.

They were now in a narrow portion of the tunnel about twenty-five feet long and two feet square, ventilated by one small hole three inches in diameter.

They were working for the first time in clothes and

for the first time without the fresh air pushed up the tunnel by the basin. They were working three in the tunnel and they were anxious about the air. They were working for the first time by the light of a torch, and in this light the tunnel seemed smaller and the earth above more solid. The prisoners had been locked in for the night and if the tunnel collapsed now they were helpless.

They all worked fast and steadily. None of them wanted to be the one to break the rhythm of the work.

At five-thirty Peter, who had a watch, called a halt. 'We'd better push up to the top now,' he whispered. 'We've got to be out in half an hour.'

John nodded his agreement and began to push the tunnel up towards the surface. It was farther than they had expected and they thought they would never get to the top. Finally John broke through – a hole as large as his fist – and through it he caught his first glimpse of the stars. The stars in the free heavens beyond the wire.

'I'll break out the whole width of the tunnel,' John whispered, 'just leaving the thin crust over the top. Then we can break that quickly and there'll be less chance of being seen.'

Peter squeezed his arm in reply and squirmed back to Philip to warn him to get ready. On his way back he brought John's kitbag which Philip had tied to his ankle. He then went back for his own. Philip pushed his along the tunnel in front of his nose.

At exactly six o'clock they broke through to the open air, pulling the dry sandy surface down on top of them, choking and blinding them and making them want to cough. As they broke through they heard the sound of the diversion coming from the huts nearest the wire. There were men blowing trumpets, men singing, men banging the sides of the hut and yelling at the top of their voices.

'The silly bastards will get a bullet in there if they're not careful,' John whispered.

'Go on! Go now!' Peter said. He was scared. It was too light.

Quickly John hoisted his kitbag out of the tunnel and rolled it towards the ditch. He squeezed himself out of the hole and Peter saw his legs disappear from view.

Peter stuck his head out of the tunnel and looked towards the camp. It was brilliantly floodlit. He had not realised how brilliantly it was lit. But the raised sentry boxes were in darkness and he could not see whether the guards were looking in his direction or not. He could not see the guards outside the wire. He lifted out his kitbag and pushed it towards the ditch, wriggling himself out of the hole and rolling full length on the ground towards the ditch. He expected every minute to hear the crack of a rifle and feel the tearing impact of its bullet in his flesh. He gained the ditch and lay listening. The diversion in the huts had reached a new crescendo of noise.

He picked up his kitbag and ran blindly towards the pine forest on the other side of the road where John was waiting for him.

THE SECRET OF THE WELL

J. Meade Falkner

ohn Trenchard has a price on his head for smuggling. He has fled his home village of Moonfleet with his friend Elzevir, and now they are on the trail of a great diamond hidden by one of the Mohune family. They have tracked down the treasure to the well of Carisbrooke Castle, and they bribe the gate-keeper, or turnkey, to let them look for it . . .

As soon as we were entered the turnkey locked the door from the inside, and when he let the key drop to its place, and it jangled with the others on his belt, it seemed to me he had us as his prisoners in a trap. I tried to catch his eye to see if it looked bad or good, but could not, for he kept his shifty face turned always somewhere else; and then it came to my mind that if the treasure was really fraught with evil, this coarse dark-haired man, who could not look one straight, was to become a minister of ruin to bring the curse home to us.

But if I was weak and timid Elzevir had no misgivings. He had taken the coil of twine off his arm and was undoing it. 'We will let an end of this down the well,' he said, 'and I have made a knot in it at eighty feet. This lad thinks the treasure is in the well wall, eighty feet below us, so when the knot is on well lip we shall know we have the right depth. 'I tried again to see what look the turnkey wore when he heard where the treasure was, but could not, and so fell to examining the well.

A spindle ran from the axle of the wheel across the well, and on the spindle was a drum to take the rope. There was some clutch or fastening which could be fixed or loosed at will to make the drum turn with the tread-wheel, or let it run free, and a footbreak to lower the bucket fast or slow, or stop it altogether.

'I will get into the bucket,' Elzevir said, turning to me, 'and this good man will lower me gently by the break until I reach the string-end down below. Then I will shout, and so fix you the wheel and give me time to search.'

This was not what I looked for, having thought that it was I should go; and though I liked going down the well little enough, yet somehow now I felt I would rather do that than have Master Elzevir down the hole, and me left locked alone with this villainous fellow up above.

So I said, 'No, master, that cannot be; 'tis my place to go, being smaller and a lighter weight than thou; and thou shalt stop here and help this gentleman to lower me down.'

Elzevir spoke a few words to try to change my purpose, but soon gave in, knowing it was certainly the better plan, and having only thought to go himself because he doubted if I had the heart to do it. But the turnkey showed much ill-humour at the change, and strove to let the plan stand as it was, and for Elzevir to go down the well. Things that were settled, he said, should remain settled; he was not one for changes; it was a man's task this and no child's play; a boy would not have his senses about him, and might overlook the place. I fixed my eyes on Elzevir to let him know what I thought, and Master Turnkey's words fell lightly on his ears as water on a duck's back. Then this ill-eyed man tried to work upon my fears; saying that the well is deep and the bucket small, I shall get giddy and be overbalanced. I do not say that these forebodings were without effect on me, but I had made up my mind that, bad as it might be to go down, it was yet worse to have Master Elzevir prisoned in the well, and I remain above. Thus the turnkey perceived at last that he was speaking to deaf ears, and turned to the business.

Yet there was one fear that still held me, for thinking of what I had heard of the quarry shafts in Purbeck, how men had gone down to explore, and there been taken with a sudden giddiness, and never lived to tell what they had seen; and so I said to Master Elzevir, 'Art sure the well is clean, and that no deadly gases lurk below?'

'Thou mayst be sure I knew the well was sweet before I let thee talk of going down,' he answered. 'For yesterday we lowered a candle to the water, and the flame burned bright and steady; and where the candle lives, there man lives too. But thou art right: these gases change from day to day, and we will try the thing again. So bring the candle, Master Jailer.'

The jailer brought a candle fixed on a wooden triangle, which he was wont to show strangers who came to see the well and lowered it on a string. It was not till then I knew what a task I had before me, for looking over the parapet, and taking care not to lose my balance, because the parapet was low, and the floor round it green and slippery with water-splashings, I watched the candle sink into that cavernous depth, and from a bright flame turn into a little twinkling star, and then to a mere point of light. At last it rested on the water, and there was a shimmer where the wood frame had set ripples moving. We watched it twinkle for a little while, and the jailer raised the candle from the water, and dropped down a stone from some he kept there for that purpose. This stone struck the wall half-way down, and went from side to side, crashing and whirring till it met the water with a booming plunge; and there rose a groan and moan from the eddies, like those dreadful sounds of the surge that I heard on lonely nights in the sea-caverns underneath our hiding-place in Purbeck. The jailer looked at me then for the first time, and his eyes had an ugly meaning, as if he said, 'There – that is how you will sound when you fall from your perch.' But it was no use to frighten, for I had made up my mind.

They pulled the candle up forthwith and put it in my hand, and I flung the plasterer's hammer into the bucket, where it hung above the well, and then got in myself. The turnkey stood at the break-wheel, and Elzevir leant over the parapet to steady the rope. 'Art sure that thou canst do it, lad?' he said, speaking low, and put his hand kindly on my shoulder. 'Are head and heart sure? Thou art my diamond, and I would rather lose all other diamonds in the world than aught should come to thee. So, if thou doubtest, let me go, or let not any go at all.'·

'Never doubt, master,' I said, touched by tenderness, and wrung his hand. 'My head is sure; I have no broken leg to turn it silly now' – for I guessed he was thinking of Hoar Head and how I had gone giddy on the Zigzag.

The bucket was large, for all that the turnkey had tried to frighten me into think it small, and I could crouch in it low enough to feel safe of not falling out. Moreover, such a venture was not entirely new to me, for I had once been over Gad Cliff in a basket, to get two peregrines' eggs; yet none the less I felt ill at ease and fearful, when the bucket began to sink into

that dreadful depth, and the air to grow chilly as I went down. They lowered me gently enough, so that I was able to take stock of the way the wall was made, and found that for the most part it was cut through solid chalk; but here and there, where the chalk failed or was broken away, they had lined the walls with brick, patching them now on this side, now on that, and now all round. By degrees the light, which was dim even overground that rainy day, died out in the well, till all was black as night but for my candle, and far overhead I could see the well-mouth, white and round like a lustreless full-moon.

I kept an eye all the time on Elzevir's cord that hung down the well-side, and when I saw it coming to a finish, shouted to them to stop, and they brought the bucket up near level with the end of it, so I knew I was about eighty feet deep. Then I raised myself, standing up in the bucket and holding by the rope, and began to look round, knowing not all the while what I looked for, but thinking to see a hole in the wall, or perhaps the diamond itself shining out of a cranny. But I could perceive nothing; and what made it more difficult was, that the walls here were lined completely with small flat bricks, and looked much the same all round. I examined these bricks as closely as I might, and took course by course, looking first at the north side where the plumb-line hung, and afterwards turning round in the bucket till I was afraid of getting giddy; but to little purpose. They could see my candle moving round and round from the well-top, and knew no doubt what I was at, but Master Turnkey grew impatient, and shouted down, 'What are you doing? have you found nothing? can you see no treasure?'

'No,' I called back, 'I can see nothing,' and then, 'Are you sure, Master Block, that you have measured the plummet true to eighty feet?'

I heard them talking together, but could not make out what they said, for the bim-bom and echo in the well, till Elzevir shouted again, 'They say this floor has been raised; you must try lower.'

Then the bucket began to move lower, slowly, and I crouched down in it again, not wishing to look too much into the unfathomable, dark abyss below. And all the while there rose groanings and moanings from eddies in the bottom of the well, as if the spirits that kept watch over the jewel were yammering together that one should be so near it; and clear above them all I heard Grace's voice, sweet and grave, 'Have a care, have a care how you touch the treasure; it was evilly come by, and will bring a curse with it.'

But I had set foot on this way now, and must go through with it, so when the bucket stopped some six feet lower down, I fell again to diligently examining the walls. They were still built of the shallow bricks, and scanning them course by course as before, I could at first see nothing, but as I moved my eyes downward they were brought up by a mark scratched on a brick, close to the hanging plummet-line.

Now, however lightly a man may glance through a book, yet if his own name, or even only one like it, should be printed on the page, his eyes will instantly be stopped by it; so too, if his name be mentioned by others in their speech, though it should be whispered never so low, his ears will catch it. Thus it was with this mark, for though it was very slight, so that I think not one in a thousand would ever have noticed it at all, yet it stopped my eyes and brought up my thoughts suddenly, because I knew by instinct that it had something to do with me and what I sought.

The sides of this well are not moist, green, or clammy, like the sides of some others where damp and noxious exhalations abound, but dry and clean; for it is said that there are below hidden entrances and exits for the water, which keep it always moving. So these bricks were also dry and clean, and this mark as sharp as if made yesterday, though the issue showed that 'twas put there a very long time ago. Now the mark was not deeply or regularly graven, but roughly scratched, as I have known boys score their names, or alphabet letters, or a date, on the alabaster figures that lie in Moonfleet Church. And here, too, was scored a letter of the alphabet, a plain 'Y', and would have passed for nothing more perhaps to any not born in Moonfleet; but to me it was the *cross-pall*, or black 'Y' of the Mohunes, under whose shadow we were all brought up. So as soon as I saw that, I knew I was near what I sought, and that Colonel John Mohune had put his sign there a century ago, either by his own hands or by those of a servant; and then I thought of Mr Glennie's story, that the Colonel's conscience was always unquiet, because of a servant whom he had put away, and now I seemed to understand something more of it.

My heart throbbed fiercely, as many another's heart has throbbed when he has come near the fulfilment of a great desire, whether lawful or guilty, and I tried to get at the brick. But though by holding on to the rope with my left hand, I could reach over far enough to touch the brick with my right 'twas as much as I could do, and so I shouted up the well that they must bring me nearer in to the side. They understood what I would be at, and slipped a noose over the well-rope and so drew it in to the side, and made it fast till I should give the word to loose again. Thus I was brought close to the well-wall, and the marked brick near about the level of my face when I stood up in the bucket. There was nothing to show that this brick had been tampered with, nor did it sound hollow when tapped, though when I came to look closely at the joints, it seemed as though there was more cement than usual about the edges. But I never doubted that what we sought was to be found behind it, and so got to work at once, fixing the wooden frame of the candle in the fastening of the chain, and chipping out the mortar setting with the plasterer's hammer.

When they saw above that first I was to be pulled in to the side, and afterwards fell to work on the wall of the well, they guessed, no doubt, how matters were, and I had scarce begun chipping when I heard the turnkey's voice again, sharp and greedy, 'What are you doing? have you found nothing?' It chafed me that this grasping fellow should be always shouting to me while Elzevir was content to stay quiet, so I cried back that I had found nothing, and that he should know what I was doing in good time.

Soon I had the mortar out of the joints, and the brick loose enough to prise it forward, by putting the edge of the hammer in the crack. I lifted it clean out and put it in the bucket, to see later on, in case of need, if there was a hollow for anything to be hidden in; but never had occasion to look at it again, for there, behind the brick, was a little hole in the wall, and in the hole what I sought. I had my fingers in the wall too quick for words, and brought out a little parchment bag, for all the world like those dried fish-eggs cast up on the beach that children call shepherds' purses. Now, shepherds' purses are crisp, and crackle to the touch, and sometimes I have known a pebble get inside one and rattle like a pea in a drum; and this little bag that I pulled out was dry too, and crackling, and had something of the size of a small pebble that rattled in the inside of it. Only I knew well that this was no pebble, and set to work to get it out. But though the little bag was parched and dry, 'twas not so easily torn, and at last I struck off the corner of it with the sharp edge of my hammer against the bucket. Then I shook it carefully, and out into my hand there dropped a pure crystal as big as a walnut. I had never in my life seen a diamond, either large or small – yet even if I had not known that Blackbeard had buried a diamond, and if we had not come hither of set purpose to find it, I should not have doubted that what I had in my hand was a diamond, and this of matchless size and brilliance. It was cut into many facets, and though there was little or no light in the well save my candle, there seemed to be in this stone the light of a thousand fires that flashed out, sparkling red and blue and green, as I turned it between my fingers. At first I could think of nothing else, neither how it got there, nor how I had

come to find it, but only of it, the diamond, and that
with such a prize Elzevir and I could live happily
ever afterwards, and that I should be a rich man and
able to go back to Moonfleet. So I crouched down in
the bottom of the bucket, being filled entirely with
such thoughts, and turned it over and over again,
wondering continually more and more to see the
fiery light fly out of it. I was, as it were, dazed by its
brilliance, and by the possibilities of wealth that it
contained, and had, perhaps, a desire to keep it to
myself as long as might be; so that I thought nothing
of the two who were waiting for me at the well-
mouth, till I was suddenly called back by the harsh
voice of the turnkey, crying as before –

'What are you doing? have you found nothing?'

'Yes,' I shouted back, 'I have found the treasure;
you can pull me up.' The words were scarcely out of
my mouth before the bucket began to move, and I
went up a great deal faster than I had gone down. Yet
in that short journey other thoughts came to my
mind, and I heard Grace's voice again, sweet and
grave, 'Have a care, have a care how you touch the
treasure; it was evilly come by, and will bring a curse
with it.' At the same time I remembered how I had
been led to the discovery of this jewel – first, by Mr
Glennie's stories, second, by my finding the locket,
and third, by Ratsey giving me the hint that the
writing was a cipher, and so had come to the
hiding-place without a swerve or stumble; and it
seemed to me that I could not have reached it so
straight without a leading hand, but whether good or
evil, who should say?

As I neared the top I heard the turnkey urging the
donkey to trot faster in the wheel, so that the bucket
might rise the quicker, but just before my head was
level with the ground he set the break on and fixed

me where I was. I was glad to see the light again, and Elzevir's face looking kindly on me, but vexed to be brought up this suddenly just when I was expecting to set foot on *terra firma*.

The turnkey had stopped me through his covetous eagerness, so that he might get sooner at the jewel, and now he craned over the low parapet and reached out his hand to me, crying – 'Where is the treasure? where is the treasure? give me the treasure!'

I held the diamond between finger and thumb of my right hand, and waved it for Elzevir to see. By stretching out my arm I could have placed it in the turnkey's hand, and was just going to do so, when I caught his eyes for the second time that day, and something in them made me stop. There was a look in his face that brought back to me the memory of an autumn evening, when I sat in my aunt's parlour reading the book called the *Arabian Nights*; and how, in the story of the *Wonderful Lamp*, Aladdin's wicked uncle stands at the top of the stairs when the boy is coming up out of the underground cavern, and will not let him out, unless he first gives up the treasure. But Aladdin refused to give up his lamp until he should stand safe on the ground again, because he guessed that if he did, his uncle would shut him up in the cavern and leave him to die there; and the look in the turnkey's eyes made me refuse to hand him the jewel till I was safe out of the well, for a horrible fear seized me that, as soon as he had taken it from me, he meant to let me fall down and drown below.

So when he reached down his hand and said, 'Give me the treasure,' I answered, 'Pull me up then; I cannot show it you in the bucket.

'Nay, lad,' he said, cozening me, ''tis safer to give it me now, and have both hands free to help you getting out; these stones are wet and greasy, and you

may chance to slip, and having no hand to save you, fall back in the well.'

But I was not to be cheated, and said again sturdily, 'No, you must pull me up first.'

Then he took to scowling, and cried in an angry tone, 'Give me the treasure, I say, or it will be the worse for you'; but Elzevir would not let him speak to me that way, and broke in roughly, 'Let the boy up, he is sure-footed and will not slip. 'Tis his treasure, and he shall do with it as he likes: only that thou shalt have a third of it when we have sold it.'

Then he: ''Tis not his treasure – no, nor yours either, but mine, for it is my well, and I have let you get it. Yet I will give you a half-share in it; but as for this boy, what has he to do with it? We will give him a golden guinea, and he will be richly paid for his pains.'

'Tush,' cries Elzevir, 'let us have no more fooling; this boy shall have his share, or I will know the reason why.'

'Ay, you shall know the reason, fair enough,' answers the turnkey, 'and 'tis because your name is Block, and there is a price of £50 upon your head, and £20 upon this boy's. You thought to outwit me, and are yourself outwitted; and here I have you in a trap, and neither leaves this room, except with hands tied, and bound for the gallows, unless I first have the jewel safe in my purse.'

On that I whipped the diamond back quick into the little parchment bag, and thrust both down snug into my breeches-pocket, meaning to have a fight for it, anyway, before I let it go. And looking up again, I saw the turnkey's hand on the butt of his pistol, and cried, 'Beware, beware! he draws on you.' But before the words were out of my mouth, the turnkey had his weapon up and levelled full at Elzevir. 'Surrender,' he cries, 'or I shoot you dead, and the £50 is mine,' and never giving time for answer, fires. Elzevir stood on the other side of the well-mouth, and it seemed the other could not miss him at such a distance; but as I blinked my eyes at the flash, I felt the bullet strike the iron chain to which I was holding, and saw that Elzevir was safe.

The turnkey saw it too, and flinging away his pistol, sprang round the well and was at Elzevir's throat before he knew whether he was hit or not. 'I have said that the turnkey was a tall, strong man, and twenty years the younger of the two; so doubtless when he made for Elzevir, he thought he would easily have him broken down and handcuffed, and then turn to me. But he reckoned without his host, for though Elzevir was the shorter and older man, he was wonderfully strong, and seasoned as a salted thong. Then they hugged one another and began a terrible struggle: for Elzevir knew that he was wrestling for life, and I daresay the turnkey guessed that the stakes were much the same for him too.

As soon as I saw what they were at, and that the bucket was safe fixed, I laid hold of the well-chain, and climbing up by it swung myself on to the top of the parapet, being eager to help Elzevir, and get the turnkey gagged and bound while we made our escape. But before I was well on the firm ground again, I saw that little help of mine was needed, for the turnkey was flagging, and there was a look of anguish and desperate surprise upon his face, to find that the man he had thought to master so lightly was strong as a giant. They were swaying to and fro, and the jailer's grip was slackening, for his muscles were overwrought and tired; but Elzevir held him firm as a vice, and I saw from his eyes and the bearing of his body that he was gathering himself up to give his enemy a fall.

Now I guessed that the fall he would use would be the Compton Toss, for though I had never seen him give it, yet he was well known for a wrestler in his younger days, and the Compton Toss for his most certain fall. I shall not explain the method of it, but those who have seen it used will know that 'tis a deadly fall, and he who lets himself get thrown that way even upon grass, is seldom fit to wrestle another bout the same day. Still 'tis a difficult fall to use, and perhaps Elzevir would never have been able to give it, had not the other at that moment taken one hand of the waist, and tried to make a clutch with it at the throat. But the only way of avoiding that fall, and indeed most others, is to keep both hands firm between hip and shoulder-blade, and the moment Elzevir felt one hand off his back, he had the jailer off his feet and gave him Compton's Toss. I do not know whether Elzevir had been so taxed by the fierce struggle that he could not put his fullest force into the throw, or whether the other, being a very strong and heavy man, needed more to fling him; but so it was, that instead of the turnkey going down straight as he should, with the back of his head on the floor (for

that is the real damage of the toss), he must needs stagger backwards a pace or two, trying to regain his footing before he went over.

It was those few staggering paces that ruined him, for with the last he came upon the stones close to the well-mouth, that had been made wet and slippery by continual spilling there of water. Then up flew his heels, and he fell backwards with all his weight.

As soon as I saw how near the well-mouth he was got, I shouted and ran to save him; but Elzevir saw it quicker than I, and springing forward seized him by the belt just when he turned over. The parapet wall was very low, and caught the turnkey behind the knee as he staggered, tripping him over into the well-mouth. He gave a bitter cry, and there was a wrench on his face when he knew where he was come, and 'twas then Elzevir caught him by the belt. For a moment I thought he was saved, seeing Elzevir setting his body low back with heels pressed firm against the parapet wall to stand the strain. Then the belt gave way at the fastening, and Elzevir fell sprawling on the floor. But the other went backwards down the well.

I got to the parapet just as he fell head first into that

black abyss. There was a second of silence, then a dreadful noise like a coco-nut being broken on a pavement – for we once had coco-nuts in plenty at Moonfleet, when the *Bataviaman* came on the beach, then a deep echoing blow, where he rebounded and struck the wall again, and last of all, the thud and thundering splash, when he reached the water at the bottom. I held my breath for sheer horror, and listened to see if he would cry, though I knew at heart he would never cry again, after that first sickening smash; but there was no sound or voice, except the moaning voices of the water eddies that I had heard before.

Elzevir slung himself into the bucket. 'You can handle the break,' he said to me; 'let me down quick into the well.' I took the break-lever, lowering him as quickly as I durst, till I heard the bucket touch water at the bottom, and then stood by and listened. All was still, and yet I started once, and could not help looking round over my shoulder, for it seemed as if I was not alone in the well-house; and though I could see no one, yet I had a fancy of a tall black-bearded man, with coppery face, chasing another round and round the well-mouth. Both vanished from my fancy just as the pursuer had his hand on the pursued; but Mr Glennie's story came back again to my mind, how that Colonel Mohune's conscience was always unquiet because of a servant he had put away, and I guessed now that the turnkey was not the first man these walls had seen go headlong down the well.

Elzevir had been in the well so long that I began to fear something had happened to him, when he shouted to me to bring him up. So I fixed the clutch, and set the donkey going in the tread-wheel; and the patient drudge started on his round, recking nothing whether it was a bucket of water he brought up, or a live man, or a dead man, while I looked over the parapet, and waited with a cramping suspense to see whether Elzevir would be alone, or have something with him. But when the bucket came in sight there was only Elzevir in it, so I knew the turnkey had never come to the top of the water again, and, indeed, there was but little chance he should after that first knock. Elzevir said nothing to me, till I spoke: 'Let us fling the jewel down the well after him, Master Block; it was evilly come by, and will bring a curse with it.'

He hesitated for a moment while I half-hoped yet half-feared he was going to do as I asked, but then said:

'No, no; thou art not fit to keep so precious a thing. Give it me. It is thy treasure, and I will never touch penny of it; but fling it down the well though shalt not; for this man has lost his life for it, and we have risked ours for it – ay, and may lose them for it too, perhaps.'

So I gave him the jewel.

IN THE SHADOW OF THE GUILLOTINE

Ronald Welch

aris during the French Revolution is a dangerous place to be. Richard Carey, a young Englishman, has risked everything to get his cousin Armand and Armand's father out of France alive. So far all his efforts have failed, and now he has only one chance left. . .

A thin rain was falling when Richard came down to breakfast the next morning. Armand was still in bed, and he would probably stay there for another hour at least. His mood was now one of complete despair; there was no hope for his father, he was convinced, and Richard felt much the same. Their last hope was the unknown Monsieur Hervilly, and they would know how valuable he might be that evening when Richard paid his five o'clock call. Meanwhile there was a long and boring day to be passed somehow and in this weather Richard decided to find a book and spend the time in front of Duport's fire.

The same concierge greeted him in the Rue St Antoine. His manner was even more nervous than before, and Richard inspected him curiously, and with a growing uneasiness.

'What is wrong?' he asked. 'You're frightened of something?'

'But no, Monsieur, no! What could be wrong? It is

just that everyone in Paris is frightened these days.'

'I suppose so,' Richard said doubtfully. 'On which floor is Monsieur Hervilly to be found?'

'The third, Monsieur. The door on your left when you reach the landing.'

Richard went up the stairs slowly. There was something wrong. He felt it instinctively. That was something that Rupert had told him, too. You learn to smell danger, he had said; at least, some fortunate men did, and they were fools unless they took precautions. What precautions could he take, Richard wondered? He had a pistol in each pocket. He slid his hands inside the pockets and fingered the smooth butts; the mere touch reassured him, and he quickened his pace.

He hesitated outside the door on the third landing, then shrugged his shoulders, and tapped on the panel.

'Entrez!' a voice said from inside.

Richard walked inside, and the door was slammed behind him with a crash. Richard whirled round. A man was leaning back against the door, and he smiled at the startled expression on Richard's face.

Slowly Richard turned. Another man was standing by the window. In the fading light it was difficult to see their faces under the brims of their hats; both wore dark coats and white breeches with top boots; in each buttonhole was a rosette, and round each waist was a coloured sash.

There was no need for Richard to ask them who they were. He knew quite well. They were Government agents. He had walked into a neat trap.

All three stared at each other for a moment in silence. After the first shock Richard's brain had recovered very quickly, and he was able to think

about his next move. He must get away, that was
quite clear. Once arrested, there would be little
chance for him. Both the men were armed, with
heavy pistols stuck into the sash around their waist.
Not very easy to pull one out quickly, Richard
thought. But even if he reached one man in time, and
knocked him down, the other could shoot him at
leisure.

'Yes, Citizen?' said the man at the window.

'I came to see a Monsieur Robert Hervilly.' Richard
decided to brazen it out.

'Citizen Hervilly,' the man said, with slight emph-
asis on the 'Citizen'. 'Citizen Hervilly was arrested
last week. And why do you wish to see an enemy of
the Republic?'

'I'm a University student,' Richard said. 'From
Colombey-sur-Thaon in Normandy. I've never met
Citizen Hervilly. But he is an acquaintance of my
uncle. Édouard Gribeauval, and he asked me to call
on Citizen Hervilly.'

The man by the window, obviously the senior of
the two, digested this story; he was a short, stumpy
fellow, with a white and haggard face. The man by
the door was short, too, but fairly stout, with a

vacant, somewhat stupid face. He leant against the door and was listening indifferently to the conversation, but his eyes were on Richard.

'Your name, Citizen?'

'Richard. . .Cartier.' Richard hesitated for a fraction of a second over the name; he had never been asked for it before, and it did not come easily to his tongue.

'You do not seem very certain of that, Citizen,' the Frenchman said. 'Your papers.'

Richard pulled out his papers and put them on the table. He would have to watch this fellow; he had been quick enough to notice that momentary hesitation. The agent bent down to read the documents. Richard had moved two steps closer to him when he had asked for the papers, and with his long reach, Richard could have touched him at arm's length now.

'I am not satisfied, Citizen,' the man said, and raised his head. 'You will come with us.'

Richard's right caught him on the chin with a smack. He went over on his back, and the small table with him, and Richard had spun round with all the agility and speed of the trained fencer. Oh for his sword, he thought, as he leapt for the man at the door.

But his risk had been a calculated one; he was relying on that expression of stupidity on the man's face, and he had been right. The second agent had gaped for the first vital second when his companion went down, and only when Richard was nearly on him did he snatch at his pistol.

He had tugged it out when Richard's hand closed on his wrist, and the other came up in a blurred white streak and crunched into his jaw. He went back against the door, and Richard swung viciously once more. As the man went down, he reached for the door-knob and pulled.

But although the door opened, it jammed against the man lying on the floor; there was barely room for Richard to squeeze through. He grunted, and some instinct made him turn and drop to his knees. The first agent was struggling to his feet, pistol in hand. There was a bright flash and a tremendous explosion, magnified in that small room, and the bullet thudded into the door above Richard's head.

Richard turned again, felt a hand grasp for his feet, kicked out wildly, and was through the door, which he pulled behind him. And there was the key on the outside, as the two agents had left it. Richard turned it, and rushed across the landing, and down the stairs in a clatter of feet. That shot would fetch out the concierge; no wonder he had been so scared, acting under orders from two Government agents. Richard pulled out a pistol; he was not going to be stopped now, and once he reached the street he could easily escape in the darkness, for the sun was down, and the hanging lanterns of Paris did not give much light.

He thundered down to the landing below. A door opened, and a hand caught at him. Up came Richard's pistol, but it was not cocked. Too late now, and the dark figure in the doorway grasped his wrist.

'Quick, Carey!' the figure said in English. 'Through here! They've got two men downstairs in the hall!'

He pulled Richard through the open door, and pushed him across a darkened room. Richard stumbled over a chair, kicked it out of his way, but he had nearly fallen.

'Through the window!' hissed the voice behind him. 'Ten foot drop only.'

Richard was not conscious of any coherent thought. He did as he was told instinctively. He thrust his long legs clumsily through the window, wriggled his body out until he was hanging by his fingers to the sill, his feet scrabbling for a hold. But there was none.

'Let yourself go,' the voice said above his head. 'Bend your knees, and roll when you hit the ground!'

Richard drew a deep breath and let go. But there was no time to worry about bending his knees in that swift drop. His feet smashed into the ground with a jar that went through his whole body, and he sprawled clumsily on the ground, half breathless and wondering if he had broken a leg. A thud and a heavy body rolled over on him. A hand tugged urgently at his coat-sleeve.

'Quick, Carey! This way!'

Richard scrambled to his feet. Two dark figures were bending over him, and a new voice hissed at him.

'Down the alley there!' it said, and Richard pounded after the two men in the darkness, slipping and stumbling on the muddy cobbles, past blank, shuttered windows, under the creaking, swaying lanterns with their pools of yellow light, round a corner, then another, through the labyrinth of alleys

and streets that honeycombed the poorer parts of Paris.

Richard was panting loudly when they pulled up in front of a tall house, and he was pulled inside a dark hall, one hand guiding him through a door until he found himself sitting on a hard chair, head down and gasping for breath.

'Can you hear anything, Jack?' a voice asked.

Richard heard the rasp of flint, and a candle flickered, throwing a narrow circle of light over the table. But Richard was wondering where he had heard that voice before. One of the men was holding back the window curtain, and the other was standing by the door. From him came a crack, and then another crack as he tugged uneasily at his fingers.

Richard held up the candle. 'Bellamy!' he said. 'Where the devil did you jump from?'

The second man had lighted another candle, and Richard could see Bellamy clearly now. The man's long, sallow face broke into a smile as he watched Richard.

'Oh, I've been in Paris for over a year, Mr Carey. Put some wood on the fire, Jack. I'm frozen, even after that run. By the way, Mr Carey, may I introduce you to Jack Wilson?'

Richard nodded his head; he was still far too bewildered by everything that had happened in the last few minutes. He watched the two men as they lighted candles, made up the fire, and put food on the table.

Bellamy had not changed much since he had seen him last in Cambridge. He was still thin, and clumsy, and his black hair hung down over his high forehead as untidily as ever. But his nervousness had gone; so too had those irritating repetitions at the end of each sentence.

Wilson was a powerful young man with wide shoulders and large, capable hands. But to describe him would have been difficult, for though Richard could have said that he possessed a nose, a mouth, and two eyes, he could not have added that there was anything conspicuous about them, unusual or usual. His face was just a blank, and as he seldom spoke, Richard often forgot that the man was in the room at all. Jack Wilson merely faded into the background, and that, so it seemed, was his main object.

They set cold meat in front of him, some rough wine, bread and cheese, and apologized for the food. Richard ate hungrily. There were many questions he would like to have asked, but both men were behaving as if the events of the last hour were of no importance. But when he had finished, he turned to Bellamy.

'Look here, Bellamy,' he said.

Bellamy laughed. 'You want to know how Jack and I arrived so providentially, eh?'

'I certainly do.'

'Well, it's quite simple, really. We are agents for the British Foreign Office. Unofficial ones, and not connected with the Embassy in any way. They know about us, but I don't think they approve.'

Richard grinned. He could not imagine the pompous Mr Lilley approving of either Bellamy or Wilson.

'Our main job is to collect information,' Bellamy said, 'send reports of public opinion in Paris, possible moves by the Government. Most of the stuff we send to London is unimportant. But occasionally we do learn something useful, not often, but enough to make it worth our while.'

'But what were you doing at this fellow Hervilly's apartment?' Richard asked.

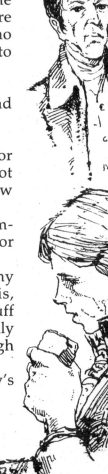

'He is one of our sources of information. I think he is almost certainly acting under orders from the *émigrés* in Germany. The King's brother, the Duke of Artois, is at their head. Anyway, Hervilly was arrested a couple of days ago, and we noticed that two agents of the Republic were watching the house. Our job was to stop our friends from going inside, in case they were arrested, too. Jack here saw you talking to the concierge yesterday. He didn't know who you were, but we decided to speak to you tonight. But you were too early for us. I saw you go in, and couldn't believe my eyes, Mr Carey. I had no idea you were in Paris. We went in by the back door, and heard the shot, and saw you come out. That's when Jack grabbed you.'

Richard finished his red wine – pretty poor stuff, he thought, but he was thirsty after his exertions.

'We would like to know two things, Mr Carey,' Bellamy said. His quiet, assured manner made Richard smile. 'What are you doing in Paris?'

Richard explained, and the two men listened in silence; they asked no questions, but there was little either of them had missed, Richard thought. Bellamy tugged at his fingers when Richard had finished, and exchanged glances with the silent Mr Wilson.

'We should have known about this man de Marillac,' Bellamy said. 'Did you take any papers from him?'

'The usual identity ones, and his special pass as an agent of the Committee of Public Safety.'

'Ah, now that might be useful, Mr Carey. The other point that puzzles me is how did you know about Hervilly?'

'I didn't know anything about him. My uncle, Sir Rupert gave me his address, and said that he might be able to help us.'

'Sir Rupert!' Bellamy smiled, and his fingers cracked with delight. 'Well, that solves all our problems, Mr Carey. Do you think you can find your way back to the Rue St Honoré? Perhaps Jack had better come with you. Safer not to ask the way at night in Paris these days.'

He stood up, and Richard did the same instinctively; but then he sat down again. 'Look here, Bellamy,' he said. 'We want help, Armand d'Assailly and I. You are just the people.'

Bellamy shook his head regretfully. 'No, no, Mr Carey. I was afraid you would say that. We can do nothing to help you.'

Richard glared at him indignantly. 'But why not?' he demanded.

'We have quite definite orders. On no account must we become involved with escapes from the prisons, or any plots against the Government. Our duty is to report, and nothing else.'

Richard grunted. There was a note of polite and very firm refusal in Bellamy's voice. 'Can't you even suggest anything?' he pleaded, and the mere thought that he was begging favours from the despised Bellamy made him wriggle his feet uneasily.

Bellamy exchanged glances with Wilson, who was sitting on the other side of the fire, perfectly still, his face a blank, and indifferent to the whole conversation, or so he seemed, though Richard felt that the man had probably missed nothing.

He shook his head slightly at Richard. 'We'll think about it, Mr Carey,' he said. 'Not easy, you know.'

'Anyway, you know where to find us,' Bellamy said. 'But you must not come here unless it is really urgent. You understand that, Mr Carey?'

Richard nodded meekly. He was being lectured by Bellamy now. But the fellow had changed in the most extraordinary manner; there was a certain force and directness about him that impressed Richard, despite his annoyance at being impressed at all.

Wilson led him back through the maze of dark streets to the Rue St Honoré. Beyond an occasional curt instruction about the various turnings they took, he said nothing, and when he was satisfied that Richard could safely be left, he nodded and disappeared into the gloom. Led like a child with a nursemaid, Richard thought angrily, as he hurried down the street; these two men were treating him in the way a trained and experienced professional agent would condescend towards a bumbling amateur. With a shock, Richard realized that this was indeed the position. To Bellamy he was probably a nuisance and a danger, stumbling clumsily around Paris, attempting an impossible task with blundering inefficiency.

For the next two days Armand went the rounds of his friends, though without any success; many of them were no longer in Paris, and those who were had no intention of risking their lives by trying to help Armand in what they considered a hopeless and dangerous task. All they wished to do was to remain in a safe obscurity, and Richard could not help sympathizing with them. The effect of all this on Armand was to reduce him to a state of bitter depression, and the news that the Convention had finally voted for the execution of the King only made matters worse.

Paris was quiet on that third day, and Duport advised them to stay indoors, though Richard was anxious to go out. He was finding this confinement and lack of action intolerably boring. But he joined Duport and Armand at the upstairs windows of the tailor's house as the street outside gradually filled with a restless and excited crowd of Parisians.

'They are taking no chances,' Armand said. 'National Guards all along the pavements.'

'I have never seen so many troops in the streets before,' Duport said. 'Every barrier out of the city is manned with a double guard, I was told.'

Richard watched the crowd; it was not a hostile one, he thought, just curious and somewhat subdued, waiting patiently in the chill mist that hung over Paris.

'What's that?' he asked, cocking his head.

'Drums,' Armand said.

From the left, far down the road, came the steady throb of sound, and then the drummers outside took up the monotonous beat, a dull, forbidding roll that filled Richard with a feeling of depression and fear.

Then he heard a different sound, the clip-clop of many hooves, and a squadron of cavalry trotted past;

the crowds swayed and pushed, and fell silent. Richard craned his head out of the window. But there was little to see, except the dense masses of horsemen, and in the centre a large green coach that rumbled swiftly over the cobbles. Richard caught a brief glimpse of a brown-coated man inside, a calm, white face and a high forehead, and King Louis had passed.

'Close the window,' Armand said harshly.

He went and sat by the fire, poking at the coals with his boot. Outside the drums had fallen silent, but they were still beating in the distance, and the sound suddenly increased, and then abruptly they stopped, while all Paris waited. For a minute Richard raised his head and Armand crouched by the fire. Then the drums rolled out once more for a few seconds, stopped again, and Armand sighed heavily, and dropped his head, his long fingers covering his face.

Armand refused to move from the house all the next day, but Richard was determined to go out. He had no idea what to do next; he could see no solution to any of their problems. The chances of helping Quentin d'Assailly were obviously quite hopeless, and the best thing that he had and Armand could do would be to try to leave France. Even that would be difficult, but the effort would at least give them something to do, instead of hiding like rats in Duport's house.

Duport had suggested that Richard should go and listen to the debates in the Convention; they met daily in the old Riding School of the Tuileries Palace, the tailor said, and there was no risk attached to such a visit. No papers were asked for in the public gallery, and foreigners and visitors to Paris went there out of curiosity, for the Convention was one of the sights of Paris now.

Duport was right, for Richard walked in with several other people through the door that led to the public gallery; nobody stopped them, or showed the slightest interest as Richard found an empty seat on a wooden bench, and looked about him curiously.

He was looking down at a long and narrow room lit by windows high up on the walls. Rows of green leather seats rose on either side of a gangway that ran the full length of the Chamber, so that the speakers faced each other, as did the members in the English House of Commons.

But there all similarity vanished. The members spoke, as Richard saw, from a kind of pulpit, and there was already a speech in progress. Richard leant forward to listen. But if he was expecting a vivid, sparkling debate such as he had often heard at Westminster, he was disappointed, for the speaker was reading his speech, a rambling, dull, and extremely vague lecture on the present system of taxation in France. The other members seemed to share Richard's boredom, for few were listening; they strolled about dressed in long overcoats, chatted loudly, and ignored completely the continual ringing of the President's bell, or the shouted 'Chut! Chut!' of the ushers appealing for silence.

The speakers who followed were no more interesting, and Richard began to examine the people sitting with him in the gallery. They were a strange mixture, varying from well-dressed and very respectable men, or foreigners perhaps on business in Paris, to obvious tradesmen of the city, and unshaven and unwashed men and women whose faces appalled Richard. Never had he seen such naked ferocity before; here at last he was looking at some of the Paris mob who had fired the Bastille, stormed the

Tuileries, massacred the prisoners last September, and who had horrified all Europe with their savagery. They were following the speeches closely, and occasionally applauding with frenzied shouts.

Richard was turning back to watch a new speaker who had just walked across to the pulpit when he noticed someone looking at him from the back of the gallery. He did not see the face for more than a second, except to notice a blue coat and a turn of the light-coloured hair. Richard frowned, and pretended to listen to the speech below. But that man, whoever he was, had been watching him. He half turned his head quickly. But the blue coat had gone. Richard shrugged his shoulders. He was imagining things, of course, he decided. Living in hiding in Paris, as he was, he always felt this uneasiness, that people were looking at him suspiciously.

But as he sat there, his long legs cramped by the

narrow benches in front, he still felt that uneasiness. Someone was still watching him. He turned slowly this time. Four or five men were standing by the door that led down to the entrance and the street outside, and one of these men looked swiftly away as Richard's head came round.

Richard wriggled sideways on the hard bench, as if attempting to find a more comfortable position, but he could watch the door now without having to turn completely round. Yes, the man was looking at him, a fellow in a dark coat with long hair falling to his shoulders.

The atmosphere in the chamber was cold and clammy, but Richard felt a wave of prickly heat pass over him, and he stared down at the scene below, his hands clenched. Well, he would not be caught here, he decided. If he could make his way outside, there would be room to use his hands, and his pistols, too, for he never came out without them.

He pushed his way past the man next to him, and made for the door. The dark-haired man was still there, leaning forward now to watch what was happening in the debate, but his eyes flickered towards Richard and then away as Richard walked past him. With a sigh Richard clattered down the wooden stairs, but stopped just before he reached the bottom. There was silence for a moment, and then he heard feet tramping down towards him.

Richard jumped the last three steps, rushed through the doorway, and swung to his left. Ahead lay the gardens of the Tuileries, open now to the public, and filled with a maze of flower-beds and tall hedges. He could lose himself in there quickly enough, or, if it came to a fight, then he could deal with this fellow in comparative secrecy.

He walked as fast as he could without actually

breaking into a run, for that would have attracted attention. There was no one about here, though, and as he dashed through the gates of the gardens, he glanced over his shoulder. Dark-coat was coming after him, but he was alone.

Richard grinned, though there was little amusement on his face. Well, this fellow was due for a violent surprise, and prospect of some action after the boring frustrations of the last week appealed to Richard. He had forgotten his sudden panic up there in the gallery, and as he darted to the left and up a narrow path between the hedges, one hand was inside his pocket and pulling back the cocking-piece of a pistol.

He could hear the hurried patter of the feet, and he moved back against the thick hedge and waited.

Dark-coat burst into view, his white face anxious, but he smiled as he saw Richard.

'Monsieur Carey?' he asked.

Richard gaped at him. This was worse than he had thought. They knew his name, then, so this fellow was an agent of the Government. He pulled out his pistol, and the long barrel glinted for a moment in the dull afternoon light.

'No, Monsieur! No!' the man said, and held up his hands as he stepped hurriedly away. 'I am a friend. I have been told to bring you to the Baron's.'

'The Baron? Which Baron?' Richard asked, suspiciously, without moving his pistol.

'The Baron de Batz, Monsieur.'

'Who the. . .' Richard broke off. He had heard that name before. De Batz, de Batz. He grinned, with genuine amusement this time. Of course, this was one of old Rupert's acquaintances. Good old Rupert! He must have got in touch with de Batz somehow, and told him to look out for Richard.

'If you will follow me, Monsieur,' dark-coat said, relief on his face as he saw the heavy pistol disappear once more.

Richard nodded, but as they set off he still kept one hand inside a pocket, his fingers touching the pistol butt. They went through the garden, across the wide Place de la Révolution, and into the streets beyond, most of them fairly respectable, and lined with shops and cafés, until dark-coat turned down a quiet road and stopped in front of a large house.

'Here, Monsieur,' he said, and tapped on the door.

There was no delay, for it swung open immediately, but only far enough for a face to peer out for a second. The head nodded, and Richard found himself inside a spacious hall. The large town house of some nobleman once, he decided; there was still a magnificent chandelier hanging over his head. Government office now, was the next thought that ran through his head. He had been trapped, after all.

ACKNOWLEDGEMENTS

The publishers would like to extend their grateful thanks to the following authors, publishers and others for kindly granting permission to reproduce the extracts and stories included in this anthology:

THE CURSE OF THE IDOL from *Raiders of the Lost Ark* by Campbell Black. Reproduced by permission of Corgi Books. Copyright © Lucasfilm Ltd (LFL) 1981.

THE ADVENTURE OF THE SPECTACLED ROADMAN from *The Thirty-Nine Steps* by John Buchan. Reproduced by permission of The Rt Hon Lord Tweedsmuir of Elsfield, CBE.

SAMPAN IN THE RIVER from *The House of Sixty Fathers* by Meindert DeJong. Reprinted by permission of Lutterworth Press and Harper and Row, Publishers, Inc. Copyright © Meindert DeJong, 1956.

TRAPPED IN HAZELL'S WOOD from *Danny the Champion of the World* by Roald Dahl. Reprinted by permission of Jonathan Cape Ltd and Alfred A. Knopf, Inc. Copyright © 1975 by Roald Dahl.

DOLPHIN TO THE RESCUE from *The Dolphin Crossing* by Jill Paton Walsh. Reprinted by permission of Macmillan Ltd. Copyright © Gillian Paton Walsh, 1967.

FELIX AND THE ASSASSINS from *Go Saddle the Sea* by Joan Aiken. Reprinted by permission of Jonathan Cape Ltd and Doubleday and Co., Inc. Copyright © 1978 by Joan Aiken Enterprises Ltd.

IN THE ABYSS by H. G. Wells. Reprinted by permission of The Literary Executors of the Estate of the late H. G. Wells.

ALL THE DOGS IN THE WORLD from *A Hundred Million Francs* by Paul Berna. Reprinted by permission of The Bodley Head. Copyright © Paul Berna, 1963.

DANGER AFLOAT from *Master of Morgana* by Allan Campbell McLean. Reprinted by permission of the author. Copyright © Allan Campbell McLean, 1960.